Sarah Thornton cast off the lines to her law career not long after being awarded Australian Corporate Lawyer of the Year in 2016. She now lives with her husband aboard a 43-foot sailing catamaran, exploring this most magnificent blue planet and chasing an endless summer. She took up writing novels as a way to liberate her imagination after twenty years in the structured confines of legal and corporate life. Her debut novel, *Lapse*, is the first of a series featuring former corporate lawyer Clementine Jones.

SARAH THORNTON
LAPSE

TEXT PUBLISHING MELBOURNE AUSTRALIA

textpublishing.com.au

The Text Publishing Company
Swann House
22 William Street
Melbourne Victoria 3000
Australia

Published by The Text Publishing Company, 2019
Reprinted 2019

Book design by Imogen Stubbs
Cover image by Terry Schmidbauer/Stocksy
Typeset by J&M Typesetting

Printed and bound in Australia by Griffin Press, part of Ovato, an accredited ISO/NZS 14001:2004 Environmental Management System printer

ISBN: 9781925773941 (paperback)
ISBN: 9781925774696 (ebook)

A catalogue record for this book is available from the National Library of Australia.

To Dean, the captain of my dreams

Saturday night and the beer was flowing as wet and free as the rain bucketing down outside the Katinga Arms. The barman positioned a plastic tub under the drip in the far corner to the boisterous jeers of a cluster of drinkers nearby.

The young man surrounded by his mates at the end of the bar accepted another glass, his friends clapping him on the back.

'Not the end of the world, mate.'

'Best medicine. Get it into ya!'

He smiled and took a swig. They thought he'd been keeping up, but he'd skipped a couple of rounds without them noticing. Still, he'd had at least three, maybe four. One more than the coach allowed. But what did that matter now, anyway?

As the rain eased, the pub began emptying slowly, but the boys were still going strong, getting rowdier with each round. He tried to laugh along, keep his chin up, but every now and then the shouted conversations and the laughter around him faded to a dull buzz, and he found himself staring blankly at the scuffed timber floor—staring and wondering what the hell he was going to do now.

He managed to slip away around eleven, sneaking out the side entrance so the boys wouldn't see and call him back. As the door swung closed on the warmth and light inside, he felt the chill in the air, and the grey mist of despair settled over him again. He made his way up the narrow lane beside the pub, decided to take a leak before the long walk home to the Plains.

As he zipped up his fly, footsteps from behind. He began to turn. Too late. Arms pinned, chest slammed into the wall with a thud, a grunt of air emptying from his lungs, his head clamped against the brickwork.

Heart thumping, he thought of his mates so close on just the other side of the wall. They wouldn't hear him call. *Shut up. Stay cool. Breathe.*

The shorter one did the talking—right up close, bourbon on his breath. 'We know you, kid.' The other guy ground his head harder against the brick wall. Sharp pain in his cheekbone. 'And we know where you and your missus live.'

The short guy took a step sideways, his arm swinging back, fist hitting him hard in the guts.

No air. Gasping. *Winded is all. Breathe.*

They wore beanies pulled low and thick scarves across their faces, only their eyes showing. The tall guy shoved him and he fell face first onto the dirty, wet pavement, long, skinny legs appearing in front of him—square-toed boots like a frickin' cowboy, one of them swinging. He got a hand up to soften the blow as it crashed into his ribs.

'Me mate here wants to kill you now,' said the short one. 'Reckon I might let him.'

He pushed himself up onto his knees, tried to stand. The next boot landed in his groin, flattening him again.

'But nah, you're a lucky prick. Someone wants you alive…for now—so long as you keep your mouth shut. Not a word, hear me? Not a fucking word!'

'Yeah. Yeah. Okay,' the young man whispered.

'I haven't finished yet, shithead. You make yourself scarce, right. Leave town.'

He felt a pressure in his back—the cold, hard muzzle of a gun.

'You got that? You feeling it?'

The next kick came hard to his stomach. A croak came out as he tried to breathe. Then the short guy held a burning cigarette in front of his face, pinched between forefinger and thumb. He wanted to shout, but the man put a finger to his lips.

'This is a test. Not a sound.'

He bit down, eyes scrunched tight, as he felt the man pushing up the sleeve of his jacket. A faint sizzling sound, the smell of his own flesh burning. He sucked air through his teeth, smothering his scream, lay there groaning.

'Top marks. A-plus,' said the man, straightening up and taking a step back. 'That's the sort of quiet we're after. You're a fast learner, kid, I'll say that for ya. Let's just hope the bub takes after you, eh?'

CHAPTER 1

Eight o'clock and the team had finished their warm-down. Bathed in the harsh oval lights, steam rose from their bodies, the smell of smashed grass and sweat filling the air.

'All right, boys, that's it for the night. Well done,' she said. 'Looking good for Saturday.'

The men made their way towards the sheds. The click-clack of their boots on the concrete seemed to give Clementine confidence. They were strong and fit, and as the season moved on they were gaining momentum, working together now like a well-practised rock band—a long way from the discordant rabble that had turned up that first day. She smiled to herself, not wanting to jinx anything, but it was hard not to predict a win this weekend against Jeridgalee.

Not for the first time, she wondered how she'd ended up with this job. Must have been the only applicant. There was no other way she could explain it.

As she bent down to pick up her backpack, the last of the players trotted past her, a small group of five. A voice came from the pack. 'Nice tits, Jonesy.'

She stiffened. A top button had worked its way loose on her shirt. 'Hey! Stop there!' she called with a ferocity she hadn't had to use for a while.

They pulled up, shuffling, dirt-spattered, sheepish.

'Who said that?' she demanded.

4

'Just a joke. Nothin' in it,' said Beasley. She knew it wasn't him, but she also knew no one would own up.

'Right then. Twenty push-ups. All of you,' she said, her voice stony.

Groans, headshakes, hands on hips.

'All right, if you want to act like high school kids, get going and keep going, all of you, and don't bother turning up to the game.' Stunned looks. 'Yes, that's right—anyone who's never seen a woman's breasts before, keep walking,' she barked. 'I only want men on this team.'

The giant ruckman, Torrens, dropped to the ground, the others falling over themselves to follow. Bodies stretched taut, hands square, Torrens keeping count through clenched teeth. She stalked off when they got to fifteen, too annoyed to speak to them again tonight.

As she walked to her car, someone called her name from the other side of the car park. Jenny Rodham—fifty-something club treasurer and business manager at the only bank in town—waving something at her.

'System's down,' Jenny called as she hurried across. 'Had to write out an old-fashioned cheque! Haven't done that since Noah was a boy!' Her raucous laugh was hard not to enjoy as she handed Clementine her weekly wage, all $140 of it. 'Oh, and by the way,' she said, 'you've been here nine months, high time you came round for dinner.' She cocked her head sideways, her neat black bob falling across the beginnings of a double chin. 'Are you free this Sunday? I do a damn fine lamb roast, and Trev does an amaaaazing gravy.'

Clementine's smile faded. Holed up in the hills, she'd stuck to the plan, never going anywhere or doing anything that wasn't mandatory—certainly not hanging around chatting in car parks like these country folk seemed so keen on.

'No thanks, Jen. I'm having a quiet one at home.'

All her evenings were quiet ones, and they both knew it.

5

One of the players, Clancy Kennedy, was jogging towards them, looking like he wanted to speak with her. A diversion from the dinner invitation. Good.

'Hey, Jonesy,' he called. 'Could I have a word with you?'

'Sure.'

His eyes darted around the remaining cars. 'It's kind of private. Can we talk in the sheds?'

\l/

Clancy sat on a red plastic chair on the other side of the fold-up table, feet spread wide and his hands resting on his knees. The biting chill of the evening air hung solid and heavy between the concrete block walls.

She was still speechless.

'I'm sorry, Jonesy, I just have to look after Mel, you know. She's nearly due, and she's a bit scared.' His voice was unusually soft—she could barely hear him.

'But there's still five weeks to go till the baby comes, right?'

He nodded, dropped his head. Something odd, she thought, something he wasn't telling her, but she couldn't put her finger on it. In fact she couldn't think straight at all. His words were ringing in her head: *Quitting the team. Quitting the team. Quitting the team.* Her star player, the key to the midfield. It didn't make sense. The bloke just loved to play, lived for footy. She was doing her best to stay calm, but it felt like she had one of those huge antibiotic capsules stuck sideways in her throat.

Clancy said nothing, staring at the grey cement floor.

'Couldn't you at least play the home games? We could have someone on stand-by ready to drive you to the hospital as soon as we get the call.'

Clancy shook his head. 'Our first kid and all. Just gotta be there. Wouldn't be right not to.'

6

The words sounded rehearsed and he shifted nervously in the chair as he spoke. If this were a negotiation she'd feel like she had only to dig a bit further, find a weak spot, and an opening would appear, a way to take a point, a win for her client. But this was a long way from the corporate office towers of Sydney and a long way from anything that smelt vaguely like business. No, this young man sitting in front of her, coiled tight like a spring—nothing could be more personal.

She stood up, walked over to the dirt-smeared window looking over the oval. The lights were off now and the car park empty. It was a clear night, and once again she marvelled at the thick smudge of stars across the midnight-blue sky. She thought of the conversation she'd had with Mrs Lemmon at the club fundraising fete. Standing at a stall packed with knitted beanies and crocheted tea-cosies, the old woman had grabbed Clementine's hand as she was leaving.

'My Tom would have loved you, Miss Jones. Yes, yes,' she crooned, 'he would have loved you. Would have called you a bottler of a girl.' She patted Clementine's hand, the soft crepe of her skin and lavender perfume reminding Clementine of her gran.

'He played for Katinga back in the sixties, you know, before he went to Vietnam. Yes, he was one of those high-flyers, full-forward mostly, deadeye Dick with the boot. Of course Tom couldn't play anymore after the war—his back was never the same. Well, I guess you can't fly high when part of your spine's missing, can you now?' She chuckled sadly. 'Oh, but did he love going to the game, though! Oh yes, he was the Cats' number one supporter for five years running.' Her eyes glazed with the sheen of Tom's memory.

'They gave him life membership, you know. That was just before he died, the year after we made the finals in '82. He was gutted when we lost in the semi, but oh was he chuffed to get the life membership.' Her voice trailed off, and she'd smiled kindly at Clementine. 'Hmm, yes, Tom would have said you were the best thing to come to Katinga since Jesus.'

Clementine didn't feel like she could walk on water right now. The town was counting on her to save them from a decades-long losing streak, and now she was going to disappoint them. She should never have taken on the coaching role. Stupid idea.

Turning back towards Clancy, she heard herself say, 'Family always comes first, Clancy. You have to do what's best for Melissa and the new bub.'

He flashed her a look and then quickly glanced away.

After he'd left she sat down with her head in her hands, the edge of the chair cutting into her thighs. The smell of thirty-four years of disappointment overwhelmed her, the echo of hundreds of men, the steam from their panting and the exhaustion in their eyes, the murmurs and bowed heads of the supporters and Mrs Lemmon putting flowers on her Tom's grave.

CHAPTER 2

Clementine forced her eyes open. Through the crack in the curtains she could see the bare branches of the plum tree in the backyard against the pale hues of dawn. Such cold winters—probably only three degrees outside. The folds of her doona felt extravagantly warm. She snuck her fingers out just enough to pull the covers up over her nose.

She had woken twice during the night, each time replaying the scene in her head. Something about Clancy's story didn't stack up. What was it? She searched her memory. Was it the way Clancy had muttered his wife's name, like he didn't want to mention her? Or maybe his eyes, darting all around? He hadn't looked at her once as they spoke. Maybe something to do with Indigenous culture, she thought. But then, when she made that lame comment about putting family first, his eyes had landed right on her.

Family first. How dare she speak of family after what she'd done? She shuddered and rolled over on her side, taking care to keep the doona over her shoulders. The cockatoos in the mountain gums were getting up a screeching chorus outside.

What was she going to tell the team? Shit. Her stomach lurched. What the hell would she say? She should have tried harder—for the team's sake, at least, and Mrs Lemmon's. God, for the whole bloody town. A kid with that much talent—the best coaches would have challenged him, persuaded him to stay.

A kookaburra let out an exuberant *guuguubarra*, the morning air carrying the echo back to her from the escarpment on the other side of the valley.

Oh, for God's sake, why are you comparing yourself with the best coaches? She sighed. *Stay out of it, Jones. Keep your head down, and people will leave you alone. That's the plan. The football is just something to keep you from going crazy, nothing more. Bloody hell, don't start believing the Jesus comments.*

She gazed up at the white meringue of plaster cornice framing the ceiling. Pieces were falling away, exposing the pulpy greyness underneath. She'd planned to paint this room but hadn't got around to it. There was so much that needed doing around the place, and she'd only scratched the surface. She'd made an energetic start, replacing the guttering and painting the kitchen, but then the place started to grow on her. The faded carpet and scuffed timber hallway spoke of the people who had lived here before her. Were they like her? Had they been hiding? Or just keeping to themselves up here in the hills? She had felt the warmth of their company, the glide of their hands on a worn doorknob, a reverberation of voices when she turned on the shower. It had stripped away her modernising zeal.

She threw the covers off and swung her legs out of bed, peeking behind the curtains to observe the whole of the new day. Pocket was bounding after a galah that had landed in the backyard. She'd chosen him as a six-month-old puppy from the Earlville pound. Spiky black fur stuck up higgledy-piggledy along the ridge of his back, white chest dappled with enough flecks of black to make it grey. He had some cattle dog in him, a touch of border collie—a bit of this, a bit of that. It didn't matter, he'd made her smile, and the cottage was different, lighter with his presence.

She padded down the icy floorboards in the hall to the bathroom, fluffy dressing-gown wrapped tightly around her waist. Hot water took ages up here, not like her flat in Sydney. She waited until the last moment to drop her dressing-gown and step in. By the time she'd emerged from the shower, the decision was made—a quick conversation with Clancy couldn't hurt. She would stop at his place before training on Thursday.

CHAPTER 3

Clementine swung the station wagon left off the highway towards Katinga. Her mobile rang. Gerard Holt.

Groan. What did he want? He must have heard about Clancy. Of course he would ring expecting Clementine to miraculously fix it. She pulled over.

'Good morning, Clementine,' he said, in his impeccably charming voice.

'Morning, Gerard. What can I do you for?'

'Just checking you're right for next Wednesday night. Got your speech ready, have you?'

Good, she thought. *He doesn't know.*

'Yes, nothing to worry about, Gerard—I've got it covered.'

'Excellent. Excellent. Now don't forget to acknowledge the sponsors. You've got the list I sent you?'

The list, yes, she had the list, with Clearham Technology & Services at the top, the primary sponsor and biggest employer in town. That's what this call was really about. Gerard's wife, Bernadette, was state manager. Gerard reported to her as Victorian operations manager. The fundraiser was another opportunity to beat the drum for CTS.

'Yes, got the list, thanks, Gerard.'

'Okay, good. Now, don't forget, six-thirty sharp. Be early. We need the supercoach to squeeze a few palms, talk to the punters, get their juices flowing ready for the auction.'

She winced. Talking to the supporters, the sponsors, fielding their questions, sidestepping their inquiries—it was getting more difficult every week. The team's success had become an albatross around her neck. There had been a time when winning was everything. It seemed so long ago now, that old life in Sydney.

'Oh, and another thing,' said Gerard. 'I bumped into Tiny Spencer at the Rotary Club meeting last night. He wants to do a feature on you for the weekend edition. You know Tiny, don't you? The editor of the *Valley News*?'

Clementine searched for a response that would nip this disagreeable suggestion in the bud. Nothing came to her. 'Gerard, I don't think that's a good idea.'

'Don't be silly. Great publicity for the team, for the sponsors, for you.'

Clementine fumbled for an angle. 'Sometimes a bit of mystery is good for business, Gerard—keeps people guessing, sparks their interest.'

Gerard laughed. 'Bullshit. I know you like to keep to yourself, but this is part of the job, I'm afraid. Besides, we haven't had this sort of success in over thirty years. We need to ride this wave, sunshine.' God, she hated it when he called her sunshine. 'I'll give Spencer your number. Gotta go, meeting with Bernadette and Crowcher. See you Wednesday, six-thirty sharp.' He hung up.

Clementine heard the self-importance in his voice as he dropped Crowcher's name. She'd researched CTS, looked up the board and executive team, financial results. Crowcher was the CEO. The company was preparing to list on the stock market, and its executives would clean up on share options. Bernadette probably had a few as Victorian state manager, but she'd need a promotion to senior executive level to really cash in. An executive director position was vacant and Bernadette might have her eye on it.

Clementine pulled back out onto the road and switched the radio on. Country music again. She flicked it off. As she headed towards Katinga Plains, thick grey clouds rolled in across the mountains in the distance. Her uneasiness about the editorial grew as she considered the kind of things Tiny Spencer might ask, the innocuous questions about birthplace and childhood inevitably leading to the prising open of her more recent past.

She ran through the exit plan that she kept at the ready, just in case, this time with a hint of sadness. She would head north to New South Wales, lie low, start learning the guitar maybe, eat takeaways and, most importantly, stay away from football altogether.

\1/

The house at 14 O'Reilly Street was a shoebox of grey concrete blocks, identical to the house next door, and the one next to that and the house over the street and all the houses in that street and the next street. Each one swivelled to face a different direction on its lot—the state of Victoria's take on variety.

The lawn was thick buffalo grass, recently mowed, with a few brown patches of dirt scattered around the straggly gums. She couldn't see a front door, so she followed the empty driveway— two narrow strips of concrete—around the side of the house to a small porch. The edges of the drive crumbled there, as if something heavy (a fridge?) had been dropped over the railing from above.

Clementine climbed the steps, hesitated, then knocked. The door slipped loose from its latch, opening just a crack. She heard voices from the house next door, where five middle-aged men were smoking around an outdoor table.

She knocked again and waited, feeling out of place and uneasy in her white skin.

A yell from next door: 'She's inside. Just go in. She won't hurt you, coach.' She heard sniggering. 'Big bad coach lady got no balls,' one of the men said. 'What that make them boys on the team, eh?' More laughing.

Clementine pushed the door open. 'Hello?' she called. There was no answer. She waited, called out again. Nothing. She stepped in. To her left was a tiny laundry, yellow lino curling in one corner, a basket of neatly folded clothes on top of the machine. Shit. She'd come in the back door. Should she go around to the front? Too late, she thought.

She closed the door behind her and took two steps into the kitchen. The afternoon light filled the room, catching the faded gold specks in the laminate benchtops.

'Hello?' she called again. The kitchen merged into a small dining room. She glanced at the photographs on the chipboard bookshelf behind the dining table. Clancy in his footy gear, Clancy and an elderly woman, Clancy and his bride and a very large group of smiling relatives.

Down the hallway past a door opening into a bedroom. Music was coming from behind a closed door on the left.

She knocked. 'Hello? It's Clementine Jones from the footy club.'

She heard the creak of vinyl, then a voice: 'Come in. But shut the door after you—it's bloody cold out there.'

Clementine entered a small lounge room. A young woman, maybe still a teenager, was pushing herself up out of an armchair. An oversized pink jumper hung loosely over her heavily pregnant tummy. A large bar heater glowed in the corner next to an empty fireplace, and the room smelled of toast.

'You the new coach, then?' said the young woman, looking Clementine up and down.

'That's right. Yes.'

'Yep. I seen you at the footy ground before. I'm Melissa.' She stood with her back arched to balance the weight of her belly. She looked like she was about to smile, like she usually would smile, but then a cloud swept across her face.

'Nice to meet you,' Clementine said. 'I just came around to check in and see how you and Clancy are getting on.'

15

Melissa looked sideways out the window and onto the street. A car with a hole in its exhaust roared past. 'He's not here. Left an hour ago. Probably won't be back till tonight.' She flicked a strand of hair from her face and looked at Clementine defiantly.

'Oh, okay. I'm sorry to have bothered you. Clancy tells me you're due soon.'

Melissa nodded. 'Yep. Feels like I'm about to pop a big football outta here, a big football filled with lead.' Clementine could tell this would ordinarily have been delivered as a joke, but Melissa seemed guarded.

The speech Clementine had prepared tumbled out in a rush: 'Melissa, I think it's great Clancy is committed to being there for you, but I was really sorry when he quit the team. I was just hoping we could talk about some way he could still play? There's only two more games and then the finals. I thought if we had someone there as a driver at every game, ready to go, Clancy could be off the field and to the hospital in thirty minutes.'

The words hung in the air, misshapen, off the mark somehow. Melissa was looking at her, confused.'Whaddya talking about? I don't need him,' she scoffed. 'I got me aunties and me cousin Tash across the road. Mum's in the next block over. It's not like I'm on me own.'

'But he told me you needed him with you. Your first baby and all. Anyone would be nervous.'

Melissa frowned and crossed her arms over her chest. Her belly bulged accusingly at Clementine. 'You whitefellas got a nerve, haven't ya?' She spoke slowly, as if Clementine were a child. 'You think I'm weak or somethin'? Think I can't have a baby without someone holding my hand? Let me tell you, my people been havin' babies on this country for thousands of years, you know. Yeah, out here in the cold and in the dark, no lights, no cars, no hospitals, no white sheets, no painkillers, nothin'. Reckon I'm scared of what my mum already did five times?'

Melissa shook her head, her eyes scornful.

Clementine squirmed, desperately wanting to crawl into the empty fireplace and escape via the chimney, but she was stapled to the floor, mystified. Something strange was going on here, something Clancy felt he needed to lie about.

Before she could respond, Melissa said, 'Clancy was so upset when he got home Tuesday night. Told me you kicked him off the team for being late to training.'

What the hell is going on? thought Clementine. 'Why would I do that? Clancy's our best player, and he hasn't been late to training all season.'

'Well, I dunno what you're thinking, but it was nothin' to do with me, and now he's lost his job he's just gunna get in my way. Geez, I wish he *would* go to footy,' she snorted.

'Clancy's lost his job?'

'Thought you would've known. The whole bloody town probably knows by now.' That defiance in her eyes again. 'Stealing. From the warehouse. So some liar said.' She looked away. 'But they don't know my Clancy. Most he ever did was pinch a Mars bar from the corner store. He loved that job. That was our money, for us...' Her voice faltered. 'For the three of us.'

Clementine suddenly felt the stifling heat of the room and a flush rose in her cheeks. She wanted to get out of there, now. 'I'm so sorry, Melissa. I had no idea,' she said. 'What about Clancy's course? He was studying, wasn't he?'

'Yeah. Diploma of fitness. Got a year to go. Dunno if he'll finish it now.'

'Is there anything I can do?' Clementine asked, silently hoping the answer would be no.

'Nope. We can get by. Don't need no one's help.' Melissa reached up and tugged at her thick ponytail.

'All right, then. But it's a hell of a blow. I'm so sorry. Let me know if there's anything I can do—anything at all.' Why did she say that? She wanted to run, get out of there, disappear for good and leave these people to deal with their own shit.

Clementine opened the door and started down the hall. Melissa followed her, one steadying hand on the wall and the other cradling her belly.

Outside, the men next door were talking quietly. Melissa stood on the porch, leaning on the railing. 'What's really going on here, eh?' she called as Clementine walked to her car.

Clementine looked back at her, confused. 'What do you mean?'

Melissa peered down, chin jutting forward. 'You come round, sticking your nose in, making up stories about Clancy. You got somethin' riding on this? Maybe you got somebody else you want on the team? Maybe a white boy?' Her eyes were burning.

Clementine's jaw dropped. 'No. Of course not.'

Suspicion clouded Melissa's eyes. 'You got it in for us or somethin'? Who are you, anyway? Where you from? Turn up here like some hero, take over the footy team. Got some sort of magic spell over those boys, they say. What business you got here in Katinga?'

The voices on the porch next door had stopped. Clementine felt five pairs of eyes burning into her back.

She got in the car, fumbled frantically with the key in the ignition and reversed too fast up the narrow driveway to the street. Stepping on the accelerator, she saw the men next door, all standing now, glaring at her as she sped off.

CHAPTER 4

It was the sound that made her scream. The screech of metal on metal. Then came the image again, a chaotic mash of memory, coloured red and black, and the fresh gleam of white bone winking through pink puffs of flesh.

'You okay in there?'

Still gripping the steering wheel, she turned her head towards the sound. A man was bending over, hands on his knees, looking at her through the car window. His face was tanned with that dry richness that comes from daily exposure to the sun.

Clementine wound down her window, but her voice was stuck, soundless underneath the crush of memories. She nodded.

He rested rough, calloused hands on the window sill.

'Cars'll be fine. Not to worry, eh.'

She switched the engine off, cleared her throat. 'So sorry. I just didn't see you. Are you sure your car's okay?' she said, looking at him vacantly. She'd hit the rear of his van as he'd stopped to give way.

'One corner's a bit smaller than it was a minute ago, but it'll blend in with the rest now.' His grin was tempered, like he didn't want to go to the effort of a full smile, and his three-day growth was dotted with the slightest beginnings of silver.

They were at the intersection where the main road headed back to town from the Plains. It had been a mistake to go to Clancy's place. If she'd just kept her nose out of other people's business this would never have happened.

Clementine reached for her handbag. 'My name's Jones,' she said, holding out her licence.

He stood up and stepped back from the window, ignoring her outstretched hand. 'Yeah, I know who you are.'

A car slowed on the crunchy gravel, pulling up alongside them. An old man leaned across and wound his passenger-side window down. 'You folks all right?'

The man turned to him. 'Yeah, all good, mate. Thanks.'

The old man gave a nod, raised a forefinger from the wheel in acknowledgement and pulled away.

The man walked to the front of Clementine's car in long, easy strides, for all the world looking like nothing at all had happened. She got out and stood up on jelly legs, noticing the writing on the side of his vehicle: *Dempsey's Handyman Van*.

He was inspecting the dent in the front grille near her shattered right headlight. 'Doesn't look too bad, but I reckon you should let me tow you home.'

Clementine joined him at the front of the car. The strong breeze blowing across the road filled her nostrils with the scent of horses in the paddock over the road.

'Oh, I don't think that's necessary. It's fine.'

'The car, maybe,' he said, standing up straight and fixing her with a knowing look. 'What about you, but?'

She assured him she was fine. He nodded and said, 'Mmm,' as if he knew more about her than anyone else on the planet. She looked away at the horses, folding her arms across her chest and squinting in the midday light. She wished she could be like them. All they had to do was eat, nothing more. God, they looked so peaceful in the lush grass.

'Well, I'll be off then,' the man said.

'Hang on, we need to exchange licence details and insurers,' she called after him as he walked off.

'Nah, no need,' he said, climbing into his van and starting the engine. With the slightest nod of his head in her direction, he rolled off up the road, leaving her standing there in the dust.

CHAPTER 5

Clem cupped her hands together in front of her face, puffed a couple of warm breaths onto her chilled fingers. She'd spent some time planning tonight's training session, coming up with a theme and downloading targeted exercises from her favourite coaching sites. She'd also practised how she would deliver the news.

The last of the players were coming out of the sheds, forming a loose cluster in front of her, jostling each other and laughing.

'Come on, hurry up, before we all freeze,' she yelled.

Her stomach tensed. She needed to keep this short, get training started before the boys could start feeling sorry for themselves.

'Okay. We've got the Eels on Saturday, and we know they're going to be tough. Physical as ever around the mids and a well-organised defensive zone at the kick-ins. We can match them physically, but the key to breaking through that zone is the second phase after Devo's kick in—that's what the focus is tonight.'

She had directed their thoughts to the game. Now to slip in the bad news.

'Before we get started, I've got something to tell you—Clancy won't be seeing out the season. Needs to be with his family.'

Stunned looks. An indignant murmuring.

'What the fuck? We're that close to finals!' said the captain, Sellingham.

'We all have to make hard choices sometimes. Clancy's got a baby coming. There's nothing more important than that.'

'Oh, come on, Jonesy, he's our best player! Surely his wife can look after herself?'

What could she say? She'd felt exactly the same. 'Look, I don't like it any more than you do, but you have to respect a man's decisions, right. None of us really knows the situation Clance is in. You think it's been easy for him?' A few heads dropped. 'No, that's right, it would have been bloody agonising. The guy loves his footy.'

A muttering from the back of the group, she just caught the end of it, something like *drinking goon with the rest of 'em*.

'Hey! Cut that shit out,' she snapped, her eyes flashing darkly across the huddle. 'Next man to make a stupid comment like that's doing five extra laps around the oval.' She let the words sink in for a second before resuming. 'Now, I'm bringing Richie Jones up from the reserves.' Richie grinned, the blokes around him slapping his back. 'And Maggot, you're going into the midfield to take Clancy's place. We'll talk about roles in a bit more detail later. Now, off you go, two laps, light jog, and back here for stretches.'

A few of the more enthusiastic in the group set off, the rest following. There was none of the usual chatter and a heaviness in the thunder of their boots as they jogged across the ground. When they'd completed their laps she kept them moving briskly through the stretches and then straight into a series of sprints followed by a complex kicking drill. Keeping their minds focused on the now and away from what lay ahead on the weekend was the only way she could think to help them through.

\\/

As soon as she'd left training that evening the encounter with Melissa flooded back, the syllables hammering inside her head, '*What-biz-ness-you-got-here-in-Kat-ing-a?*'

She'd been unhurt in the accident but everything was on edge, her jaw clamped and neck muscles wound tight, a thumping headache the result. Now, driving up the winding stretch of Makepeace Road through the state forest, she felt a tight little knot of anger forming at the top of her neck. Clancy quits on some false pretext and Melissa accuses her of white bias. It was all so ridiculous.

The thick-forested slopes loomed overhead as she swung the Commodore around the familiar corners. The half-hour drive from town was a pleasant buffer between civilisation and seclusion, and she particularly loved this stretch of dense bush—bracken and white-flowering tea-tree crowding together in the elbow of each bend, jostling for light, stately gums towering above. But tonight, she just couldn't enjoy it.

She pulled up at the front of the cottage and looked out over the valley, still seated in the car. The full moon cast a beautiful creamy light over the paddocks, and Pocket barked his impatient welcome from the backyard. She felt resentful.

Damn Clancy Kennedy. Damn the whole bloody thing.

CHAPTER 6

Clem stood gripping the railing, blue-and-white Cats scarf wrapped tight around her neck and beanie pulled low. Four exhausted bodies sat crumpled behind her on the interchange bench, eighteen more on the field, each of them bewildered, demoralised. The Jeridgalee Eels had built a steady lead over the first three quarters and were running away with it in the last, a four-goal margin ballooning to seven.

There was nothing more she could do. The Cats' structure had fallen away as the defensive effort took its toll and a few of the more volatile players had started yelling at their own teammates, pointing fingers and waving their arms in frustration.

A loyal band of supporters had travelled two hours to be there and stood in loose clusters nearby. They had begun with gusto, yelling encouragement, shouting advice, booing the opponents and howling like fiends at the umpire, but had gradually lost their heart for the fight as the game had shuffled towards its miserable end.

The final siren sounded and the players slunk off the field, the sparse Katinga crowd dutifully forming a cordon along the pathway to the sheds, slapping the sweat-soaked backs of the players as they passed by, clapping with as much spirit as they could muster.

Now, with the sun dropping, the supporters trudged up behind the team and lined the back of the shed, speaking in hushed voices. The players sat on the low timber benches, some slumped with head in hands, others staring straight ahead, jaws hanging slack, beaten.

Big Matthew Torrens was up and pacing in the empty space in front of the benches. He pulled up sharply in front of Clementine as she entered. At six foot six, he towered over her, and he was shaking with anger. 'Clancy's got to come back. You have to get him back.'

The muttered conversations at the back of the shed stopped. She felt the heat of his breath on her face, but she refused to take a step back.

'Sit down, Torrens,' she ordered. He didn't move.

'But he's right,' said Beasley in his high-pitched voice. 'We're not going to make it without Clance.'

Looking across the shed, about twenty of the club's most ardent supporters still remained. She recognised Benny Carmichael, a farmer who'd just lost his wife. Next to him was the entire Flood family. Kelsey, the eldest, was the club's leading goalkicker. His father, Steve, had been unemployed since the mine closed four years ago, as had Kelsey and Kim, the next eldest. The younger two Flood boys were still in school. Right at the back, leaning against the wall, was the man from Dempsey's Handyman Van, arms crossed, looking at her with those dark, deep-set eyes. She couldn't remember seeing him at an away game before.

Every eye in the room was on her. Every one of these people wanted something. She turned a stony gaze back at Torrens, her words slow and deliberate, 'I said *sit down*.'

Torrens did nothing for a moment, then turned and walked with leaden steps to the bench, his rage giving way to despair.

She took a breath and regarded the players. Young Wakely was still slumped but with his head raised, looking at her. Same for Sellingham and Conti, Devo and Maggot Maloney. Beasley was gripping the bench tight as if he might topple off.

'Righto, then, listen up. Some of you boys tried pretty hard today'—her voice bounced lightly around the corrugated-iron shed—'but none of you tried hard enough.' She raised her voice

26

a little louder. 'Who can put up his hand and say to me straight, "I gave everything today"?'

Silence. No hands went up.

'That's right. No one. And you all know you can do better. You all know you've got more to give.' She paused, swept her eyes across the benches. 'But what you need to understand is that you are contenders. And you know what?' she said, her voice building in intensity. 'You are winners. But you will never taste victory if you can't face up to adversity.'

A murmur of agreement came from the supporters at the back of the shed.

'Now you're a man down and you've lost a game. Next week you could be two men down—injury could hit anyone. Premiership clubs rise above it. Premiership clubs don't lie down and die. They fight on.'

A shuffling of boots on the concrete, slumped bodies beginning to raise themselves, eyes turning towards her, the hesitant green shoots of hope.

'Clancy's gone, but you blokes have to keep fighting,' she said. 'Look around you. These people are counting on you. They turn up each week because you've given Katinga a bit of its pride back, and they want to help you make it to the top. You're not just doing this for yourself, or for the team—you're doing it for them, for the town.'

Nods from the back of the room. She stood taller, took a deep breath.

'So. There'll be no more crying over Clancy. I don't even want to hear you mention his name until you hold that trophy in the air and dedicate the win to him.'

The players' heads had lifted, their spines straightening. It was like an electric current going through the bench. From the back of the shed came a spontaneous shout: 'C'arn the Cats!' Another followed, and another, the whole room full of charged voices, shouting encouragement.

She wondered what to say next. She didn't have to, as someone started singing the club song and everyone joined in. The tin walls of the shed rang with the sound. Clementine stood there for a moment, nodded her endorsement, then grabbed her bag and hurried out.

She walked quickly away from the sheds, towards the car park, the fear of letting these people down crushing her chest. She had managed to talk the team around today, but what would she do next time?

A chill evening breeze had kicked up, whipping across the back of her neck. She shivered. Someone was ahead of her—Dempsey, in faded jeans and khaki jacket. As he put the key in the door of his van he looked up, saw her walking to her car. Suddenly self-conscious, she tucked her hair behind her ears.

'You fixed the headlight then,' he said in that gravelly voice.

'Yes, yes. All good. How about yours?' She couldn't see the back of his van from where she stood.

'Not yet.'

'I really should get my insurers to pay for the repairs,' she said, a gust of wind blowing ice-cold into her face.

He snorted dismissively. 'I'm going to the pub for a drink—you could buy me one if you like.' He gave the first full smile she'd seen—like the sun emerging from behind a rocky crag.

She wanted to make an excuse, like she always did. But it was as if the bricks in her carefully constructed wall had loosened a little, like something heavy had slammed into it. The excuse just wouldn't come.

'Okay, if that's the only way you'll let me pay what I owe,' she said, surprising herself.

They had a beer each and a round of chips. His name was Rowan. Rowan Dempsey. He said he'd loved her speech to the team, the way she spoke to the players. He'd played footy himself, but coaches were different then—gruff, uncommunicative, unable to truly reach out to the players except as a barking sergeant major or a mate, nothing in between. Clementine was surprised at how much she appreciated the compliment, felt lighter inside.

He let her pay and gave her another of those smiles when they left. She listened to the country music channel the entire two-hour drive home.

\l/

Clementine hung back behind the counter, a giant vase of beautifully arranged lilies partially shielding her from the secretary, who was organising a flight for Gerard. She finished the call, returned the handset to its cradle and offered up a perfectly crafted smile.

'Hello, how can I help you, Ms Jones?'

'I'd like to see Gerard, please.'

'Hmm, let me see.' She peered at the calendar on the computer screen, her gold necklace hanging free as she leaned forward. 'How about Wednesday at three?'

'Oh no, I meant now, actually.'

'Well, that might be difficult—he's in meetings all day, I'm afraid.'

'Looks like there's no one in there now. I only need ten minutes—it's just something I need to ask him before the fundraiser on Wednesday,' she lied.

'Okay, let me check. Make yourself comfortable there for a moment.' She pointed at a chair in the foyer. Clementine remained standing.

After a string of acquisitions in the nineties, CTS had become the largest agricultural services and equipment firm in Australia. Eschewing Melbourne and the larger regional centre of Earlville, the board had chosen to show its commitment to rural Australia by establishing its Victorian head office at the regional depot in tiny Katinga. It was the biggest development there since the CTS

29

warehouses were first built forty years ago. When the mine closed, CTS became the biggest employer in the region. Strong autumn and winter rains this year had generated a bumper season for agricultural equipment sales up and down the east coast.

The secretary came out and ushered Clementine through the door of Gerard's office. 'Come through, Ms Jones.'

She stepped into the office, taking in the view from the wall of windows on the far side, over the rolling fields to the east. Three armchairs dominated the centre of the room around a small coffee table. Running along the inside wall was a long bureau with a timber-panelled bar fridge. The look was masculine and functional, luxurious enough to convey power but not so much that it would piss off the farming clientele. Gerard was seated in the far corner behind an oversized desk, in a disproportionately tall leather chair, behind him a painting—black geese, flying in a row.

'Clementine, good to see you,' he said, immaculate in a white business shirt and tie. 'Thanks for dropping in. Have a seat.'

She parked her jeans in the chrome chair in front of his desk, crossed her legs and clasped her hands in the same way she used to when she was briefing a partner back in the day—only no denim then, never denim, why did she wear denim?

She dived in. 'Clancy quit the team, and now I hear he's lost his job.'

Gerard grimaced. 'Yes,' he said with an audible sigh, his eyes on the white leather desk pad in front of him.

'Why didn't you tell me?'

He looked up and met her gaze, eyebrows raised. 'You know I can't tell you company business, much less the affairs of individual employees, Clementine.' He had a pained look, as if it were killing him not to be able to share. What he said was true, at least in a legal sense, but coming from Gerard it was bullshit. If he'd wanted her to know, he'd have told her anyway.

'I heard it from Clancy's wife—theft of company stock—so you might as well fill me in on the details.' Her voice sounded more authoritative than she felt, not so rusty after all.

'Oh, I wish I could, but it's really not possible to—'

'Listen, Gerard, I'm just trying to get him back on the team. I'm here on club business, and you're club president. I don't care about CTS or anything going on here. All I want to know is why my best player quit. I'm sure you can tell me without jeopardising any confidentiality obligations.' She had to admit she was enjoying getting back into the groove, that old Sydney swagger.

Gerard pushed back into the depths of the enormous chair. The leather gave a soft hiss. His head was fully reclined as he looked down his nose at her. Power pose, she noted.

'I don't know why he quit the team. Maybe he's too busy looking for a new job, who knows?' He shrugged.

'He told me he was quitting because Melissa needed him—the baby's due in two weeks.'

'Yes, well, I guess he would say that, wouldn't he? He's stolen from the company and lost his job—he's ashamed.'

'So he did steal something then?' Again, she felt the familiar thrill as she gained an inch of ground.

'Clementine, I said I wasn't going to discuss company business, and I meant it.'

Clem decided to ease off, see how much she could tease out by appearing chastened. 'Yes, okay, okay, you're right,' she sighed. 'It's just that it seems so out of character. Apparently he's never stolen before. Why would he start now? Why risk his job with a baby on the way? He's so devoted to his family, and we all know how much he loved his job.'

'I know,' Gerard said. 'I find it odd too. I really don't know why he left, and it's a terrible blow for the rest of the team.' He leaned forward in an avuncular way, his hands clasped on the desk in front of him. 'So this is where you really need to shine, Clementine. Your speech at Jeridgalee, it was inspirational. That's

31

what the team needs now—you've got to focus on the flock, not the lost lamb.'

She stared at his white teeth, mirrored his posture, clasping her hands in front of her. 'That's exactly why I'm doing this, Gerard—for the team. I have to try to win him back. He's so important. I can rally the troops and keep them going, of course, but if I can get Clancy back as well, think of the boost for the finals.'

'Okay, fine. Do what you need to do—but I can't help. You know that. It's not worth my job to stick my neck out.'

She went in for the kill. 'Tell me who reported the theft.'

Gerard gave an exasperated huff. 'I can't help you, Jones.'

Clementine leant over the outrageously large desk. 'Tell me, or I'm on the phone to a lawyer now to get started on an unfair dismissal claim.' Her voice was quiet, calm and confident, but inside she couldn't believe what she was saying. So many months under the radar, and here she was threatening one of the most powerful men in town.

Gerard's jaw locked into a perfect square as he placed his hands palm down on the desk in front of him, his eyes narrowed. 'You really are persistent, aren't you, Jones? I guess that's what makes you such a good coach.' He leaned back, clasping his hands behind his head and puffing out his chest. 'But don't push your luck around here. Small towns don't like overly inquisitive people. We mind our own business, and so should you.'

Clementine reached for her mobile phone and starting scrolling through her contacts. 'Paul Quincy at Quincy & Fleming is a friend of the family,' she lied. 'Let's see if he's got time to see me and Clancy tomorrow.'

A look of fury flashed over Gerard's face as she called her own home number and raised the phone to her ear. 'All right,' he said. 'I'll give you a name, but that has to be the end of it.'

She tapped the 'end call' button. 'Of course, Gerard, I understand.'

'Frank Cranfield,' he said, begrudgingly.

'Who's he?'

'I said I'd give you a name. That's the name.'

Clementine stood up. 'Thank you, Gerard. I really appreciate it.'

'He's a good worker, Frank. Been with us over ten years. Best thing you can do now is help Clancy write a resumé.' She heard him swear under his breath as she walked away. 'Don't go making it any harder for the team, Jones,' he called. 'They're hurting. And I damn well expect you to make sure they get up off the floor and win this bloody thing.' His voice softened. 'After fifty-three years, the whole fucking town does.'

\1/

Clementine walked past the well-kept gardens around the office and across the car park dividing the head office from the warehouse. Gerard's BMW, a few up-market SUVs and a large cluster of hatchbacks gave way abruptly to rows of Holdens, Fords, utilities and off-road four-wheel drives, mud-splattered and dinged.

Gerard had been more helpful than she'd expected. If he'd been her client she would have told him to keep his trap shut. And why had he felt it necessary to tell her that Frank was a good worker, a good man?

Her mobile phone rang—Tiny Spencer from the *Valley News*. 'Sorry, Tiny, I can't make it tomorrow...No, I can't make it any time tomorrow...Well, there doesn't seem to be any rush...How about we aim for next week?...Okay, Tuesday it is.' She hung up, tapped the appointment into the calendar on her phone, fully intending to postpone when the time came.

She walked over to the first of the three hulking sheds that made up the warehouse complex, heading for the small office just inside. Approaching the yawning opening, she could make out an arsenal of enormous equipment—spiralling blade ploughs, giant rakes and brutish-looking tree spears. To her left, a forklift stacked high with a pallet of boxes whirred and spun on its stumpy rear, and two men guided a massive yellow drum swinging weightily from a crane, shouting instructions as it was lowered towards the tray of a flatbed truck.

An enormous '*Safety First!*' sign hung outside the office enclosure, another sign above it proclaiming, '*CTS...Powering the agriculture of the future*'. Inside, at a desk below a large service window, a grey-haired woman wearing an olive cardigan was deftly stamping a stack of dockets, her body completely still apart from the flick of her fingers as she turned the page and the snap of her wrist as she stamped. She looked up as Clem's shadow fell over the desk.

'Can I help you?' she said blandly, peering over the top of her bifocals.

'Yes, thank you. I'd like to see Frank Cranfield, please.'

Behind the woman, in a glass-walled fishbowl of an office, a man sat signing documents. Clementine recognised him as one of the players' fathers. The nameplate on the door caught her eye: *John Wakely, Warehouse Manager*. Ah yes, Todd's father.

Before Clementine could speak, Wakely was up from behind his desk. 'Hello, Miss Jones, good to see you,' he called from inside his office. He was at the door in two long strides and out into the main office area. 'Marjorie, this is Clementine Jones, coach of the footy club,' he said, extending his hand to Clem. 'What brings you here?'

In his beige slacks, and with that grey V-neck woollen jumper over a tightly-packed collar and tie, he reminded Clementine of her father.

'Good morning, Mr Wakely. Sorry to interrupt your day, but I was hoping to have a word if I may.'

'Not at all. Come in—I was just about to get a cuppa. And it's John, by the way.'

He opened the door to the outer office and waved her through.

Marjorie returned to her dockets as Clementine followed Wakely through a door next to his glass office that led to a staff kitchen. There were new vinyl tiles on the floor and a gleaming row of microwave ovens and toasted sandwich makers on the bench. Beyond the kitchen, in the crib room, were two long tables with shiny new chairs neatly huddled around. It was quiet, waiting for smoko to roar into life.

'Bad loss at Jeridgalee last week, but maybe it'll wake the boys up and get them firing for the finals?' He spoke with his back to Clementine as he took two mugs from the cupboard. 'Tea or coffee for you, love?'

'Tea, thanks. White, no sugar.' Wakely hadn't mentioned Clancy's absence, she noticed. Most people were into it in their first breath.

He put tea bags in the mugs, held one under a tap in the sink, pressing a button on top.

'Gee, all mod cons here, then—push-button boiling water. You'll have a barista making lattes soon,' she joked.

'Ha, yes, the place has changed a bit over the last couple of years, that's for sure. All of it's cheap stuff, though. You know— looks good for investors but doesn't hurt the bottom line too much. It's all about the float these days, of course. Got to keep the mob out there happy too.' He nodded his head towards the warehouse as he set the mugs down on the table in the crib room. 'Especially with a brand spanking new ivory tower next door. Don't want any industrial activity making things awkward right before the listing.'

They both pulled up a chair and sat down. 'So what can I help you with, love?' Wakely said.

Clementine took a sip of tea. 'It's Clancy. I'm worried about him.'

He sighed. 'Yes, I'm struggling to make sense of it all, to be honest.' He reached a hand to his spectacles, put them down

35

carefully on the table. 'He seemed fine to me. You know, worked hard, reliable, seemed to get along okay with the rest of the crew here. Never missed a day of work, except for that time a couple of years ago when he broke his wrist. First game of the season. We didn't win a game for ten weeks after that, not until he came back.' He took a sip from his mug.

'What about this stealing business?'

'Lord almighty, I have no idea,' he said, raising his palms heavenward. 'That just came out of the blue, from bloody nowhere.'

'Maybe he needed money for the new bub?'

'Maybe that's it, but I'd be surprised. He told me not so long ago he'd been putting a bit away every week and he'd just given his wife half of it to buy a few things. She bought a cot from the Salvos. They were thrifty like that. I even had a laugh with him, told him once the bub came along he'd be bleeding cash, Melissa wanting a thousand-dollar pram and so on. He just laughed, told me she'd already got one for forty bucks from a garage sale.' He sighed again. 'I remember thinking that's how it was in my day— all about making the money stretch. Should be more of it. But now I guess it turns out Clancy's no different to the next young gun, wanting everything now.' He shook his head ruefully.

'It must've been a shock when he was caught stealing, then.'

'Oh, too right it was. I couldn't believe it. I was away for the long weekend with the grandkids at the time. When I heard, I rang Frank from Melbourne to get him to copy all the CCTV footage. Gets deleted every two days, you see.'

'Frank Cranfield?'

'Yeah, he's the supervisor. He's the one who found the gear in Clancy's car.'

'So, anything interesting on the CCTV tape?'

'Well, that's the problem, you see. I got back on the Tuesday and the warehouse footage was all good, couldn't see anything untoward there, but the car park footage had disappeared. It was supposed to be locked in my drawer, but it's not exactly Fort Knox here—lots of people know where the keys are. Even still, I wasn't too happy with Frank, I can tell you. He should have taken it up to head office for safekeeping.'

'Why wouldn't Frank have put the CCTV tapes somewhere safer?'

'Well, he probably didn't think—it was pretty busy here last week, and with me away, Frank was doing his job as well as mine. Don't be fooled by the fancy boiling water and new decor'—he swept an arm around him—'this is all capex. Only shows on the balance sheet—window-dressing for the unions. But every penny of opex they're all over like Scrooge McDuck, despite the boom this season. Staff costs, all of it hits the bottom line, hurts the sale price.'

A bell clanged loudly from the warehouse. Wakely took a swig from his mug and stood up. 'Smoko,' he announced. 'I better clear out—the boys like to have the place to themselves. Best they let off steam without the boss hanging around.'

Clementine got up and sloshed the remainder of her tea down the sink. 'John, which one's Frank? Do you reckon he'd mind if I spoke to him? I'd love to get Clancy back on the team, even if he's lost his job—might lift his spirits to be around his mates.'

'And ours too, love. Todd was devastated when we lost last week. He said you gave them a spray after the game, though—set them all straight.' He winked at Clementine—one manager to another—and led her back out into the office. 'You know, after Todd left school he never got out of bed before midday, not till this season. Now he's applying for jobs, got a resumé, even managed to get himself an interview for an apprenticeship. I don't know how that'll go, though—he's not the sharpest crayon in the box. But good on you, Miss Jones—they bloody needed a kick up the arse, these blokes. Just 'cos the mine's closed, that's no excuse for healthy young bodies not to be working.'

Standing at the service window, he flicked his head towards

a group of men walking over to the crib room. 'That's Frank, the one with the orange cap.' He stepped out into the warehouse. 'Frank,' he called, beckoning him over.

Cranfield was maybe late forties, big, dark beard, barrel chest, a little fat around the waist. He broke away from the group and headed over to the office, flipping open the flap on his breast pocket, his fingers searching for something.

'Yeah, boss, what's up?' He had a booming voice.

'Frank, this is Clementine Jones, the new coach. She wants to have a chat with you about Clancy. Did you know he'd quit the team?'

Clementine thought she saw something flicker in Frank's eyes as he glanced her way. 'Nope, didn't know that,' he said.

'I can come back after smoko if you like, or after work if that's more convenient,' Clementine said. *Convenient.* Why had she said that? Made her sound like a big-city wanker, seeking an appointment with some government minister.

'Nah, now's good. But you'll need to come outside—I gotta get me smokes, left 'em in me car. Tryin' to make it easier to give up— it's not working, but.' He looked at Wakely. 'How about you bring me a coffee, boss, so's I don't miss out on my break?'

Wakely snorted. 'Cheeky bugger. You wouldn't try that shit on if there wasn't a good-looking woman around. Go on, I'll get Marjorie to bring you one.'

'Thanks, boss,' Frank grinned. 'White with two.'

Wakely stepped back into the office, waving his hand in mock offence.

\\//

Frank Cranfield took another drag on his cigarette and blew out a thin stream of smoke. He was leaning against the back of his new Toyota Hilux, staring across the car park. The conversation had been cordial—Clementine had admired his new car, and they'd exchanged jokes about giving up smoking—but Cranfield was clearly irritated now.

'Listen, lady, all I know is, I saw the stock in his car, right. Three of them, brand new angle grinders and electric drills, in their boxes, sitting on the back seat.' Was he holding something back? She looked for a sign in his face, but there was nothing to see in those dark eyes but his growing impatience.

'Why would he leave them in full view, Frank? It just doesn't add up.'

'How the fuck would I know? 'Scuse the language, love, but I really wouldn't have a clue what was going on his head. He's a young fool from the Plains with a wife and a baby on the way— maybe he just freaked out.'

'Did you see him put the power tools in the car?'

'Nope.' Cranfield took a short, hurried drag on his cigarette, then exhaled, sending the smoke streaming towards her. Rude boofhead, she thought. 'All I did was report what I saw to the boss, okay. The guys in the big chairs make the decisions, not me.'

'So you mean you reported it to Wakely?'

'Wakely was on leave. I spoke with Holt.' Cranfield flung open the door to his car and threw his cigarettes onto the front seat. The passenger-side floor of the sparkling new ute was already buried beneath McDonald's wrappers and beer bottles.

'So you didn't just ring Wakely? You went straight to the top?'

'I spoke to the only manager who was here at the time. Wakely was on leave, for Christ's sake.' He was openly hostile now, not bothering to hide his anger.

'What about the CCTV, then?' she asked. 'Where did the tape go?'

Cranfield threw his cigarette butt on the pavement and ground it savagely beneath his boot. 'If I knew that, it wouldn't be lost, would it, Einstein?'

As he pushed past her, heading for the warehouse, Clementine held out her hand to stop him. He angrily thrust it away, sending her staggering, off balance. What a brute.

Out of the corner of her eye she saw Gerard leaving the office. Cranfield saw him too. Gerard looked across from the other end of the car park. The briefest of glances before he opened the door of his silver BMW. Was there some sort of exchange between the two men? She couldn't tell—she was too far away. Cranfield was halfway across the car park now, still heading for the warehouse. Clementine ran after him.

'Frank, did you give that CCTV footage to Gerard for safe-keeping?'

He stopped, turned around.

She tried again. 'Gerard, he's the manager, he's the one who does the firing, so did he ask to see it?'

Frank's eyebrows were low, and she could see a scowl behind his beard but his voice was calm, measured. 'Yes, he did. So what?'

'You gave him the copy, didn't you?'

'Lady, he can have whatever he damn well wants—he runs the joint.'

'But now it's lost, and you told Wakely somebody stole it.'

'I told Wakely nothing—he wasn't even here.' Gerard's car was rolling out of the driveway and onto the street. 'Look, we're busy here. It's friggin' full on. We can't hire anyone because of the float. They're not replacing Clancy. I don't even have time to take a piss, that's how flat out we are.'

'But you and Gerard talked it over, didn't you? You gave him the copy?'

'I don't recall giving him a copy, no.' He took a step towards her, pulling himself up to his full height. 'Jones, isn't it? Well, you ask a helluva lot of questions, Ms Jones.' He moved in closer. 'But let me ask you something—how would you like it if I started snooping around in your business, digging up things you'd rather forget?'

Clementine gasped, her mind racing to the scene of the accident, the woman's head resting on the steering wheel. Oh God, oh God, what does he know? She felt the asphalt of the car park rising up at the edges, curling in like the corners of a mouldy linoleum floor towards her.

Cranfield bent at the waist, looming over her. 'I had to fucking dob in one of my guys. Yeah, okay, I had no choice—it's my job. But that doesn't make it any easier. Then they sack the poor bugger. How do you think I feel now?'

The warehouse bell clanged and he stormed off. She stood alone in the car park, hands clenched, feet rooted to the ground. For the first time that morning she noticed the ice in the air. A cloud passed across the sky, blocking the sun.

CHAPTER 7

Clementine sat down on the edge of the escarpment. Her home was nestled between two hills, hunched like shoulders around the little cottage. Looking out at this view, she liked to think that perhaps the valley hadn't changed all that much since the first Australians were there, picking their way along well-trodden paths, sitting in that same spot watching the changing hues of the forest below.

Yesterday morning's confrontations flooded into her head again. She'd been carried away with her big-city lawyer act, charging on from Gerard's office to track down Cranfield, putting herself in the line of fire. Cranfield's challenge was, she realised, not a threat after all. But it was close, very close, a warning of sorts. Her escape plan was becoming more detailed now. She could pack up and move on, hire an agent in Earlville to find a tenant for the cottage. She could even save some money from the rent if she lived lean.

She imagined Clancy feeling like his life had only just begun before it started falling apart. She had felt like that—like her entire world had drained away overnight, leaving a brown sludge of sump oil, a stain on the concrete.

But it wasn't just her world...there was a family, a child. She felt the panic creep in, her heart rate rising. She did the exercise in her head, the one the counsellor had taught her, took a few deep breaths.

Pocket arrived back from his scouting mission at a run, tongue hanging out. He skidded to a halt in the gravel on the path, looked up at her and sped off again. She watched him disappear into the scrub.

She gazed out over the view, drinking in the eucalypt greens and the calm of the valley. *Everybody needs one break in life.* That had been her dad's saying. She, of course, had enjoyed every opportunity that growing up white and middle-class could offer. She didn't deserve any more chances. But Clancy did. And Melissa. And their child.

Something was going on. Something dark and hidden that Clancy, a guy who'd given her his all on the footy field, felt he must lie about. Someone had to find out what the hell was going on to turn his life upside down like this. It might as well be someone with as little to lose as she had.

\!/

She dumped her groceries on the passenger's seat and shut the car door, locking it for good measure. Relaxing deeper into the seat, she let out a sigh of relief. Every trip into town these days was an ordeal, everyone wanting to know if the Cats could win without Clancy. She felt like a magician who'd lost her assistant, expected to pull a rabbit from the hat.

The *Valley News* had published its usual Monday morning report on the game. It had been careful not to catastrophise the loss, not to crush the hopes of its readers. Towards the end it had noted, in passing, the fact that there were no Indigenous players in the seniors now, after the loss of Clancy Kennedy, who had left the team for 'personal reasons'.

Clouds were gathering as she drove up Main Street. There'd been more rain overnight and there was more on the way. In Sydney she had undercover parking, took a lift from the basement to her seventh-floor apartment. Rain didn't mean much there: an umbrella between taxi and office, car and coffee shop, taxi and club. Out here it affected everything, everyone. The farmers had been cautious when it first started six weeks ago, then jubilant when it continued. Up at the cottage, the backyard was a series of brown puddles, and the ground around Pocket's kennel had turned into a thick cake-batter sludge. Every time he came through the dog door there'd be another trail of paw-prints to clean up in the kitchen.

Not that it worried her. Nobody on this dry continent would begrudge the farmers rain. The dams were full and the livestock grazed on great pillowed clumps of grass, almost knee-height. CTS had benefited, of course, recording its highest revenues ever as farmers invested in new equipment and serviced the old. A few of the out-of-work miners had picked up jobs there, she'd heard, all as casuals, with many more lining up at Centrelink. She thought of Clancy and Melissa, trying to get by on the dole.

The light was fading. A man was walking out of the hardware shop. She recognised his gait—the long, loping strides of a tall man. Rowan Dempsey from Dempsey's Handyman Van was a slow mover, his hips swinging languidly with each step. She felt something flutter in her stomach, tapped her thumbs on the steering wheel nervously. All the things that needed doing around the cottage began flying into her head. The drip from the shower was slowly getting worse, she could no longer open the kitchen window, and the front door latch had given up the ghost. She'd had to jam the door shut with a wedge of timber. Worst of all, she was pretty sure the stink she could smell when the wind blew from the west was coming from the septic tank.

She jumped out of the car and jogged over.

'Rowan,' she called as she approached. He turned towards the voice. 'Hi,' she said. 'Just saw you walking past and remembered my septic stinks.'

He chuckled.

Shit. Going from awkward to downright embarrassing. 'I mean,

44

I didn't mean you remind me of...Oh, far out...I mean, I thought maybe you could come by, look at a few things need doing around the house.'

'Yeah, no worries,' he said. 'Tomorrow all right?'

CHAPTER 8

He swept up the sawdust from around the front door and then tested the latch, opening and closing the door three times. The sun streamed through each time, and she liked the soft click the door made when it closed. He'd been quick and efficient with the taps and the window, and then he'd told her that the septic tank needed emptying. Regularly. A more embarrassing moment she could not remember.

'There you go. Nice and smooth,' he said. He was in faded dirty jeans again, and a tight T-shirt that bulged across his tanned biceps.

'Thanks. What do I owe you?' she said, looking away.

'Two hundred'll do it,' he said, squatting down to pick up his tools and return them to his battered red toolbox. Pocket tried to get his nose inside it. Rowan shooed him away gently with a grunt.

'Okay, I'll just get my wallet,' she said. Pocket trotted along behind her as she went to the kitchen.

When she came back Rowan was outside, loading his toolbox into the van. He rolled the side door shut and turned to face her as she approached.

'I didn't want to say anything when we were at the pub last week,' he said, reaching for the cigarettes in his top pocket.

'About what?'

'The Clancy thing,' he said, in a way that didn't invite a response. She handed him the cash and waited while he lit up a cigarette.

'Lot of racism in this place, you know.' He stood with one finger cocked over the waistband of his jeans as he blew a long stream of smoke from the side of his mouth. 'Sure, they like 'em to win footy games, but the rest of the time they prefer 'em out of sight, out at the Plains.'

Still not finished, thought Clementine.

'Heard a couple of blokes from the Plains at the pub last night. They'd had a few, got a bit rowdy. They reckon you should've replaced Clancy with some other Indigenous kid from the reserves.'

She rolled her eyes. 'I pick whoever is most suited to the position. Simple as that—doesn't matter what colour they are,' she snapped.

Rowan didn't move, just raised one eyebrow. 'I wouldn't have a clue either way—just thought you oughta know what people are saying.'

'Yeah, well, I get plenty of advice about what I should and shouldn't do. I'm not about to start listening to a few punters with a gutful of beer.'

Rowan shrugged. 'I should get going,' he said, and took out his keys.

As he walked to the front of the van she followed him, not wanting to miss an opportunity to talk to someone who knew people around town. 'Do you know Clancy at all? Do you know anything about why he might have quit the team or lost his job?' she asked.

'Nah, don't know him. Plenty of people I know who wouldn't be sad to see him gone, though. You know he testified, don't you?'

'No. Testified about what?'

'The bashing. He was the only one of the victims to stand up in court and say who was there.'

'Bashing?'

'Yeah, Earlville, a few years back, around the time of that Adam Goodes drama. Bunch of teenagers set upon three blackfellas, beat the shit out of 'em.'

She felt her stomach turn. 'I'd hoped that whole Goodes affair might have changed things for the better,' she said.

'Wishful thinking out here. Just turned up the heat,' he said kicking a large chunk of mud off the rim of the front tyre on the van.

'Anyone convicted?'

'Don't make me laugh,' he snorted. 'They gave each other alibis.' He got into the cab, turned the key in the ignition and hung an elbow out the open window. 'Let me know if you want me to fix that flapping roof on the shed. Might lose it if it blows.' He gave her another of those half-smiles, and with that Rowan Dempsey was off.

\I/

Clementine sipped the cheap bubbles fizzing idly in her glass and looked around the room. The high ceiling of the school gym made it look half-empty, but it was a good turn-up for a country footy club. She had delivered her speech and spent what seemed like an inordinate amount of time cosying up to the eager crowd of sponsors under Gerard's watchful gaze, finally managing to escape to the ladies', where she'd sat in a cubicle for as long as she thought she could get away with it. Emerging some fifteen minutes later, she'd sat herself in the shadows at an empty corner table, wondering if it would be bad form to leave before ten o'clock.

The band from Earlville was well into 'Shake a Tail Feather' and a dozen players were gyrating beneath the garish lights with their dates. Torrens sat in the far corner, his legs spread wide and a young woman in red draped around his neck. A large group of parents and relatives were gathered around a few tables in the centre of the room, half-empty jugs of beer in front of them, talking loudly over the music as two waiters (high school students?) cleared away plates smeared with cheesecake remains. At another table, to Clementine's right, were the families of the six Indigenous players on the reserves team.

Towards the back of the room stood a cluster of men in suits and women in expensive evening gowns: Gerard telling a story, John Wakely to his right, Tiny Spencer to his left with a young woman standing close by his elbow—surely not his wife?—and next to her the boss from the IGA supermarket—what was his name? Nicholls? Yes, Bob Nicholls—and, presumably, Mrs Nicholls, in a low-cut green dress. Directly opposite Gerard was his wife, Bernadette Holt, tall, slender and regal in black, with a silver necklace around her long neck.

Clem had spoken with her earlier in the night, the first opportunity they'd had for a real conversation other than small talk at a few football games and that time Clem had been summoned to present to a club committee meeting at the Holts' house. Tonight Bernadette had made an effort to engage, asking insightful questions about Clementine's strategy in the lead-up to the finals. They had moved on to discuss Clancy's departure from the team. Bernadette was adamant that no individual was indispensable, that an outflow of talent would create a vacuum for others to fill. She believed women in leadership roles had a knack for finding talent and allowing it to flourish.

This was the first and only mention of gender throughout the conversation. It seemed it was just as irrelevant to Bernadette as it had been to Clementine and yet, in the presence of this powerful woman, she had felt a wave of energy, a feeling of camaraderie, like she wasn't alone in this caper—the leader of an organisation jam-packed with men.

It was at that point that Bernadette leaned forward, touched Clementine on the arm and said, 'You know sharks can only swim forward, don't you? We're sharks, Clementine, you and I. We swim forward, every day, and we don't stop for anything.'

Clem took this as an invitation to ask something more personal.

'So do you find it difficult, being a woman in a senior role?'

Bernadette thought about it for a moment. 'In Sydney, with my peers, definitely. A room full of male egos. Katinga's different. I guess when you hold the power to fire someone, they tend to be a tad more respectful. I think half the time here, though, people are just plain flabbergasted.' She laughed, waving her champagne glass. 'I mean, a woman being the boss of her husband—my God!'

Clem laughed along. 'Yes, well, there's that! A very odd state of affairs to have husbands obeying their wives.'

Bernadette's laughter died away. She took a swig from her glass, swallowed grimly. 'Odd. Yes. The bloody odd couple. That's us.'

Clem was taken aback. She'd only just met the woman. 'I expect it must be difficult,' she said, tentatively. 'Home and work. Marriage and business...never getting a break from each other.'

A visible stiffening in Bernadette's jaw. The corners of her mouth turned down, then settled in a sour flat line. 'Never undervalue convenience and appearances, Ms Jones,' she said coldly.

Clem thought it best to change the subject. 'So tell me about the public listing,' she said. 'That must be taking up all your time just now.' Bernadette seemed relieved to move on, opening up about the challenges in the lead-up to the CTS listing—keeping staff committed, dealing with union pressures and meeting the demands of head office in Sydney for higher revenues and lower costs, so important for the sale price.

Clementine decided to risk another question. 'So are you thinking of taking on the executive director role in Sydney?'

A slight flush rose in Bernadette's cheeks. 'Well, I'm surprised you're following the happenings at CTS so closely,' she said, 'but that reminds me—I was wondering if you'd be interested in a role here at the Victorian office? We need smart women like you, and I'm all for giving other women a hand up.'

Bernadette's deft but obvious deflection of the question was enough. There was no doubt she was in the hunt for the job, a shark chasing a very lucrative bait.

\1/

It was after ten-thirty, and a few people had started to shuffle out the doors, which were now propped wide open, the cold rushing in like a late guest. Good, she thought, safe for her to slip away as well.

Her eyes swept the room. Every person here was so much a part of this town, so much more a part of it than Clementine. What did they know about Clancy? Someone here must be hiding something—but who? Whose secrets was Clancy protecting?

On the other side of the room Bernadette was deep in conversation with Mr Nicholls.

She turned her gaze to Wakely. Why hadn't he made more effort to secure the CCTV footage? And even more concerning, why hadn't he investigated further? He'd treated it like it was just one of those things, and yet a young man's livelihood was on the line. He looked trim and neat in his somewhat dated double-breasted suit and waistcoat, holding a red wine and listening intently to Gerard telling a longwinded story, nodding and chuckling at the right moments.

And Gerard, in his tuxedo with his perfect hair? Well, his resistance to her inquiries, though appropriate in a legal sense, felt unnatural, like a coat he seemed unused to wearing. She had a sense too that there might have been something in that look he'd given Cranfield across the car park. But then again, maybe she was reading too much into things.

She moved towards her table to collect her handbag. Jenny Rodham turned to greet her.

'Fine speech tonight, my lady. Dollars are rolling in. Never seen so many pledges in all my time as treasurer, and Bob Nicholls from the IGA just told me he's going to give a grand for every man of the match to the end of the season. A grand! I remember when he used to give a box of breakfast cereal.' Her neat bob above her shoulders bounced with the beat of her laughter.

Clem smiled. 'That might be just the lift the boys need for the finals.' She tried to sound enthusiastic, but Bob Nicholls' generosity was just another reminder of how much the team's success meant to the town—and the disappointment they'd feel if she failed them. It was her job to make this money mean something.

'Ah, come on, Clem. Don't get scared on us now.'

How did Jen know? Am I that transparent? thought Clem. 'Yeah, yeah, I know—you're counting on me too, right?' she said.

'Actually I'm not, you know.'

Clem raised an eyebrow.

'You've already changed lives around here, Clementine Jones, and all I'm asking is that you see out the season. Don't go shooting through.' God, it was as if this woman knew her thoughts. Clementine hoped she didn't look too stunned.

'Just stick around to the end, win or lose,' Jen said. 'You can tell us we won anyway, you know—the journey, the struggle, all that jazz. Trophy or no trophy, that's all we need you to do, honey.'

For the second time that evening, Clementine felt the strength of the women of Katinga, a warmth and solidarity she realised she'd been missing since she left the firm.

'By the way,' Jen said, 'you're coming to our house for dinner, madam. No more putting it off—you can't hole up there in the hills on your own forever. We're free every night this week—pick one.' Clem's mum had bossed her like this. There was something comforting about it.

'Yeah, thanks. I'll think about it,' Clem mumbled, and changed the subject. 'You know, I met Bernadette tonight. I mean, I've met her before, but I'd never really spoken with her, not properly. Amazing woman. But do you think it's strange she's with Gerard?'

'Ha! Not at all. Gerard's a known social climber. And he's probably the most ambitious man I know, but geez, he puts in, Clem. And you need that sort of energy in a club president. God knows nothing happens otherwise. Bloody handy he's married to the boss lady too. You know the sponsorship deal with CTS is seventy per cent of our revenue?'

'Really? Impressive,' said Clem. Jen was a talker, and one of those locals who seemed to know everyone.

'Gerard's having a great night, eh?' Clem flicked her head towards him just as he was landing another funny line, Wakely bursting into a round of laughter at his elbow. 'Seems like he and John Wakely get on well.'

'Oh, yes, they go back a while. Wakely used to be club president, but it was him who got Gerard on board. Thought he might be able to bring in more sponsorship. Well, he was spot on there!' Jen took another swig from her wineglass. She'd obviously had a few drinks and was even chattier than usual. Clem decided to spring something from left field, see what turned up.

'And what about Frank Cranfield, Gerard's mate? I don't see him around much. What's his caper?'

Jen's smile disappeared and her face set solid. 'Cranfield? A mate?' she asked, incredulous.

'They're not friends, then?'

There was a momentary pause as Jenny appeared to hold herself back. 'No, Clem, Gerard is not mates with Cranfield. For one, Gerard doesn't mix with the plebs.' Her tone was sharp, bitter. 'And certainly not with Frank Cranfield.'

'Oh, well—I guess I had that wrong,' said Clem. The band were still playing, and the drummer started on a deafening solo. She turned to watch the frenzied young man, hair flying, sticks a blur, the beat chaotic for a moment, then blending back into the rhythm of the song.

Jen turned back to Clementine. 'You're curious all of a sudden.

What's got you interested in Gerard?'

'Oh, nothing specific, just that—' She felt a shove in her back and almost fell forward onto Jenny.

'Oh, geez. Sorry, Jonesy. Tripped on that cable. Sorry.' It was Todd Wakely who'd sent her flying. He was looking particularly awkward in a pair of navy trousers a size too small for him, his tie skewed to the left like a noose.

'You had too much to drink, Wakely?' Clementine shot him an accusing look.

'No, Jonesy. No way. Just the three beers, like you said. I swear. Look'—he pointed to a loop of power cable arching up from the floor—'I got my toe stuck under there.'

'Well, watch where you put your clumsy feet, all right,' she said, smoothing down her dress. 'Anyway, I'm off. Good night, Jen,' she said, 'and thanks for your support.' She turned to leave, but Wakely stepped in front of her.

'I've been meaning to speak to you, Jonesy,' he said.

The band was getting louder again. She raised her voice. 'Well, I'm here, man. Let her rip.'

Todd stood up taller, squared his shoulders. 'It's about Clancy. I just wanted to say, because you're not from round here and all, well, me and most of the rest of the blokes, we're not worried or anything about him not being on the team.'

'Oh, really. Well, that's good.' She was alert, wondering what might be behind this unsolicited reassurance.

'Yeah, the less darkies the better.'

He'd shouted these words above the sound of the band. She glanced sideways, but it seemed only she had heard. Jen had already moved away to join the big group in the centre of the room. Was Wakely joking? Clementine looked at the young man, searching for some sign of humour in his eyes, but saw only an earnest intensity.

He saw the look of confusion on her face and rushed on, thinking he hadn't explained himself properly. 'I mean they run

54

hot and cold, you never know if they're going to show up or not—'

'Shut up, Wakely,' she said urgently. 'Shut the fuck up. I don't want to hear this. It's not true. In fact it's the biggest load of bullshit I've ever heard. Clancy was our best player and you know it.'

A frown swept across Wakely's brow.

Clementine swallowed and gripped the handbag strap on her shoulder. Todd was the stand-out for most improved this year. If you made him feel important, pumped him up to believe in himself, he was a line-breaking defender, clever at covering his opponent but able to create the play up forward.

She didn't want a scene with this young buck, not here, so she decided to let it slide, turn it into a coaching opportunity, 'Hey, I hear you've stepped up your training at home during the week. Well done. I need you to run all day, yeah?'

He relaxed his stance slightly. 'Yep, that's what I'm aiming for, coach.'

'The more you run at home, the easier it'll be to break through in the final quarter. Your opponent just won't have the fuel in the tank. So good work, Wakely.' She patted his shoulder. 'Keep it up. I want to see you bursting into the midfield with the ball under your arm and your man left standing there with a stupid look on his face.'

Todd had a smile from ear to ear, so proud he looked like he might burst as she turned to walk away.

The band started up the first of the slow songs, 'My Island Home', and Clementine felt a hot rush of shame at how she'd handled the situation. She thought of Clancy, working, studying for his future, and on the field—the way he dominated the midfield, his grace and precision. He should be here tonight, with Melissa. Her thoughts ran to their neat home, the worn carpet and the forty-dollar pram; to Melissa's pride in the strength of the women of her family through the ages, the certainty of support from her community. The high school gym suddenly felt smaller, the band out of tune, and indigestion from the cheap bubbly formed an uncomfortable plug of pain in her chest.

Damn Todd Wakely, damn this town and damn its small-minded people. She strode off towards the open door. She would swim forward, all right—she'd finish the season and then tell the whole lot of them what she thought of their racist shit. *I may have denied you in this moment, Clancy Kennedy, but I am not giving up on you, you and your secret, whatever it is.*

CHAPTER 9

She had rung Rowan to see if he could work on the shed roof this week. He said he could make a start next Tuesday. She was bursting to know more about Frank Cranfield. Jen's reaction suggested there was something to find out. She decided to stick a toe in the water with Rowan while she had him on the phone.

'Don't happen to know a bloke called Frank Cranfield, do you?'

'Cranfield? Whaddya wanna know about him?'

'I bumped into him in town, never met him before. Just seemed a bit of an oddball, a bit strange. You've lived here a long time...I thought you might know him.'

Rowan cleared his throat. She waited, sensing he would fill the silence if she kept quiet and didn't push.

'I dunno what he does for a crust now, but he was a chippie, worked for himself. Had a car accident. Took to drinking pretty heavy. Lost his business.'

She heard him take a drag on a cigarette and the soft pop of his lips releasing the smoke.

'It was a bad one. A bloke called Steve Mason was killed,' he said.

Mason. Where had she heard that name before? That's right, the Masons owned a big dairy farm north of Katinga. Harry Mason, Jenny's nephew, had played on the wing for the first few games before she'd dropped him back to the reserves.

'Oh, yes. Jenny Rodham was a Mason, wasn't she?'

'She might've been. There were lots of Masons. Steve was the youngest. Jack runs the property now.' He paused again, and she waited. 'Yeah, I think there was a sister, Jenny. Works in the bank, married Trev Rodham.' Another pause. 'Steve was dead in the driver's seat. Family claimed Frank was driving, had too much to drink, put Steve in the driver's seat to cover it up.' There was no emotion in his voice, no blame. Clearly Rowan was not a willing participant in the shift and grind of tensions and history underpinning life in this small town.

Clem sensed that Rowan was nearing the boundary where harmless chat tipped over into an emotional no-man's-land, a place he did not care to visit. She ignored it, pushed on.

'So was he ever charged?'

'Nah.'

'Must have been a terrible time for everyone.' Emotion again, risky. Rowan gave a noncommittal grunt. *Okay, too far*, she thought. *Back to the facts.* 'And where's he at now?'

'Well, I know he drinks a helluva lot more these days, now his wife and kids have shot through. There were a lot of 'em, too.'

'Kids, you mean?'

'Yeah. Bloody house full of rug rats. I reckon what he doesn't drink goes on child support.'

Clem immediately thought of Cranfield's shiny new ute.

\\/

Clementine shoved the last piece of roast lamb into her mouth. *Damn, this woman can cook*, she thought. And she'd never been partial to gravy, but Trev was clearly some sort of culinary genius.

He was leaning across from his chair at the dining table, pointing his fork at the TV. 'So you see how the whole team pushes back in defence, and you get a kind of wall across halfback?' The Cats were due to play the Bursley Tigers next week and Trev had driven all the way, two hours, to Bursley to record the Tigers' last game. It was amazing what these Katinga folk would do to support their team.

'Yeah, I see it. But look how slow they're getting in the last ten minutes of the quarter. They don't have the fitness to keep it up for the full twenty-five minutes. That's when we'll sting them. Play steady and tight in the first part of each quarter, stick to our zones, not run ourselves ragged chasing the man, use the width of the ground. Then we bust them open, straight up the corridor, run like mad, two and three at a time taking the ball up.' She'd had too much red wine, spouting off like a garden hose.

Clem scooped the last forkful of crispy-skinned roast potatoes into her mouth and looked around the room. It was just like she'd imagined it would be, jammed full of dated furniture, tacky ornaments on lacy doilies and crocheted cushion covers. Jen had told her about her mum and grandmother, how she couldn't bear to part with all their things after they'd passed. The kitchen had recently been renovated, though, with Miele appliances and lots of stainless steel—the sort of clash you'd never see in Potts Point. Her mind wandered back to her flat on the seventh floor with its minimalist style, everything white other than the pistachio green carpet in the bedrooms, so soft and deep beneath her bare feet.

Trev turned off the video as Jen took the empty plates into the kitchen. He brought the open bottle of red over from the sideboard, topping up Jen's glass and hovering over Clem's. She waved him away and poured herself a water from the jug in the centre of the table.

'Don't mind me, folks, but I've got to put my feet up.' Jen sank into a brown suede armchair and pressed a button on the side. The chair reclined, raising her chubby legs up to horizontal. She kicked off her shoes with a loud sigh and let them fall to the floor. Trev had picked up the newspaper and was reading the back page through the bottom of his bifocals.

Clem sat opposite Jen in a vintage armchair covered in a faded pink floral fabric. On the walls around the room were a collection of photographs. On the shelf beside her was a large, wooden-framed picture of a group of teenagers in a paddock, clustered around a tractor, the girls in hand-knitted jumpers and 1980s-style high-waisted jeans—Jen and her siblings—next to it, in a smaller frame, another of a young man, probably Steve, the youngest brother. Then Jen's two kids in their school uniforms, all gap-toothed smiles and freckles, a wedding photo from the seventies—the men in frilly shirts, hair ballooning out over their ears, a flower girl in the front who may have been Jen—and a portrait of two women with Jen's eyes—her nan in the purple pillbox hat and her mum in a wedding gown?

It was so long since she'd spoken to her own family. Clementine had emailed her parents after she got out, just to let them know she was safe and she was going to start again somewhere. They didn't even know where she was. It hurt to think about it as she sat there, in someone else's home, with the warm currents of their family history sloshing around the edges of the room, lapping gently around her feet.

She closed her eyes for a second, took a deep breath in. Time to get down to business.

'So, Jen, tell me, how long have you been club treasurer?' she said, easing into the conversation.

'Oh gawd, too bloody long. Must be coming up to ten years next year.'

'That's dedication. And how many of those with Gerard as president?'

'Almost two years now. This is his second season,' Jen eased the angle of the backrest down a little, closed her eyes. Her plump form seemed to be completely at one with the chocolate-brown suede.

'He's not a local, is he?'

60

'No, city boy.' Her eyes snapped open. 'What's this? Twenty questions or something?'

'I just find the Holts intriguing—you know—El Presidente and the first lady of Katinga.'

Jen laughed. 'I'll do you a deal,' she said. 'I'll tell you about the Holts and anyone else you'd like to know about in this town—but only if you'll tell me about Clementine Jones.'

'I guess that's only fair,' she said. She'd planned for this eventuality, and after downing two glasses of red, it felt like it was now or never.

Jen smiled like the cat who'd got the cream, and launched forth.

'Well, Bernadette was a Walker. Wealthy squatters, been in this country for generations. They own a couple of sheep properties and got into property development—shopping centres and unit blocks, that sort of thing—and a fancy homestead out west of Echuca. When the GFC arrived, they took a hit, I heard, sold off a fair bit of property.

'So anyway, Bernadette went to university in Melbourne—got her degree and a fiancé, Gerard. I don't know much about his background, but I've always had the impression that marrying into the Walker family was a healthy step up for him.'

Clem nodded, not that Jen needed any encouragement.

'They have a son, Nathan, but no one ever sees him anymore. He tried to commit suicide a few years ago. It was during the drought, and we'd had a bad run of that sort of thing—mostly farmers blowing their brains out. Dreadful times.' Jenny shook her head sadly. 'Apparently Nathan's an addict. Shocking, that ice stuff, truly shocking,' she said. 'Or was it heroin? Thank God our two aren't into any of that drug culture, isn't that right, love?'

'Oh my word, love, my word,' said Trev, his voice gentle, like purring. He was doing the crossword now.

Clem felt her mouth drying out as the Holts' hidden pain spread across the room. She picked up her glass. 'Just getting another

61

water, Jen—would you like one?'

'Oh God no, bring me that wine bottle, Jones—I'm not driving tonight!'

Jen's laughter followed her to the kitchen. She filled her glass and came back out to the dining room, picked up the wine bottle and refilled Trev's and Jen's glasses before settling herself into the old armchair.

'Thank you, my dear, and good health to us all!' Jen raised her glass and took a sip. 'So here's what I know about Gerard. He moved here with Bernadette when she got the state manager job about five years ago. He's very well connected, so I believe, and I reckon he's played a big part in Bernadette's success. Workaholic, does a lot for the community too. Not so sure about their marriage, though. I've heard a few things over the years...'

'Oh, really?'

'Just gossip, I'm sure. But Bernadette, so I hear, has a roving eye,' said Jen, giving Clem a conspiratorial wink. She hardly took a breath before rattling on. 'So anyway, Bernadette started with CTS straight out of university, worked her way up, got Gerard a job there at some stage. I believe she's got her eye on one of the top jobs at head office in Sydney. They say she could be CEO one day, and a good thing too—God knows we need more women at the top in this world, especially people like Bernadette. I've seen her in action at some of the Women in Business functions in Earlville, and she's amazing—a natural leader. A lot of the young women look up to her—probably the blokes too, for that matter—and the numbers the Victorian division has produced over the last couple of years are phenomenal. She'd be turning heads at head office, that's for sure—in more ways than one, I'd bet.' She chuckled to herself.

'It's good for Katinga too,' Jen said. 'Not just our profile, but when CTS are doing well there's more jobs. It's taking a while to absorb the job losses at the mine, but people are gradually getting work on the farms or in the other businesses around town that feed off CTS. I mean, the rains have helped her financial results, that's true, but all of the eastern states have had decent rain these last two years too and our Bernadette is still kicking butt compared to New South Wales and Queensland. Oh, and of course every time a farmer wants to invest something back into the farm—a new tractor, new fencing or whatever—well, they borrow, don't they! And who doesn't love to see the bank doing well, hey?'

Jen laughed so hard she snorted red wine out her nose. Clem couldn't help but laugh too. Trev just gave a wry smile and kept scratching away at the crossword puzzle, apparently used to Jen cracking herself up with her own jokes.

'Ah, Jen,' said Clem. 'I've been needing a good laugh, what with the Clancy thing and everything,' she sighed. 'Speaking of Clancy—do you know much about him?' she asked, casually—hoping Jen would continue on.

'No, I don't know much about the Plains mob. They tend to stick to themselves, and not many of them apply for bank loans.'

'And the Wakelys—what's their story?'

'Hey, hang on a minute, girl, my turn to ask you a question,' Jen snapped.

'No way. You have to answer all mine first. You should have read the small print before you accepted the deal.' Clem didn't have a sister but she was sure this was the silly banter they would have enjoyed. It was different with her brother. He was so much younger, she'd sort of protected him and mothered him all those years really—it got in the way of just letting it all hang out.

'Bloody hell, are you a lawyer or something? Sheesh.'

Clem's heart skipped a beat, but she needn't have worried. Jen took a swig of her wine and put it down on the table by her elbow. 'Well, here you go, but this isn't for free—it's your turn after this.' She shook her finger at Clementine. She clearly had no idea how close she'd come to the truth.

'Yes, yes, of course—just get on with it, will you?' Clem said, curling her legs up underneath her. The odd clutter of furniture felt warm, like a nest formed by a line of women through the generations, each reaching their arms out and around her. She took a deep draught of the water to wake herself up—she must be on her guard, her turn was coming up soon.

'So, the Wakelys,' Jen said. 'Well, Johnno Wakely's worked his whole life at CTS. Married to Janine for thirty years before she passed. Only three years ago now. Very sad. Brain tumour. And young Todd, he's been a bit lost since he lost his mum. He's an only child. They'd tried for years before they had him. IVF and all. Then, after Janine died, Todd started hanging around with a pretty unsavoury crowd from Earlville. I'm not sure whether he's still involved with them, but he was part of a nasty incident a couple of years back.'

'The attack on the boys from the Plains?' Clem asked.

'Yeah, that's right. Todd and a few others were charged with assault—had to go to court. They got off, but it was a bad time around here. Really awful. A lot of tension, bad blood. I don't think it's ever really gone away, to be honest, just simmering in the background.'

Jen reached for the glass of wine. 'So, my lady, your turn. Shall we start with where you grew up?'

Clementine sat up a little straighter. *Well, here goes: the price of knowing is to be known.* She rested her glass on the shelf beside the photo of the Mason siblings and started on the make-believe tale she'd been crafting all day, ready for this moment.

She thought of the little house in western Sydney, and her bedroom, the same room she'd slept in for twenty-two years before she left for her inner-city corporate life. 'Well, nowhere in particular, really. We moved around a lot. Dad was in the air force. Mostly Queensland, I suppose you'd say. Townsville, then Oakey, west of Brisbane, back to Townsville, Williamtown near

Newcastle for a short bit, then up to Darwin, and then Oakey again.'

It felt easy, the lies crawling out like cockroaches from behind a fridge.

'So where's the family now?'

'Mum and Dad died a while back.' She sent a silent prayer into the night: *So, so sorry, Mum and Dad*. 'I've got a brother in Sydney. That's it really.' This was the truth, the only truth she had spoken so far.

'You see him much?' Jen was letting her ease into her story, leaving condolences for her lost parents for some other time.

'Nah, we're not close. We ring each other on Christmas Day—that's about it.' *Joshua, her beautiful Josh*. It couldn't get much worse from here—no longer even able to acknowledge the people she loved.

'Hmm, so what brought you to Katinga, Clem?' Jen said, trying to keep things upbeat.

Clementine was ready for this question, had practised her casual tone all afternoon. 'I had a shit job in Sydney, working my arse off as a paralegal at a city law firm. The partners were bullies, the pay was crap and I'd had enough, so I just up and left.'

'Aha! I knew it, from paralegal to famed football coach—it's all starting to fit together now!'

'Sarcasm is very unbecoming on you, Jen. I'll have you know I'm the two-time grand-final-winning coach of the Easton Bay under-sixteens,' she declared.

'So is that it? That's all your experience?'

'Born into the game, Jen, the whole family lived and breathed it. I was a pretty handy player myself until work got in the way. Anyway, you're on the committee, you tell me—was I the only applicant?'

Clem remembered when she'd posted the application—it had been a particularly boring day, even for this slow-moving life in the country. It was little more than something to do to pass the time—she hadn't come close to thinking she might actually get the job.

'Well, I wasn't part of the selection process, but…ahem,' said Jen, clearing her throat. 'Yes, you were it. Turnover's been pretty high these last ten years. Lord, the last guy was a complete disaster— hip flask of Jim Beam at every training session!' she laughed.

'What's wrong with that?' said Clem with mock indignation.

'Nothing, nothing at all!' Overcome with laughter, Jen could hardly get the words out. 'Good lord, there were games I wished I had a whole bottle!'

They chatted about the series of coaches that had passed through the Katinga Cats' revolving door until finally Clem saw an opportunity to excuse herself.

'Well, Mrs Rodham, it's almost eleven, and I think that's enough questions for one evening.'

'Fair enough, as long as there'll be a part two to the life and times of Clem Jones? You haven't tried Trev's lasagne yet.'

'It takes a lot to coax me from my hilltop lair.' Clem eased her way out of the chair and picked up her bag. 'But if Trev's lasagne is anything like his gravy, then maybe I will,' she lied.

CHAPTER 10

The magnificence of the mountain forest on the drive home from the game felt all the sweeter after the team's victory. Only three points in it, wobbly without Clancy and against a mediocre team in the Tigers, but a win was a win. Trev had given her a full-on bear hug when the siren sounded. She'd mentioned him in her post-game speech: 'And to Trev Rodham, genius-of-the-week award. Wonder why our strategy worked up the corridor at the back end of each quarter? Thank Trev, who drove all the way to watch the Tigers and record their game last week. Bloody legend, Trev.' Everyone had cheered, and Trev, standing there in his camel-coloured duffel coat, looked as chuffed as if he'd just invented the paperclip.

The players had been exuberant. The tiny seed of hope they'd held in their chests had sprouted leaves. At the end of the game, the sheds were crammed with people as they'd belted out the team song. Mrs Lemmon had held Clem's hand the whole way through, chirping away in her quavering little soprano.

The win had propelled the Cats to third on the ladder with still one more week of the home-and-away season before the finals— time enough to get Clancy back.

A wombat trundled across the road up ahead, not even bothering to speed up in the headlights. She slowed as its round bottom disappeared into the undergrowth, then planted her foot down hard on the last of the straight stretches before the climb up Katinga Hill. A rabbit dashed out from the right, leaping into the headlights. She gasped but held the wheel firm, kept driving straight. They said swerving was dangerous. The bump was hardly noticeable. She checked the rear-view mirror—little more than a smudge on the road in her tail-lights. She was thankful—a quick death, no need to stop and make sure of it. Something else in the mirror. A glimpse of headlights at the start of the long straight stretch behind her. She checked again—definitely headlights. It was rare to see any cars on this road, especially at this time of night. Must be her neighbour, Jim, from the sheep property next door.

She relaxed into the driving, felt the gentle roll of the car as it climbed around the sharp bends, the dark weight of the huge eucalypts forming an impenetrable canopy overhead. Then out into the rolling paddocks and the starry night again, before a sharp right onto her dirt driveway. As she walked across the path to the front door, she stopped to look up. She would never get over how thick the Milky Way was out here in the country. Thousands of faint, distant stars, joining together in a creamy glow, and the closer ones big and bright—like a smear of spangled butter across the sky.

She could hear Pocket going off in the backyard—his usual welcome. As she closed the front door he rushed inside and started an excited circling around her feet, sniffing the meat pie she'd trodden in at half-time.

She poured herself a half-nip of the cheap Scotch in the pantry and took Pocket outside to his kennel for the night. He strolled out, then suddenly stopped in his tracks, tail straight up in the air, looking right, growling. Something moved in the bushes along the fence.

'It's just a fox, crankypants. Go on, off you go.'

Pocket paused, the fur on his neck still bristling, then trotted over to his kennel, his eyes trained on the bushes, but all was dark and silent.

She locked the back door and, with the Scotch warming her stomach, headed for bed. She did not hear Pocket barking in the backyard about half an hour later.

She found the note the next day, pinned to the front door, made up of letters cut from the *Valley News* glued onto a grubby manila folder:

No more questions BITCH One and only Warning before we do some real Damage up here

CHAPTER 11

Nine o'clock in the morning and the sun had disappeared again behind thick tufts of cloud. Clementine punched the number into the phone and leaned forward at the dining table, a pen, a notepad and an open laptop in front of her. The note had consumed her thoughts all of yesterday and she'd agonised over its source. Someone who knew she'd been asking questions. Someone who didn't want her to know about Clancy. Cranfield? Gerard? John Wakely? Or maybe Todd Wakely and his cronies, wanting to make sure Clancy stayed off the team? Whoever it was had missed their mark—the threat had done nothing but spur her on.

'Hello, Jenny Rodham speaking.'

Clementine rested her elbows on the table. 'Hi, Jenny—it's me, Clementine. Thanks for a great night on Friday.'

'Our absolute pleasure, honey.'

'Have you got a minute to talk?'

'Sure, what's up?'

'I was hoping you might do me a favour—I need you to look something up for me.'

'Of course, Clem—is it something to do with the club? I banked the takings from the fundraiser today. We made $7432—a record, three times last year's total. Good, eh?'

'Outstanding, Jen. People are so generous. I wonder if I should ask for a finals bonus?' She was only half-joking.

'Well, at $140 a game, I'm not sure how you're getting by. Must have a sugar daddy somewhere…something you're not telling us, girl?'

'I have no need of a man, Jen—too complicated.'

'Humph, stop being so selfish. It would be a lot more interesting for me if you had a man in your bed.'

'I'm sorry I'm so boring.'

'So what was it you wanted me to look up?'

'It's about Clancy. Did you know he lost his job?'

'Yes, Trev told me on the weekend. What a shame. His poor wife, and with a baby on the way, too. Trev said he stole something from the warehouse.'

'Yeah, well, that's the official story. I've spoken to Clancy, Jen, and I just don't think he did it.'

'But you just never know, do you? I mean, people do crazy things. I don't know him that well, truth be told, seemed decent enough, but they say nothing good ever comes out of the Plains.'

Clementine decided to ignore the comment. 'Jen, I think someone was paid to set Clancy up.'

'Why on earth would you think that?' Jen whispered. 'Hang on, don't answer that—I'm going out the back where it's private.' Clementine waited. She heard a door close.

'Now what the bloody hell are you talking about?' Jen said.

'I've spoken to the bloke who dobbed him in, and things just don't add up, Jen. I need you to look up his account for me, the guy who reported him.'

There was a pause. 'Clementine, you know I can't do that. I should hang up now—I can't even be talking about this.'

'No, Jen, please don't hang up. That's why I rang your mobile. It's okay. Let me explain.'

'Explaining won't help,' Jenny hissed. 'What you're asking me to do is against bank policy. It's illegal, for Christ's sake. And who was it that sacked Clancy anyway? I heard it was Gerard Holt.'

'It doesn't matter who—'

'Who sacked him, Clementine?'

'Okay, yes, it was Gerard who sacked him.'

'Oh good God almighty, you are playing with fire, Clementine Jones. Do you realise who Gerard Holt is? I told you, he's *connected*. He's more than connected—he and his wife are everything in this town. Everything.'

'But I'm not asking you to check Gerard's account—'

Jen wasn't listening. 'Gerard is a powerful man round here—you have no idea how small towns work, girl. He's second in charge at CTS, his wife runs the joint, he's president of the footy club, he's on the board of the chamber of commerce, he's in close with the editor of the local rag, and he rubs shoulders all day long with the wealthiest cockies in the region. Oh, and don't get me started on the pollies—he's mates with the mayor, our federal member and who knows how many big knobs in Melbourne. Do you want to be on the wrong side of all of that? Don't be a bloody fool.'

Clem bit her lip. Jen was right, of course. All this time keeping a low profile, and here she was throwing herself into a fight with the big end of town. But the note had produced the opposite effect. Now she knew for sure that something sinister lay behind Clancy's sacking—and damned if she'd roll over just because someone with bad punctuation had left her a childish note.

She heard Jen sigh. 'Come on, Clem, you're going so well—the team is winning, those boys are learning some self-respect and there's optimism in this town like we haven't known since the mine shut down. Why on God's earth would you want to sacrifice all that?'

'It's important, Jen. All I need is the transactions over the last few weeks. Could you just take a quick look and then tell me on the phone? I won't even write anything down.'

Jenny snorted. 'Well, *you* might want to self-destruct—that's none of my business—but you do realise I could lose my job, don't you? It's madness, Clementine!'

Clementine waited. There was silence but for their breathing. 'Jen, he's one of our boys. He gave everything for the team, now someone's trying to take him down. We've got to do something.'

A long pause. She went in for the kill. 'Jen, it was Frank Cranfield who dobbed Clancy in. It's his account I want you to look at.' The silence came with a crash. Clementine could hear the wind outside ramp up a notch and the bar heater at her feet creaked. *Here goes* she thought. *All in now.* 'Jen, I know what Frank Cranfield did to your brother. Now he's screwing up somebody else's life. You've got to help.'

Jen's voice was strangled. 'I'm hanging up.' Click. The line went dead.

Clementine dropped the phone, shocked she'd actually said it. Jen was the closest thing to a friend she had in this town. How could she bring that up?

At that moment Pocket burst through the dog door, leaving it flapping wildly. His tongue hung out and the fur on his back was clotted together. She stared down at him, hardly seeing anything. Then a foul odour wafted past—the smell of something dead, something rotting—and she wanted to retch. 'Oh, you filthy dog, you filthy, filthy dog. Out, out.' She shooed him to the back door, trying not to touch him. Pocket had taken to rolling around on top of dead animals, the more advanced the decomposition the better. The smell was all through the house.

She heard her phone ringing from the front room, and ran back down the hall to grab it. It was Jen, calling from her mobile. She snatched at the pen and notepad.

'I warned you—remember that, Clementine, when all this ends badly. I warned you.' Jenny's voice was hushed and trembling. 'Twenty thousand dollars was paid into Cranfield's account two weeks ago. The only other deposits are his pay every fortnight. The funds came from an account in the name of BT Regional at 159 Railway Parade in Earlville. Don't you dare write that down—you'll just have to remember it. You got that?'

'Yes. Yes. Thank you so much, Jen.'

The phone went dead.

\\//

Clementine sat low in the driver's seat, watching the comings and goings at 159 Railway Parade, Earlville, about as comfortable as a cat in a puddle. She'd never set foot in a tattoo parlour before, let alone investigated one. This would definitely be a once off. In and out, quick and slick.

Half an hour ago a woman with dreadlocks and round Janis Joplin glasses had emerged, her rust-coloured dress flouncing with each stride. Another woman, wearing a black leather miniskirt and flowing white blouse, had gone in not long after. Her legs were completely covered in tattoos, from the hem of her short skirt all the way down to her ankles.

To Clementine's left a loaded freight train rattled past on the line behind the fish and chip shop. From across the street, next door to the tattoo parlour, came the intermittent clangs and hydraulic swooshes of a panelbeating shop. On the other side of number 159 was a lone house amid the commercial buildings, a single-storey postwar wreck of a place, coated in dark layers of dust.

A blue ute pulled up in front of her and a man in a red flannelette shirt and black leather vest jumped out—shortish, shaved head, Doc Martens, striding across the street to the tattoo parlour, thigh muscles bulging in black jeans.

She looked at her watch. After four o'clock. She'd hoped to get the manager alone but it had been one customer after another. Another ten minutes and the miniskirt woman came out. The website said the shop closed at five—Clementine could delay no longer. She got out of the car and crossed the street, a fluttering uneasiness in her stomach as she pushed through the door.

74

The walls inside were jam-packed with posters of tattooed people—waif-thin women and pale-skinned men. There was a chemical smell, overlaid with a kind of fleshy musk. On the far side of the shop, Red Flanno was standing bare-chested at the counter, pointing to his chiselled belly, biceps adorned with inky teeth, hollow eyes, curling tongues.

'I want a quote here. You know, writing,' he said.

A puny-looking guy was leaning on his elbows behind the glass counter. 'Sure, what did you have in mind?'

'Master of destiny.'

'Very cool,' said the guy. 'Any particular font you prefer?'

Clementine moved to the back of the cramped shop and started flicking through a display album full of skulls and demons. There was a door towards the back and two screens. *That must be where the torture takes place.* Every now and then she glanced up to sneak a look at the rippling human canvas at the front of the shop. His back was covered in an eagle with outspread wings. She couldn't quite make it out from that distance, but she thought she could see a swastika under its talons. She picked up another album.

The company search on BT Regional had shown that the owner was another company, which in turn was owned by another company, and then a parent company above that, BT Holdings. She'd printed out the directors' names and addresses for each of the four companies. One name had come up as a director on all the boards: Dwight Benson. According to Google, Benson was the founding partner of a small criminal defence firm in Melbourne. She had prepared a series of questions to try to get to the bottom of the movers and shakers at 159 Railway Parade.

Red Flanno booked an appointment, buttoned his shirt and headed for the door. The puny guy came out from behind the counter and gave Clementine a smile.

'G'day, love, can I help you?'

He wore a badge that said *Ricky*, and had one of those deeply pockmarked faces indicative of a miserable adolescence.

She tucked her hair behind her ear and said, in the halting tone she'd been practising for the occasion, 'Um, yes, I think I'm sort of interested in getting a tattoo. But it's my first one and I'm kind of nervous.'

'Sure, no worries. Got anything in mind?'

'Um, well, I was hoping to discuss a few things with you first.'

'Fire away,' said Ricky obligingly.

'I was wondering about infections, you know, hygiene and everything. A friend of mine knew someone who got hepatitis from a dodgy tatt. Place was run by bikies.'

'You've got no worries here, love. We follow the Tattooists Guild's standards. New needles for each client, sterile packs, the works. Never had a problem with infections or anything like that.'

Yet another customer came into the shop, fitted western shirt, fancy leather boots and a disturbingly large gold chain round his neck. Ricky gave him a brief glance. 'Be with you in a minute, mate.'

'That's good to know. So the owner's pretty careful then? Is he a local?' said Clementine, not willing to waste a moment.

'I don't actually know the owner. I think there's a few blokes, one of them's some big-shot lawyer in Melbourne or something.'

From the corner of her eye she could see the guy in the fancy boots preening himself in the mirror to her left.

'Oh, a lawyer? Owning a tattoo parlour? That's odd.'

'Never met the guy. I only ever deal with the manager,' said Ricky, tapping his fingertips on the counter, eyes darting across to the guy with the gold chain, who seemed to be coming to the end of his grooming session.

This was going nowhere. She needed to keep Ricky talking, find out how he'd come to work here, for how long, who else worked there, who did the books and whether he knew Frank Cranfield. So much ground to cover.

'Oh right, is the manager local?' This was all coming out wrong. She'd meant to ease her way in. Ricky just looked at her from under raised eyebrows. The guy had finished at the mirror and had taken up a position right behind her at the counter now, one fancy leather boot stuck out wide, arms crossed.

Hurry up. You're never coming back here again, Jones.

'Yeah,' said Ricky reaching across to a laminated card at the end of the counter, 'Listen, love, here's an info sheet.' The card was headed *Everything You Need to Know About Getting a Tattoo.* 'How about you have a read, and I'll come back when you're ready.'

Shit. She'd found out exactly zero. It was after four-thirty and Fancy Boots could take up the rest of the available time. There was only one thing for it...

'Oh, no! ' she said, a little too hurriedly. 'I mean, I think I'm ready. In fact, yes, I'll have a butterfly.'

'You sure?' he said.

'Yes, I'm sure. And I want to do it now, before I change my mind.'

'All right. Well I've got nothing booked, so I can fit you in. You pick something out,' he said, handing her an album from beneath the counter, 'and I'll just see to this fella.'

Ricky spoke to Fancy Boots, booking him for an appointment next week, and returned to the other end of the counter, where Clementine was staring blankly at the album.

'Okay, any thoughts?'

She had no thoughts, other than the pain she was about to suffer and the fact that she'd be stuck with this tattoo for the rest of her life. Ricky began flipping through the pages, discussing the ins and outs of the various offerings in the butterfly section and the time required for each, Clem barely managing to comment. He was talking up a butterfly he'd done for a young woman—'Her first one, just like you, came out real nice.' He found the page he was after. 'Ah, here it is—'

Clementine didn't hear what Ricky said next. The design was huge, big enough to cover an entire scapula and surrounds—multicoloured, lavish wings, looping tendrils, the butterfly itself sitting on an elaborate twig complete with carefully etched leaves.

'Oh, perhaps something small and, um, discreet?'

'Oh, yeah, of course, no worries,' said Ricky, realising his mistake. They flipped through a couple more pages, Clem's stomach twisting in ever more contorted knots.

Ricky seemed to sense her lack of enthusiasm. Finally he said, 'How about you have a think about it and pop back in when you've decided on the design.'

Oh God. Now or never.

'No, no, I'm good to go,' she said. 'I'll have this one.' She pointed at a design just big enough to give her half an hour with Ricky.

'You sure, love?' Ricky looked doubtful.

'Yes, I'm sure...on my lower back, please.'

Lower lower back, so no one but lovers will ever see it...

'Righto, then. Why don't you just take a seat over there behind that screen and I'll be with you in a moment.'

She sat behind the screen, in utter disbelief at where she was, what she was about to do. Above her was a brass lamp on a long boom, there was a bench with a sink on the back wall, more framed pictures of tattoo models and to the right, above her head, loomed a decidedly unnerving reindeer head, its glass eye reflecting the light on the ceiling, antlers casting a tree-like shadow on the wall behind it.

She heard Ricky locking the door to the shop, drawers opening and closing, then his light-footed steps, and there he was beside her, smiling. She felt sick.

'Right,' he said, rubbing his hands together. 'Ready?'

She nodded. He went to the sink at the bench, his back to her, and began washing his hands while she lay face down on a massage table, looking through the narrow slit to the tiled floor below, her shirt pulled up high and just her underwear beneath a sheet draped over her bum. Ricky approached the massage table. She felt his fingers on the sheet—he was gently easing her panties lower. *Oh God.*

More hand washing, the squeak of surgical gloves and Ricky began dabbing some sort of solution on her skin.

'I'm so nervous,' she blurted. 'I should have asked more questions, shouldn't I?'

'No pressure,' he said, ceasing the dabbing for a moment. 'We can call it off now, no charge, but once I start, that's it. You sure you're okay?'

'Yep. Good as gold,' she said, her voice an octave too high.

He finished the dabbing, then there was a rattling sound, like stirring a spoon in a cup.

'So, Clementine, I'm going to stencil the design onto your back here. Just like drawing on your skin.'

'Make sure you tell me when the needles are going to start, yeah?' she said nervously.

Ricky was gentle, but it was only the drawing stage, and she was so tense her jaw was aching already. By the time he'd fired up the machine, she was sweating, and when the first needles pierced the thin layer of skin above her sacrum she let out a tiny, surprised yelp. She forced herself to ask her questions through gritted teeth and deep breaths as the needle hammered against her spine.

He had a great bedside manner, chatting away as he worked, answering all of Clem's questions. She discovered that Ricky had worked there two years, had been interviewed for the job by a really great guy named Ambrose ('Brose' for short) who lived in Earlville and rode a motorcycle. Ricky loved his job and did watercolour painting on the side and he found her completely fabricated story of breaking up with her ex, Frank, hilarious.

'Wait, maybe you know him?' Clementine said. 'Frank's the

one who suggested I come here. He's got loads of tatts. Frank Cranfield.'

'Never heard of him,' Ricky said. 'But it sounds like you're better off without him, love.'

It was after five when she stepped out onto the pavement. She wore her jeans low, way low, beneath the screaming red patch of mortification just above her butt crack.

CHAPTER 12

'Look, Jones, I'm only doing my job. I received a complaint about you—I have to follow up on it.' Gerard had called Clementine to his office on 'urgent club business'. She sat opposite him now, scarcely able to believe what she was hearing.

'Just because his name's Jones doesn't mean we're related, for Christ's sake! Surely I don't need to tell you that?'

'I know, I know. I'm not—'

'And he's had a blinding season in the reserves, kicked twenty-eight goals. He's the obvious choice to cover for Maloney so Maloney can take Clancy's place in the midfield.'

'Clementine, calm down. It's perfectly understandable. The Plains community are hurting. Clancy's gone, and they've lost their champion. They desperately want to be part of the success of the team—God, the whole town wants to be part of it—it's no surprise they're disappointed. They want another champion on board and carrying their flag.'

Clementine blinked, took a sharp breath. It pained her that Gerard had commandeered the moral high ground—she wasn't used to it. She stared at the painting of the wild geese flying away from the lake behind Gerard's head. Black geese with white wing tips.

'You know, I've often thought about a quota system, Jones. Diversity's more than just a buzzword, you know. There's real proof that it brings significant benefit to an organisation. We could have a certain number of places for Indigenous players at each level.'

Clementine sighed. 'You're not going to cave to this bullshit complaint, are you, Gerard? There's absolutely no substance to it, and to introduce a quota system now would totally cock everything up. We can't do it, not with the finals knocking on the door.'

'Hold your horses, sunshine. I'm in complete agreement. It'd be next year if we were to do anything like that. Now, take a deep breath, and I'll tell you how we deal with this.' He clasped his hands together on the desk and leaned forward.

Don't call me sunshine.

'You're going to write a report for the monthly committee meeting next Monday night, detailing the selection process you followed to find a replacement for Clancy. You will fully describe the proposed reshuffle and Richie Jones' suitability for the vacant role up front. You will also explain that you are not, in any way, related to Richie or his family.'

Clementine snorted—was she supposed to provide a complete family tree going back to the Old Country?

'I will support you,' said Gerard, ignoring her disdain. 'The committee will find the complaint unjustified, and your selection will be endorsed. The last thing any of us want is a bloody anti-discrimination case.'

She couldn't help herself. 'Simple defence on the facts...' she muttered. As soon as it was out she regretted it.

'Eh?' Gerard was staring at her intently. 'My goodness, Jones, you do seem to know a lot about the law. Unfair dismissal, discrimination claims...' Gerard paused, waiting for Clementine to react. She didn't. He moved on, but the information was out there and she could never take it back.

'So,' Gerard continued, still appraising her closely, 'I'll move a motion to have another position added to the committee: a diversity officer, with responsibility for developing a diversity policy and implementing it next season.'

She couldn't deny this was a good plan—she understood now how Gerard had worked his way up the ranks within CTS, something of a 'fixer'. 'Okay, fine,' she said, rising from her chair, 'I'll write the report.'

'Please sit down, Jones—I haven't finished.'

She sighed and slumped back down in the seat.

'About Clancy. I hear you've been poking around, stirring up trouble.'

It was a simple statement, but it immediately sent her mind racing back to the note on the door, *No more questions BITCH*. Was Gerard responsible for the note?

'What trouble?'

'Well, that's where this whole complaint came from, didn't it? You sticking your nose in out at the Plains? They say you were out there harassing Clancy's wife, asking all sorts of questions, and then left in a hurry driving like a lunatic, and smashed into someone further up the road. People are going to start doubting your judgement if you keep carrying on like that.'

How did he know about the crash? She'd well and truly left the Plains before she'd hit Rowan's van—no one there could have seen it. Who had started the story circulating? Not Rowan, surely? Maybe the old guy who'd stopped to ask if they were okay. Suspicion leaked into her mind like a drop of ink in water.

'Frank was upset too. Came to see me. Said you'd accused him of some sort of cover-up.'

Clementine didn't miss the opportunity. 'Is there a cover-up, Gerard?'

Those eyes. Blue. Blank. Nothing at all.

'Jones, you know as much as I do. The kid stole from the company. Simple as that. There's no cover-up.' He sighed and reached for a file in the cabinet behind the desk. 'Here, see for yourself.' He slapped the file down in front of her.

She opened it to find a series of photographs. A red hatchback, its registration plate visible, parked in the warehouse car park. A shot of the interior of the car, the back seat laden with boxes. A close-up of the boxes, angle grinders and drills. Another photograph, the front passenger's side door open, showing Clancy's footy boots and training gear on the floor. The next showed the opened boxes, revealing an array of shiny new power tools still in their plastic packaging.

The last three photographs showed the inside of the warehouse, grainy and dark. A shadowy figure was walking out with an armful of boxes. Clementine remembered Wakely saying that the footage from inside the warehouse didn't show anything.

'Well, these look pretty inconclusive—that could be anyone. How about you show me the CCTV footage of the car park?'

'You know it's not available, Jones. Frank and Wakely told you that.' So he had spoken to them both. Her mind started running faster.

'But where is it, Gerard? Haven't you tracked it down yet? I'd like to see it—set my mind at rest.'

He shook his head and sighed. 'Look, I shouldn't be telling you this, Jones, but it seems you're not going to let it go unless I do.' He paused, looked her straight in the eye. 'Clancy confessed.'

The words hit her like a slap, took her breath away. She'd assumed the allegations against Clancy were false. She'd imagined him fiercely denying them.

She stared at the black geese again, at the graceful arc of their flight. It calmed her. Come on, Jones—did a confession change things? It might have been coerced. If they had something over him, he might have had no choice. Or maybe Gerard was lying. These were all possibilities, but doubt had crawled in now. Maybe she didn't really know Clancy after all. Maybe he was a thief.

She dropped her head, a look of defeat plastered across her face. 'Okay, okay, I'm out. I'm done with Clancy,' she heard herself say.

'I'll have the report on your desk by Thursday.'

Gerard knew better than to speak. He had conquered. He rose to see her out.

She'd put herself out there, risked her low-profile existence, and now people were complaining about her. It had seemed a simple plan—hide, be anonymous, be someone else or nobody, anyone other than that person she was—but it was proving awfully difficult to execute. Definitely time to pull her head in, go to ground again, think of herself for a change.

She looked up, her gaze holding Gerard there as he stood behind his desk. 'Gerard, I'd like a finals bonus.'

'You what?'

'A finals bonus. A five-hundred-dollar game fee for the first final, and then keep doubling it for each one after that if we win.'

'Where has this come from?' Gerard looked dumbfounded. She was glad. She wanted him to feel her power as well as her submission.

'The fundraiser was a breakthrough success—we're up three times on our annual revenues. It's the first time in thirty-four years Katinga has come close to actually making the finals, and I'm responsible for both these miracles. I deserve it.'

Gerard threw back his head and laughed. 'Ha! That's the shot, Jones! This is what I keep telling people about you. Aggression, insisting on success, demanding it. No doubt about you.'

'And?'

'I'll recommend it to the committee, but fifty per cent of it should be contingent on you signing on for another year.'

He was already bargaining—this deal was done. 'Sounds reasonable. Thank you, Gerard.'

She stood up to walk away, knowing she would sign the contract, and knowing also that she would walk away from it as soon as the season was over and the money in her account. *So sue me, sunshine.*

The winter air came from Clementine's lungs in short, steamy puffs as she closed the gate behind her and walked across the paddock. The white trunks of the mountain gums to the east of the bush near the cottage were resplendent as the sun emerged from the top of the hill. Clementine stopped to run her hand along a silky trunk.

Twenty minutes later and she'd made it to the top of the rise. Standing on a rocky ledge, she gazed down at her cottage in the saddle between the two ridges, Jim's sheep dotting the fields next door. The mint-green weatherboard looked peaceful beneath its corrugated-iron roof, patchy with rust. The mountain gum in the backyard looked much bigger from this angle, the green of its leaves obscuring the corner of the house above her bedroom. A pair of black cockatoos screeched below her, emerging from the treetops, their tails long and straight behind them. The black minority in the cockatoo world.

She knew the pursuit was over. It was dragging her deeper into territory she did not want to occupy. As much as she was suspicious of Gerard and Cranfield and the Wakelys, the community was now getting suspicious. If someone found out about her...She shivered. She would have to leave if it came to that, but leaving seemed out of the question. She wanted to stay for the finals.

For now, she must do what Gerard asked to keep him off her case, fade back into the background. Just the coach, nothing more.

How had she ended up in this predicament anyway? She thought about the Tuesday nights she'd put in at the Community Legal Centre in Redfern that last summer before the incident. She'd advised a few Indigenous clients, pro bono, in her own time. Didn't that count for something? *No, be honest with yourself, Jones, you were only doing it to impress the partners back at the firm, advance another rung in the race up the partnership ladder.*

She sat down in the dirt, her legs stretched out, boots hanging over the ledge. A kookaburra landed in the tree to her right, cocked its head, staring at her for a moment, then swooped low to the base of the tree to her left and grabbed at a caterpillar with its beak, pounding it into the dirt. That could be me later today when Tiny Spencer calls, she thought—an insect, writhing in his beak. The bird tossed its head back and she watched the caterpillar disappear down its throat.

And really, how could she claim to understand? She sneered at herself, realising how remote she'd been, in her glittering tower in Potts Point, how insulated from the cut and thrust of black and white in real life. And now she could see the two hundred plus years since colonisation stretching out in front of her, a yawning divide in which suspicion and bitterness grew, spawning distrust and violence. She was on the wrong side of that divide, and all the good intentions in the world were irrelevant.

CHAPTER 13

Torrens had just landed his first-ever real job as a boner at the meatworks outside of Earlville. He'd insisted on taking Clementine out for a drink tonight after Tuesday-night training to thank her for giving him a place on the team and starting his journey back into the community. It had been a big day for her, what with Gerard in the morning, then the afternoon dancing around Tiny Spencer's questions before taking the team through their Tuesday-night training run. She could do with a drink.

Clementine watched Torrens as he lumbered to the bar. The Katinga Arms was a block of a red-brick building, standing two storeys tall in the main street for almost one hundred years. She sat at one of the tables beneath a wall pinned with souvenir beer coasters, close enough to the open fire to feel the right side of her leg start to tingle with heat. Patronage had peaked at about six-thirty, but there were still a few drinkers loitering. Matthew Torrens towered over the bar, chatting to a local she didn't know as he waited for their drinks.

What a find he'd been, she thought. They'd already won two of their first four games of the season when twenty-four-year-old Torrens had asked her if he could join the team. He was fresh out of jail for she knew not what. When a six-foot-six giant asks if he can play, you don't ask why—you just invite him to training.

He was way behind on fitness at that point, but he'd worked hard to catch up, meeting with Clementine on Monday nights to train on his own and playing his first game three weeks later. His size and power had been decisive in the ruck for the Cats and the rest of the team grew in confidence with him in the centre of the ground, scowling down at the opposition. He'd blown up early in the third quarter, and she'd taken him off. The team had played out the rest of the game without him, but the lead they'd established by that stage was enough and they won the game by a two-goal margin.

'Here you go, one for you and one for me,' said Torrens, easing into the chair opposite. 'Who would have dreamt I'd be drinking fucking lights, eh?' he chuckled. 'A changed man, thanks to you.' He parked his frame on the wooden chair at the table and raised his glass. 'To you, Jonesy, for giving me a start.'

She clinked her glass on his and drank to his success. 'No, you did it yourself, Torrens. You had the guts to join the team, and you've worked your arse off ever since. Good on you.'

'Ha, only 'cos you turned up every Monday to whip me into shape, you bloody slavedriver!' He laughed again, slapping his meaty fist on the table.

They drank their beers while Torrens explained a few of the finer arts of boning meat using the hotel cutlery and a napkin to demonstrate. It was just after eight when they made their way towards the side door onto Main Street. As they passed the doorway to the dining room, Clementine glanced inside. Two tables of Tuesday-night diners. No one she knew on the first table, but then, over in the back corner, she gasped as she recognised their faces: Rosemary Jenner, in what looked like a wheelchair, and Andrew Hewitt, and opposite them, with their backs to her, Gerard and Bernadette Holt.

Clementine shoved past Torrens and rushed for the door, bumping into a man crouched over the pool table, cue poised. 'Sorry, mate,' she mumbled as she made for the exit.

Torrens followed her out, chasing her up the street. 'What the hell was that about? D'ya see a ghost or something?'

Clementine couldn't speak. She kept walking towards her car, parked further ahead.

'Hey, Jonesy, what's going on?' Torrens shouted after her.

She spun around. 'Shhhh. Keep your voice down.'

'Well tell me what this is about?' he hissed, hurrying after her.

'Nothing. Nothing. Just need to get home,' she said, quickening her pace.

This was a disaster—Rosemary and Andrew, sitting there, and with the Holts! Her old colleagues, they knew everything—the incident, her conviction. Just one word from them and her entire past would be known in Katinga.

She imagined Gerard hearing about what she'd done. Worse, Bernadette and Jen, Torrens, the team. It was unthinkable. *Shit, shit, shit.* She felt heat rising in her cheeks even as the night air blew in icy gusts onto her face.

The last time she'd seen Rosemary was the deal-closing party on the night of…A shiver swept across the back of Clementine's neck as the memories arrived, unbidden: techno music blasting, trays of canapés, young associates—chests thrust forward boisterously, the clink of champagne glasses, a waiter topping up her drink. And then there it was again, the image of the woman. The darkening scarlet oozing on white, and the eyes, the eyes. Eighteen months on and she had not found a way to stop it appearing.

Torrens caught up to her, put his big paw on her shoulder. 'Hey, hey, slow down.'

'No, no, Torrens, I have to go. I have to go.' She fumbled in her backpack for her keys.

'But mate, you're pale—you're shaking. What the hell happened in there?'

Her keys tumbled out and fell on the pavement. Torrens was quick for a big man, kicking them away as she reached for them and holding her back with one hand as he scooped them up in the other.

'Torrens, this is serious, I'm...I have to...' Her voice was trembling.

Torrens put both hands on her shoulders, turned her round and walked her towards her car. He unlocked the car, opened the passenger's side door and gently pushed her in. She did not resist. He came around to the driver's side and got in.

'Righto. You're gunna have to tell me now, because I'm not getting out of the car until you do.'

She looked over her shoulder back towards the hotel. 'Okay, okay, just drive me up the street and around the corner, where we can't be seen.' If Andrew or Rosemary saw her, just a glimpse, it would take just one word...

Torrens idled the car forward and turned into Chester Street. They sat for a while in silence while her breathing slowed.

'I can't tell you anything about what just happened,' she mumbled.

'I'm not letting you drive home until you tell me. You helped me, Jonesy. You really turned my life around. I'm not leaving you in this state, and I'm not getting out of this car until I understand what the hell is going on here.'

\|/

Up ahead of them, Andrew Hewitt was driving a black Audi, and in front of him was Gerard's silver BMW. Torrens hung back, careful not to get too close. They had taken his car so Gerard wouldn't recognise it. Clementine slunk down low in the passenger's seat beside him. He'd convinced her to follow them home. She hadn't told him much—just that she'd seen some people she was afraid of, people who could make her life very difficult, and that their presence in town was enough to make her think about leaving. He had returned the favour she had granted him that first night when they met and not asked questions. And now, despite herself, she was grateful, after everything that had happened that week, to be in this giant of a man's car, following his lead.

They had waited about half an hour before they saw the two vehicles pull out of the hotel car park and then followed them up to Katinga Heights. Gerard was turning right now, into a street with sweeping views of the valley, then he slowed in front of a large house with a grand, pillared entrance and high fence. Torrens kept driving straight ahead, did a U-turn and then parked at a point a little higher up, where they could see down the street. An automatic gate in the tall fence had opened and Andrew Hewitt's Audi was disappearing up the driveway as Gerard pulled the BMW up on the street. Inside the yard, under the glow of a street lamp, Clementine could see a manicured hedge rising above the six-foot-high fence and a grove of young trees. Behind that was a series of neatly ordered garden beds. Gerard and Bernadette headed up the driveway on foot. The gate began to close behind them.

Before Clementine could say anything, Torrens was out of the car and running down the street. *Oh Christ! He thinks he's James Bond.* He reached the automatic gate just before it closed and snuck inside.

She didn't like it up here in foreign territory, so far from the sanctuary of her cottage. After the accident she'd heard that Andrew and Rosemary had become a couple. But how did they know the Holts? And why were they here? Clementine waited. The minutes ticked by. A cat sauntered across the road, stopping at the gutter to sniff, then disappearing through a line of shrubs in the front yard of the house opposite.

She jumped as she heard the driver's side doorhandle click. Torrens. He'd come from the other direction. He eased into the seat, panting.

'Suitcases, Jonesy, big ones. Looks like they're here to stay.'

The picture on the front page wasn't too bad, she thought, and the headline carried the predictable pun: *New Coach the Cats' Whiskers*. She had managed Tiny Spencer quite well, she thought, drawing on the lies she'd already crafted for Jenny, but she flipped to the main story on page three quickly, fearing Tiny may have done some research of his own. She needn't have worried. Tiny was your typical sixty-year-old journo running a country newspaper while he waited till he could get his super. She had steered him away from her personal life and given him plenty of material on her coaching philosophy and the inner workings of the Cattery.

Her coffee arrived and she took a sip. It was a long sight better than the plunger at home but still a bull's roar from Sydney standards. Torrens was late. He wasn't due at work until the afternoon shift and they'd agreed to meet at nine am.

She'd never been to this little strip of shops out near the old mine, but she had to avoid the town centre for now, with Rosemary and Andrew around. The Wombat Cafe was a cheery place, with its yellow-painted walls covered in black-and-white photos of Katinga over the last hundred years and a bookshelf with a sign saying *Please take one*. When the mine was open, the cafe would have been busy with workers, she thought, early in the morning and again after knock-off. Now, sitting at an aluminium table in the corner, she was the only one there. An old fellow with a cane had bought an apple teacake about twenty minutes ago, but there had been no one since. He'd recognised her on his way out and shuffled over to her table to reminisce about the grand final win in '62, his teacake in a string bag hanging from his elbow. He'd been twenty-five years old at the time, working in the mines. It was the best day of his life. Now he wanted to see it happen once more before he died. 'We're countin' on you, love,' he said, patting her shoulder as he left.

Torrens finally arrived, placed his order at the counter and sat himself opposite Clementine. Immediately the table felt too small.

They'd discussed the wheelchair last night and what it might mean, Rosemary having been able-bodied when Clem had last seen her. Torrens said he thought perhaps she might have had her leg in a cast, but he couldn't be sure. They both agreed it had to be an injury or some sort of surgery or both.

'You reckon her boyfriend brought her here to stay for a bit while she recovers?' he asked.

'Maybe. I can't imagine them doing a driving holiday with Rosemary in a wheelchair. Andrew'll probably head back to work while Rosemary takes in the country air.'

'There were two huge suitcases, though, he might be here for the long haul too,' said Torrens as the waiter brought out his order—a latte and two doughnuts, steaming hot and covered in a fine dusting of sugar. He offered Clementine one, she declined.

'Yeah, but I wouldn't be surprised if the luggage was all Rosemary's. She always fancied herself as a bit of a fashion plate. Either way, I don't think I'm going to be able to hang around,' she said.

'Eh?' said Torrens, his eyes screwed up in disbelief. She shouldn't have said it. Why did she have to let on to Torrens? She could just slip away one night, never to be seen again.

'Hang on a moment! You can't leave us now! There's no fucking way on God's fucking earth you can fucking leave us now,' he said, his voice filling the cafe.

The waiter came out from behind the counter, began wiping a

94

table nearby, watching Torrens warily.

'Don't get your knickers in a twist, big fella, it was a joke. Where's your sense of humour?' she said, giving the waiter a smile to let him know all was well.

'Not funny. Not bloody funny at all,' said Torrens.

She swallowed the last of her coffee and pushed her cup to the side of the table. Everywhere she went these days, every conversation she had reminded her of the suffocating pressure—Mrs Lemmon and her Tom, the old man with the teacake, the young man sitting in front of her. All of them depending on her.

As he wolfed down his second doughnut, Torrens came up with a plan. He said it was the best way, and if they waited for a cloudy night, no moon, no one would ever find out. She didn't like it at all—it made her feel sick, in fact—but Torrens was determined to go through with it, whether she liked it or not. She felt trapped, drained, tired, and it was comforting to have someone else be the strategist for a change. She simply could not think of an alternative other than leaving Katinga, and that just didn't seem right. But she couldn't let him risk it alone.

CHAPTER 15

Clementine pulled up in the car park. It was just after five o'clock. The warehouse sheds to her left were quiet, the cavernous doors closed for the evening. A few people were still trickling out of the office into the car park, including one she recognised: John Wakely. She hadn't seen him since the loss to the Eels. He hadn't been there for the last home game, which was odd, as he was such a big supporter—anyone who'd ever had anything to do with the Cats had been there.

She got out of the car and hurried across to talk to him, the report for the committee under her arm. 'John!' she called out.

He stopped and turned towards her. His face looked grey, but maybe it was the late-afternoon light. He gave her a stiff smile.

'We missed you at the game last week,' she said. 'Everything all right?'

He was standing by a white Toyota Camry, one hand in his pocket as she approached. 'Yeah, yeah, all good. Todd tells me it was a ripper of a game.'

'I didn't think we were going to get there midway through the last quarter. It was touch and go. Really tough doing it without Clancy.' Having heard Todd's views on the subject of race, she wanted to test Wakely Senior.

'Oh yes, he's a big loss. Yes.' Agreeable, but not his usual talkative manner, she thought.

'Can I ask you something, John?' she said, squinting into the sun. 'Would anyone have wanted Clancy off the team?'

He jammed his other hand in his pocket, arched his back away from her. 'Couldn't say, really. Why do you ask?' Definitely less talkative than the first time they'd met.

'I was just wondering if anyone would have wanted Clancy off the team. Maybe some of Todd's old mates from Earlville wanted to settle the score with Clancy?'

'Nope,' he said. 'Todd's changed since then. He's not the same lad anymore.'

'Yes, I can see that. I just thought perhaps his old friends...'

Wakely shifted his weight from one foot to the other, glanced across the car park, turned back towards Clementine. 'Look, Todd got sucked into a bad crowd back then—thugs they were. It was a tough time for Todd. They were a ruthless bunch, seriously nasty. If they had an idea like that, to get revenge for Clancy taking them on in court, well, yes, I wouldn't put it past them to do it. But Todd's out of it—he doesn't have anything to do with them anymore. He's out running and doing weights half the bloody day—no time to drive over to Earlville.'

'Are you sure that's what he's doing, John, working out?'

Wakely looked uncertain for a moment. 'Yes. Yes, I'm sure. Why would you say that? Has he done something?'

'No. Todd's doing really well. I think his fitness is one of his stronger points, and it's improved as the year's gone on. But it could just be the training I'm giving him—with the team, I mean. These boys have never worked harder. We're dead serious about winning this thing, John. So just because he's fitter, it doesn't mean he's been lifting weights in his spare time, does it?'

'Well, no, I guess not. I just assumed he was...well, that's what he told me...' There seemed to be an argument going on in Wakely's head. His eyes narrowed. 'He's done something, hasn't he? Tell me what it is.'

Clementine hesitated, but felt the moment was right. 'It's just

Todd said a few things the other night, and I thought maybe he was keen to have more, well, more white people on the team.'

'Oh, for Pete's sake. The flaming idiot. Look, Todd's not the sharpest tool in the shed, and he's got a big mouth. Those Earlville mugs filled his head with that rubbish back then, and he's too much of a young dickhead to shake it off. Yeah, he's probably glad Clancy's gone so some whitefella can take his spot, but there's no way he had anything to do with Clancy leaving.'

'But you think maybe the Earlville heavies might have been involved?'

Wakely shrugged. 'From what I know, Clancy left of his own accord, to be with his wife and new baby...'

'We both know that can't be right, though, John—it just doesn't make sense.'

'Look, I can't speak for that bunch of hooligans. They might have. It's definitely possible and it's just the sort of thing they enjoy. Seeing the Cats have a good year, yes, they'd see that as an opportunity, the bastards—a good time to make Clancy pay for his part in court, threatening him so he'd leave. Who the hell knows? But one thing I do know, Clementine—my Todd has no part in anything that mob does these days. He's finished with all that.'

He was getting worked up, she needed to keep him on side—she had another line of questions to pursue. 'I'm sure you're right, John,' she said. 'Todd's doing so well. It's really been a breakthrough season for him. I couldn't be happier. You must be proud of him.'

Wakely looked relieved. 'Oh, yes. I'm very proud. It's a shame his mother isn't here to see it. Wish he'd get a job, though. I'm stuck with him at home until he does.' He laughed awkwardly.

'So he didn't get the apprenticeship, then?'

'No, missed out on that one, but he's got another interview next week down at the meatworks. Not his cup of tea—beneath him, he reckons—but I think it's his best chance now the mine's closed.'

'No jobs going around here at CTS, then? I hear you're not replacing Clancy?'

'No, there's nothing open here. Keeping the headcount tight for the sale.'

'Must be difficult to manage.'

Wakely grinned. 'Nothing an old dog like me can't handle.'

She sent out another probe. 'I guess with your share options it's worth it, though. Could be lucrative, hey?' She smiled, trying to sound cheeky rather than nosy.

'Options!' he snorted. 'I think you have me placed a bit too high up the pecking order, Miss Jones. It's them folks in the ivory tower have the options'—he flicked his head towards the office—'not the likes of me.' There was a hint of resentment in his voice but mostly just resignation.

'Oh, that's a shame. I expect Bernadette and Gerard are a rung below the serious money too, though.'

He seemed to think it over for a moment. 'Yes, I suppose you're right—I wouldn't really know. Ask me a question about the warehouse—that's all I know about.'

\ı/

In the time she'd spent in the car park with Wakely the sun had almost disappeared behind the hills. The office was quiet, only a few cars left in the car park. She headed down the corridor towards Gerard's office, her report under her arm setting out the reasons why Richie Jones, with his bag of twenty-eight goals in the reserves, deserved a place in the seniors. She stopped. Raised voices coming from Gerard's office. She took two more steps, hung back behind the secretary's desk. The frosted-glass door to Gerard's office was closed, but she could tell from the voices that it was Bernadette and Gerard, arguing.

Gerard's voice was faint—she couldn't quite catch what he

was saying, only certain words clear enough. Something like: 'All because...couldn't keep...shut.'

Bernadette was nearer to the door, easier to hear: 'Oh and you're the saint, then? One rule for men, another for women?'

'Spare me...fucking timing...'

Silence. A static in the air, making her skin prickle.

Gerard began again: 'Anyway...coming again...more...next...'

'Not our place, you fool. Go somewhere private.'

Clementine could just make out a few words of Gerard's reply, indignant, angry: 'what...expect...can't control'.

Bernadette: 'We can't...until...' The sound of her voice was trailing off as she moved away from the frosted glass, then increasing again. *Pacing?*

Gerard again, from the back of the office, his voice calmer. Clementine caught the tail end of it: '...how much?'

'I'm not sure yet,' Bernadette replied, the rest of her words too faint to hear.

Clem strained to hear above the thump of her heart pounding in her ears. The tone was lower, they were finishing up. She couldn't be sure, but she thought Gerard said the word 'million'. She saw a shape—Gerard this time, purposeful, very close, moving towards the door. She stepped out from behind the secretary's desk, pretending she was just coming in.

As he opened the door Gerard's eyes widened, his mouth dropping open just a fraction before, in an instant, he had composed himself.

'Ah, Jones, come in—you've got that report, I take it?'

They had parked Torrens' rusty station wagon around the corner, up the hill, at the point between two streetlights where it was darkest. Between them and the Holts' house was a vacant corner block, overgrown with long grass and a messy scattering of stunted trees and patches of scrub, flat at the top then falling away sharply towards the street. Clem could see Andrew Hewitt's black Audi on the street in front of the Holts' at the edge of the streetlight's beam. Torrens had checked earlier that day—there was only room for two cars inside the fence, and Gerard and Bernadette's his-and-hers BMWs occupied both spaces.

Her stomach folded itself over and over into a tightly packed wad as she watched Torrens creeping across the vacant block, using the trees and scrub as cover. He carried a small black backpack with the gear in it wrapped in towels to stop any clanging. In the side pocket was a hunting knife.

A hunting knife. She could scarcely believe it. She'd argued with Torrens about the risks. He had insisted. So here she was, playing getaway driver and lookout. It was bad enough that she'd gone along with the idea, allowed it to bloom in her mind. Now she felt dirty, disoriented, like she was in someone else's skin.

She'd stayed awake last night, arguing with herself for hours. In fact she hadn't slept well at all since the discussion in the cafe. But whichever way she looked at it, she couldn't leave Katinga, could not leave the team, nor could she abandon Clancy and Melissa.

But neither could she stay in Katinga while Rosemary and Andrew were here. One chance sighting, one word, and the malignant genie was out of the bottle. It was bad enough already—she couldn't even go to the supermarket and she was nearly out of frozen dinners.

She thought about Torrens. She was taking advantage of his gratitude, letting him put his new life in danger just months after it had started to come together for him. And all while he was still on parole! If they were caught, she would make sure she took the blame.

A dog barked. She saw Torrens freeze behind a tree. The noise came from a house further up the street. Three more barks, then it stopped. The clouds had been thick all day and now blocked out the moon and stars. After a minute or two she saw Torrens move out from behind a tree and swiftly cross to another. He was making good ground.

She gripped her wetsuit gloves tighter around the steering wheel. He'd told her to wear all black with no skin showing. She'd managed to cover everything except her face. She didn't own a balaclava and had drawn the line at shoe polish. But with her beanie pulled down low and her black scarf high over her mouth and nose, only her eyes were showing. Pocket had growled when she'd put him outside before she left.

She watched the street. All the lights were out in every house. The whoosh of the wind in the trees, the noisy bustle of the leaves the only sounds. She could see Torrens more clearly now as he reached the outer edge of the streetlight's beam. He was creeping down the steep part of the block where the grass gave way to gravel and loose rocks, carefully placing his feet. Only about twenty metres to go before he would reach the Audi. Then it happened. As if in slow motion. She watched in horror as Torrens slipped, his feet sliding out from under him. He stretched out his hand to break his fall but she heard a loud crack as his head hit the ground. The dog started up a steady, high-pitched bark. Torrens didn't move.

She opened the car door and tiptoed through the scrub, her hands trembling. She expected lights to come on in the houses at any moment, but she kept her eyes locked on Torrens. At last he moved, rolling over onto his side. She felt like crying.

There was a dark patch on a large rock and another on the back of his balaclava.

'I'm okay, I'm okay,' he mumbled. 'Just lost it for a second.'

Leaning over him, she could see the whites of his eyes as they rolled in their sockets.

'You're concussed—we have to get you back to the car.' Her voice was barely audible over the wind, but it still sounded braver than she felt. She checked the street—still no lights in the houses.

Torrens tried to protest, but she shushed him, helped him up to his feet, shaky and wobbling against her arm. They moved together, Clem with the backpack slung over her left shoulder and Torrens leaning on her right side as they crept awkwardly between the trees and scrub.

The street was quiet again now. The dog had stopped barking. Torrens was woozy, but the wind covered the sound of his unsteady feet as they scrabbled to gain traction on the loose gravel. They moved further away from the streetlight towards the car and she could no longer see her own feet in the pitch black. The darkness, the muffling effect of the wind—it was perfect. And in that moment she knew: it had to be done tonight.

She bundled Torrens back into the passenger's seat. He clearly wasn't fit to drive, so there'd be no quick getaway. She gently pushed the door closed as he leaned back against the headrest.

She made her way across the block again without incident, surprised at how strong she felt, how single-minded. Then she was there, crouching behind the last of the bushes, only metres from Andrew's car. She carefully laid the backpack on the ground and pulled out the hunting knife. It felt heavy in her hand. She held it upside down, the blade flat against the inside of her arm so it wouldn't flash in the streetlight. She moved deftly, cat-like, plunging the tip of the knife into the tyre and pulling back to leave a long gash. The sound of the air whooshing out sounded much like a puff of wind in the treetops.

She repeated the exercise on the next two tyres, and then, as she plunged the knife deep into the final tyre, the wind suddenly died to nothing. When she tugged back on the blade, there was an enormous rush of air, almost deafening in the lull. The dog started barking furiously again. She ran and knelt behind the bush, waiting, her breathing fast and shallow. It seemed like forever before a light came on two doors down. She heard someone yell, 'Shut up!' The dog whimpered and then was quiet. She heard its claws clacking on pavers in the front yard of the house opposite as it returned to its bed. The light went off. The wind picked up again, louder this time.

She looked back at the car. The tyres were spread wide, ballooning flat on the road. It looked beaten, defeated. Taking an envelope from the front of the backpack, she tiptoed to the mailbox, keeping herself well below the fence line. She dropped it in the letterbox and crept back to the bush. Her mind danced back to the note on her front door. Who had put it there? Whoever it was, she was no better than them. She had sunk to a new low.

She started unzipping the backpack—her wetsuit gloves were awkward—removed one of the cans from its towel wrap, slowly, so as not to clink it against the other. The cap was bright yellow.

She was ready. She took another look at the Audi from behind the bush and felt a twinge at what she was about to do to this beautiful black beast. Swallowing back a sudden rush of fear, she slunk to the front of the car and started spraying the hateful words on the bonnet. She did the same on the driver's side and then ran out of paint. She returned to the bush, took the second can out. It felt heavier than the first and she finished the job, repeating the words again over the boot and passenger's side.

Hidden behind the bush, she put the empties in the backpack, the towel in between them, and took one last look at the despicable lie she had scrawled on the car's shiny black paint. She gulped. The yellow stood out fiercely, reflecting the streetlight and shouting out to the world: *Child molester inside.*

CHAPTER 17

She had only just finished showering when she heard the knock at the door. *Oh God, the police already!*

She'd woken at four, spent the hours before sunrise punch-drunk from beating herself up, running over and over the events of last night, pummelling herself with guilt. It had seemed the only rational thing to do, the only reasonable path forward, but she still couldn't believe she'd actually done it, and it horrified her, sickened her. It felt like another person, another universe. And the pain she'd inflicted on Rosemary and Andrew! She imagined their confusion, their humiliation, their rage.

And now the police were here. Of course. She would be arrested. A criminal, again. It's what she deserved.

Pocket was barking in the backyard. She didn't rush. She pulled on her jeans and a jumper, a pair of socks, and walked slowly up the hallway, her hair still wet and chilling the back of her neck. She took a deep breath, steadied herself, opened the front door.

'Oh my God, Rowan,' she exclaimed, her hand to her mouth.

He was in a coat and a beanie, his hands thrust deep in his pockets. 'Guess you're pleased to see me, then,' he said, with that smile again, like the sun coming up.

'Oh, yes, no—I mean, it's just that I wasn't expecting anyone. What are you—' Then it dawned on her. 'Oh, of course, of course, the shed roof...Come in, it's freezing outside.'

'Nah, gotta get cracking. Probably take me most of the day,' he said as Pocket came charging through the dog door at the back and skidding up the hall.

They headed across the sprawling yard to the shed, Pocket bouncing around them excitedly. The clouds of the night before had disappeared but the early sun struggled to make an impression on the thick frost covering the ground. In the morning light the stands of gum and wattle along the fence cast long, gentle shadows across the patchy grass.

Pocket stuck his nose in at the shed door to make sure he was the first through when it opened. They examined the shed roof together while he sniffed the perimeter. The strong wind over-night had further dislodged a large sheet of corrugated iron, now hanging by a few rusty nails, its edges sharp and threatening. Clementine watched Rowan set up his power tools and a ladder— competent, efficient, no movement wasted. When he reached overhead, his jumper pulled up, exposing a washboard stomach. She looked away, reminding herself as she went back to the house: *Keep your distance, no connections and definitely no relationships.*

At eight she came out with mugs of tea and biscuits. Rowan had removed the loose sheets of corrugated iron and was measuring up replacement pieces. They sat in the shed on rickety chairs amid the possum poo. She asked him how long he'd been in Katinga.

'Grew up here, married a local girl, Kate. She died,' he said, lighting a cigarette.

'I'm sorry,' Clem said.

'Breast cancer.'

He looked down into his mug, studying its milky contents before taking a swig. He had really long, dark eyelashes, she noticed.

'It's hard to know what to do after something like that,' she said. A statement, intended as a question—perhaps he could help her.

'Yep,' he grunted and took another sip of tea. 'I went off the rails a bit, shot through, did some things I'd rather forget.'

Me too, she thought, pictures of her family, Rosemary, Andrew flashing into her mind.

'I kind of thought you might be in the same situation,' he said, looking at her now, gripping the mug in both hands, but when she didn't reply, he let it go, like he understood there should be no questions.

Rowan got back to work, and she took Pocket for a walk to the ridge. She imagined Rosemary and Andrew reading the note, the demand that they leave town if they wanted to avoid an escalation of the vile accusations. How long had it been before they'd noticed the car, she wondered? She felt her stomach lurch again. For a moment she wondered if this was all a nightmare, something she would wake up from.

Arriving at the largest of the mountain gums in the thick cluster leading up the slope, Clementine stopped and looked up. The sky between the branches was that rich, royal blue before the sun has hit its straps and started washing everything out. She stroked the trunk. It was something she'd always done, for as long as she could remember—touch the trees, feel their energy. The bark was so white and smooth, and the trunk so straight and simple, with one purpose only: reach for the sky. She pressed her hand flat, felt the warmth of the sun in her palm, and then a moment of release. The turmoil of the last two weeks disappeared up the silky surface of the trunk into the canopy of leaves.

She stood there for a moment before walking on, Pocket racing ahead.

The peaceful state lasted only until she arrived back home forty minutes later. It was as if the cottage had absorbed the memory of each of her contemptible actions, and she felt sure whoever had lived there in the past was shaking their head. Clem had defiled this quiet, decent place.

She checked her phone. A text—Torrens, asking her to call.

She rang him back. He was off sick from work, of course, with concussion.

'Did a drive by Katinga Heights this morning.' His voice was hushed.

'You idiot, Torrens. You shouldn't be anywhere near Katinga Heights today—the cops will be everywhere.'

'Chill, Jonesy—they would've been long gone before I went past. Besides, I drove Mum's Subaru and wore a hat.'

Clem was incredulous. 'Your mum's six foot six as well then?'

Torrens ignored her. He said the Audi hasn't been there on the first drive-by, so he'd gone for a scout around town. He'd caught a glimpse of a black late-model vehicle at Cooney's Panelbeating but couldn't be sure it was the Audi. On the second drive-by, later in the morning, he'd hit the jackpot. The gate at the Holts' place was open and the Audi was in the driveway, with new tyres and a professional cut and polish. No sign of yellow paint. Gerard and Andrew had been packing suitcases into the boot.

\//

She ate lunch with Rowan in the kitchen. He'd packed his own roast beef sandwiches, but he accepted another cup of tea. They talked football again.

'Hopeless we were back then,' he said. 'Hardly won a game a season. The other teams were bigger, stronger.'

'Bit different these days, eh? We've got some tall timber now,' she said.

'Yeah, that Torrens kid's huge.' He shook his head in disbelief. 'I was a young fella when I played with his dad. He retired after a year or so. Good bloke, Mick Torrens.'

'Yeah, I couldn't believe my luck when Matthew turned up at the club wanting to play.'

Rowan grunted, shook his head again. 'What a mongrel that

109

kid was,' he snorted. 'Bloody mountain of a boy, turned into a complete head case. Nightmare for poor Mick.' He took a bite of his sandwich. 'Wouldn't have been so bad if he'd stopped at the pranks, I suppose.'

'What pranks?' Clementine asked, forcing a casual tone.

'Blowing up letterboxes, that sort of thing.'

Clem pushed her chair back with a scrape, went to the sink and rinsed her mug. 'I never wanted to ask him about his past—it didn't seem polite,' she said.

Rowan went on as if he hadn't heard her. 'Even the graffiti, you could cop that...'

Her heart skipped a beat.

'...but the standover stuff for those dealers from Earlville—threats, intimidation, pay up or I'll smash your car, break your legs...' He chewed for a moment. 'Poor Mick couldn't hold his head up after that, had to leave town.'

Clementine kept her back to Rowan, gripping the edge of the sink and staring out through the kitchen window. Torrens had seemed so confident in his plan. Now she knew why. She'd taken him straight back to his rotten roots. She was bad luck, bad karma blowing around Katinga like a foul odour. Everything she touched was a disaster. She wanted to vomit.

Afterwards she tidied away the lunch stuff. Rowan left at about three. At four the police car rolled up the driveway.

\\/

She offered Sergeant Phillips and Constable Miller a cup of tea. They politely declined.

She could hardly concentrate. The night she'd spent in the Kings Cross watch house kept coming back to mind. The humiliating strip search. The feel of the surgical gloves on her skin. An alcoholic blur at the time, a leaden thud of realisation the next morning.

She blinked, trying to focus on what the sergeant was saying.

Apparently there'd been an incident in Katinga Heights over-night, some sort of malicious damage, threats made. They had questioned one Matthew Torrens, recently released from Loddon. He had a history of this sort of thing.

Each piece of information was like a crushing wave, pushing her deeper.

Torrens had been very cooperative. Had provided his mobile phone to the police to check his phone calls and text messages.

'He said he trains with you on a Monday night.'

'Yes,' she said. 'Matthew is behind in his fitness, but he's keen. He asked if I'd help him with extra sessions.'

'And did you?' Phillips' voice was a deep baritone. He was tall and lean, but with a middle-aged paunch beginning to spill over his belt. With his 1980s Tom Selleck moustache, he reminded her of her high school principal, standing here in her kitchen, by her pantry.

'Did I what?'

'Give him extra training sessions?' Sergeant Phillips had the look of someone who had heard enough lies to last a lifetime.

'Yes—yes, I did. Every Monday night.'

'So last night, then?' asked Constable Miller, flipping to a new page in his notebook. Despite the winter cold, Miller was in a short-sleeved shirt. Clementine couldn't help noticing his biceps as he wrote in the notebook. Miller was ripped. Some sort of gym junkie. *He should be on the team*, she thought. *Shut up, Jones. Concentrate, stay sharp!*

'Yes, last night too,' she said.

'What time was that, do you think?'

'Well, by the time we got started it would have been about six-thirty or maybe seven o'clock.'

'Bit dark at the oval that time of night?' Miller looked sceptical.

'Oh, we weren't at the oval. We went out to the scout hall. It's lit up pretty well at night, and they've got the kids' play equipment. I made him do thirty chin-ups on the monkey bars.' She hoped to God Torrens had remembered the details of the story they'd rehearsed.

'You've certainly got these boys primed, Ms Jones,' said Miller. 'Never seen such a bunch of dropouts so fit.' His tone had a sinister note, as if she were training them all to become paramilitaries in Syria or something.

'Well, I wouldn't call them dropouts, constable. They're working pretty hard for the team at the moment.'

'Some of them are dropouts, Ms Jones. And some of them are worse than that. Nasty histories in that mob.'

Clementine said nothing.

'So what time did you call it quits?' said the sergeant, steering the interview back on track.

'Um, I think it was around eight o'clock by the time he'd finished his warm-down.'

'Do anything after that, then?' Phillips asked.

'Well, he wanted to shout me a slap-up dinner for giving up my time for him. I didn't let him, of course, but we did go to the pub for a salad.'

Miller snorted. 'I bet Torrens had a bit more than salad.'

'Yeah, as a matter of fact he had a steak.' They had eaten at the pub, but the exercise session was a lie.

'Anyone see you there?' Phillips was trying to get them back on track again. Professional, she thought. She liked that in a person, but here, with two policemen in her little kitchen, it was all wrong.

She found a calm voice: 'Well, yes. Whoever was serving in the bistro, I guess, and a few drinkers at the bar—I think I saw that guy from the servo, Kenny something, having a beer with someone. Oh, and Jack and Judy Simpson were eating there too at the time.'

Miller was scribbling in his pad.

'And what time did you leave the pub?' asked Phillips.

'Probably just after nine, I reckon.'

'Did you go straight home?'

'No, I followed Matthew home—'

'So he'd had too much to drink then?' Miller was quick on the draw with his snide questions.

'No, actually. He was sober. He'd had one mid-strength beer. Team rules—three mid-strengths per week. That's it.'

Miller looked up from his notebook, surprised. 'Bloody hell! You have got them buckled in!' He laughed and turned to Phillips. 'We might just go on and win this thing, sarge!'

'Jesus, constable. Don't go putting the mockers on us now,' Clementine said, smiling. It felt like she'd been holding her breath this whole time. 'We've got a long way to go yet. You ought to join us for training. A hunk of muscle like you could do some damage, you know.'

Miller drew his shoulders back. 'Nah, not my kind of game, Aussie Rules.' He shook his head, but he was grinning stupidly.

'So, you followed him back home because...' said Phillips, losing patience.

'He fell off the monkey bars. Hit his head. He seemed fine, but I just wanted to make sure.'

'And was he okay?'

'Yes. Looked as if he was. Drove straight home, no erratic moves, and walked to the front door. He looked fine.' Phillips looked tired. Was he sick of listening to her lies?

'And so you said goodbye and went home?'

'No, we said goodbye at the pub. Torrens didn't know I followed him. They're a proud bunch, sergeant, especially Torrens. He's trying to fit in, you know, show he's up to it. Doesn't want anyone thinking he needs looking after. God knows there's always some dickhead who wants to have a go, you know. The other teams call us mummy's boys on account of me being a woman.'

'What? Which teams?' Constable Miller had swung entirely to her side.

'If you want to make them pay, constable, come to training. I'm always after strong fellas like you. God knows we need the firepower around the packs.' She gave Miller a keen look, as if she was sizing him up for a key role, like she believed in him.

'Nah, I'm totally unco,' he said, with a laugh. 'I stick to my weights and a bit of a run on my days off.' He was definitely standing taller now, and she could see his shirt strain across his pectoral muscles as he flexed.

'Hmm. It's not all about ball skills, constable, not at this level. When there's five blokes all wanting the same ball, it's all about brute strength.' She saw a glint in Miller's eyes—he believed her. Maybe he'd even show up for training?

'Oh, I can vouch for this one. He's totally without skill or brains,' Phillips said. 'You should concentrate on the blokes who can actually play.' He didn't smile, but his tone was playful. 'Well, thanks for your time, Ms Jones—we'll see ourselves out.'

They headed down the hallway. Clementine wondered if she should ask what had happened in Katinga Heights, make it look like she was curious. But before she could get the question out, Phillips stopped and turned. 'I don't suppose you can account for Torrens after you saw him off home, then?'

A chill swept over her. 'No, sorry—I went home myself after that. I expect he went straight to bed, though. He was exhausted after the training session.'

'Yes, I suppose he would have been. Thanks again, Ms Jones.' Phillips was giving nothing away. He opened the front door and strode towards the car, Miller close behind him.

She watched them drive off. Phillips wouldn't let it rest that easily, she thought. God, she wanted to speak to Torrens, find out if their stories had matched. She resisted the urge and hoped he wouldn't be crazy enough to call.

Her mobile rang.

She ran back to the kitchen and picked up the phone. It was

Gerard. Oh Lord, what must be going on at his house this morning?

He'd rung to congratulate her on the feature article from last week—he'd forgotten about it when she'd dropped the report off. He sounded like he was going through the motions, bereft of his usual energy. Clearly the incident had shaken him, but he was soldiering on, doing his job.

'Thanks, Gerard. I'm just glad it's yesterday's news now.'

'You're way too modest, Jones, but anyway, it's excellent coverage for the club. I've already had two phone calls from local businesses wanting to kick in some sponsorship funds.'

'Well, I'm happy about that bit. Should help with my bonus.'

Gerard ignored her comment. 'So the article said you worked in Sydney, for a law firm?'

'Yeah, nothing special. Clerical work, mainly.'

'That must be where you picked up your legal knowledge, then.'

Shit, Jones, he's suspicious now—why wouldn't he be? She'd been such a git.

'Oh and by the way, could you send me your resumé? Just for the file. Which firm was it again?'

'White, Shale & Jervis. A small practice out at North Sydney.' It was real—he could google it—but if he dug any further, he'd find they'd never heard of her.

'Oh, right. Just that my good friends work at Crozier Dickens. They come out for weekends sometimes. They've just gone back to Sydney, though. Perhaps when they're out this way again I should introduce you.'

CHAPTER 18

Clementine flicked the pencil torch on, shielding the tiny beam of light with her hand, flicked it off again and started scrubbing. Torrens' two-day-old blood had stuck fast.

She switched the torch on and off again. Damn. Tiny crusted patches of dark brown clung to the cracks and ridges of the rock. She pulled out her pocketknife, started picking at them.

Her fingers were clumsy with the cold, and the chill bit at her face, exposed between beanie and scarf. *At this rate I'm going to have to invest in a balaclava*, she thought.

The police might have found the blood already, of course, but she was counting on them being under-resourced, no time to do the detailed work. But what if she was wrong? She couldn't risk leaving the blood there, couldn't risk implicating him. God, how could she ever have involved him in the first place? *He's on parole, for Christ's sake.*

She picked away with the knife in the darkness, too afraid to use the torch again.

The dog barked from a house a few doors up. She stopped scraping and waited, gripping the torch so hard her fingernails bit into her palms. The moon was hidden behind the clouds, only the faintest glimmer betraying its position. The barking stopped and she went back to her work, scratching at the tiny scabs.

A door opened, a light came on. The Holts' house next door. She dropped flat to the ground, pressing herself into the cold earth, hiding the pale of her face behind a patch of long grass.

In the glow of the porch light, she could see two figures. By his stance, she knew one was Gerard, but she couldn't see the man who stood behind him. Their voices carried in the still night air, fading as they made their way down the front steps, out of view.

A light flicked on at the side of the house. Clementine held her breath. A woman's silhouette appeared at the window—Bernadette, staring out across the vacant block, her gaze hovering over Clementine's motionless form. Clementine felt the blood pulse in her ears, sharp grains of gravel digging into her cheek. It seemed like an eternity. She had to breathe—a tiny puff of steam as she exhaled. Surely she would be seen. Holding her breath again. Then silhouetted arms reached out wide, grabbed the curtains and drew them shut.

Clementine gulped at the air, sucking specks of dirt into her mouth, pushing them out with her tongue, her heart thumping into the earth beneath her.

She could still make out male voices in the front yard behind the fence. She eased herself up on her elbows and crawled forward, low to the ground like a goanna, close to the fence, and looked through a crack, no more than a thumb's breadth wide. Gerard was standing with his back to her only a few metres away, facing the other man, who was partially obscured by the branches of a tree.

'Yeah, well, I'll have someone look into it,' said the man.

'Who?' asked Gerard.

'You don't need to know that.'

'Good point,' said Gerard.

The man nodded. White, short, stocky. She strained to see his features between the leaves of the shrub. Possibly bald.

'I should take the tapes,' said the man.

'No. I need to hang on to them. For now, anyway,' Gerard said.

'Give 'em to me. Safer that way.' The man walked back up

towards Gerard, standing on the front steps. He didn't sound like he was used to accommodating objections.

'No, no.' Gerard held up one hand. 'They're my insurance. He's just as likely to do something stupid. Get pissed, start running off at the mouth if I don't give him more money. I want to be able to show him the footage, make him realise how it will look to the police. It's best I have it on hand.' Gerard's voice had a deferential, entreating tone Clementine had never heard before.

The man grunted and started down the steps. 'Your funeral,' he said. Then, as he walked towards the front gate, he said, 'See you next week.'

'Right. Not here though, Brose. I don't want you coming here.'

The overheard conversation in the office. Bernadette objecting to someone coming to their home. And that name—Brose. Where had she heard it before? The tattoo parlour...the guy who'd interviewed Ricky for his job. Ambrose.

'If you pay on time, I won't have to come chasing you, will I?'

The man, Brose, opened the gate. Gerard followed, stuck his head out and checked the street. Clementine was safely behind the side fence separating the house from the vacant block.

She heard a motorbike start. Gerard closed the gate and walked towards the front steps as the motorbike roared up the street. She inhaled sharply, not even aware she'd been holding her breath again. A tiny flying creature of the night flew into her mouth, hitting the back of her throat. She gagged silently, saliva dribbling from her lips. She despised herself, crawling about in the dirt like an insect, like a cockroach.

But through her insect eyes she could see the strands of a web in front of her and a spider, Gerard, at the centre.

CHAPTER 19

She'd been thinking about the tapes when the phone rang. She jumped, dropping her jam toast on the floor.

Jenny Rodham. 'Just ringing to let you know Gerard's on a business trip to Sydney, so he asked me to pass on that the committee met yesterday and supported your selection report,' she said.

'Thank God for that,' said Clem. It had been almost a week since she'd dropped it off, and she'd almost forgotten about it by now, after all that had happened. She watched Pocket licking up the jam from the floor, his pink tongue chasing it underneath a slit in the old lino as Jen related the details of the committee discussion. Clem had thought about replacing the lino, but she'd grown accustomed to it, like the rest of the house. Something about its idiosyncrasies and imperfections made Clem want to keep it how it was. The previous owners had probably dropped a sharp knife there decades ago and never considered it important to fix it, or perhaps couldn't afford to.

Finished with the jam, Pocket turned to the toast, wolfing it down with huge, feverish gulps.

'Don't get too comfortable, though,' Jen said. 'You're not going to like what's coming next.'

'What's that?'

'One of the committee members, Les Bridges, thought it would be a good idea if you helped out with the Indigenous Knowledge Centre event.'

'The what?'

'It's a community project. Gerard and Les are trying to get a government grant for it. Gerard's tight with Sally McIntosh.' *Oh God*, thought Clem. Sally was the local MP and Minister for Aboriginal Affairs. 'It's a publicity thing at the school. They thought if you're speaking, they'll get a better turn-up from the parents and extra press—'

'Speaking?' she groaned. 'Surely he doesn't expect me to speak?'

'Look, honey, there's no use complaining to me about it, and I suggest you don't complain to Gerard, either. He stood up for you at the committee, you know, got your report endorsed. Besides, it's good for Katinga.'

Clem started clearing the kitchen bench, put the jam back in the pantry, slamming the door.

'Anyway,' Jen said, 'Gerard's going to get started on the diversity officer job, so we should be able to kick that off in a week or two. And not a moment too soon.'

'What do you mean?'

'You didn't hear about the fight, then?'

'No.'

'The Earlville gang were here last night, down at the service station—there was a brawl with some boys from the Plains. Animals, these young blokes. Bashed the bejesus out of each other. Half a dozen taken to hospital, I heard.'

Clementine's neck stiffened. 'Who was injured?'

'I can't remember the names in the paper this morning but I didn't know any of them. I was just relieved it wasn't poor Clancy. From what I heard, half of the injured were white. It's beyond me why they do it. Kenny at the servo said the Plains mob were angry about Clancy leaving the team, accused the Earlville blokes of being behind it.'

Clem felt a sudden wave of tiredness. She leaned against the kitchen sink. 'Jen, I shouldn't have picked Richie Jones, should I?

120

None of this would have happened.'

'Bulldust. He was the best man for the job. You're being ridiculous—it has nothing to do with you.' Jen paused a moment, waiting for a reply, but there was none. 'But enough of that,' Jen said. 'I want to know how you got on with Frank Cranfield. I've been wondering all week if you've found out anything more.'

Clem told her little more than what she already knew: Cranfield had received a large deposit and he had a new car, but she hadn't uncovered anything else yet that might connect the two events.

'I'm sorry, Jen. I know how much it means to you.'

'Yeah,' she sighed. 'Steve was a beautiful boy. We all miss him dreadfully, even after all these years.' Clem listened while Jen spoke of her youngest brother and the horrific car accident that claimed his life almost twenty-five years ago. He'd been twenty-one, Cranfield three years older. The family had been shattered, convinced Cranfield had been driving, but the police were unable to produce any compelling evidence.

'So if you do find anything on Cranfield, you have to let me know,' said Jen, a hardness in her voice now. 'If we can't get him for what he did to Steve, I'd love to see him go down for something else.'

Clementine assured her she would.

'Anyway, apparently you've asked for a bonus, you cheeky bugger,' said Jen, changing the subject. 'It's been approved provided you sign on for another year.'

God, thought Clem, *I won't be here next year. I shouldn't be here now.* 'Great,' she said.

Jenny moved on to the work function she'd be attending that evening for the bank. The annual Katinga customer event. All the bank's biggest commercial customers would be there.

'I'm going to wear a black dress,' she said. 'Not the one I wore to the club fundraiser, a different one. It's full length, low-cut to show off my favourite pearls...oh, and the necklace Trevor gave

121

me.' She exploded with laughter.

Clem chuckled too but her mind was whirring. 'So is CTS a big customer, then?' she asked.

'The biggest. Bernadette's at the head table with the bank VIPs down from Sydney.'

They chatted some more about the dress, until finally Clem saw a chance to ask the question burning a hole inside her.

'So Gerard's away overnight, then, for this Sydney thing?'

'Yes,' Jenny said. 'He'll be back tomorrow afternoon.'

A few minutes later Clementine made her excuses and hung up. She would need all afternoon to prepare.

It was the only course of action available to her. It wasn't sensible, and it wasn't wise, but she had to know what it was that had turned Clancy and Melissa's young lives upside down. Whatever it was, she was sure it was on the tapes.

\l/

She drove towards town. It was raining again. The whirr of the wipers and the sweet *tick tock* as they reached the end of their arc eased the jangling in her head. The paddocks along the flat rolled by, cattle huddling under lone gum trees. She reached the top of the descent, twisting into the fresh green bends, the ferns glossy and glistening in the wet.

Maybe what was left of Torrens' blood would be washed away by the rain, she thought. Torrens had told her at training that he'd not heard anything further or received any more visits from the police since Tuesday. It looked like they might have got away with it.

She ran through the plan for tonight in her head. When she went through the steps one by one, it felt like any other project, just a series of tasks to execute. But when she visualised herself there, putting it all into action, she was appalled. It was becoming a familiar feeling. And yet in the background, somewhere deep in her subconscious, there was a hardening too, a sense that the choice was getting easier. *Is this what happens?* She pressed on the brake for a hairpin bend, taking it super slow so she could look down the steep slope to her right into the eucalypt columns.

Approaching the main road T-intersection, she turned her left indicator on and slowed to give way to a car heading towards Katinga from Earlville. A blue Falcon ute sped towards her, spray flying from its wheels. As it drew near she could see the driver, the bulk of his shoulders, a shaven head. It was the man from the tattoo parlour with the eagle tattoo. Red Flanno. As the car flashed by she could just make out a familiar face in the front passenger seat, baseball cap back to front. Todd Wakely. Definitely Todd Wakely, coming back from Earlville with his mate.

\\/

The rain was easing when she pulled up in front of the newsagent, but the overcast sky maintained its gloomy grip on the day. The streets were busy, lots of farmers and farm workers taking advantage of the rainy weather to do their banking and shopping.

She parked in the angle parking bays and stepped straight out into a puddle, water squelching in her sneakers as she made her way to the newsagent. She read the article about the fight sitting on a bench on the big wide verandah that ran the length of the commercial strip on Main Street. It didn't tell her anything more than she already knew.

Clementine wished she could speak to Sergeant Phillips or Constable Miller, find out who was involved, whether Todd Wakely was part of it all. But given what she had planned for tonight, that wasn't a good idea.

She rang John Wakely, but he didn't answer. Next she tried Todd's phone, but it went straight to message bank. Across the street Mrs Lemmon was pulling her tartan shopping trolley down the pavement, heading towards the IGA, with her permanent smile.

As Clem headed across the road towards the steps up to the verandah in front of the post office, Clancy was coming out. He tried to change direction as if he hadn't seen her, so she hurried over, calling his name.

He turned around reluctantly. 'G'day, Jonesy.'

'Good to see you, Clancy. How's things?'

'Yeah, all right, thanks,' he said, warily.

'How's Melissa? She must be very close now.'

'Yep, less than two weeks to go.'

'Exciting!' she said.

'Yeah. Looks like I'm not going to be there for it, though. The birth, I mean.'

He was trying to look indifferent, hands thrust deep into his pockets, stomach jutting forward. She recalled what he'd told her about leaving the team to look after Melissa and be there for the birth. He was so mixed up he hadn't even attempted to keep his story straight.

'Oh, no. How come?' she asked.

'Got a job in New South Wales,' he said. 'Starts Monday week.' He forced a smile.

'Oh, Clancy, that's a shame. Although I suppose it's great that you've found a new job. Where are you off to?'

'Wheat property out near Yass. Just some farmhand work, labouring, you know. Used to do a bit of it in my school holidays.'

'And they can't wait a week?'

'Nah, seasons don't work like that. You gotta get going at the right time. Manager told me if I'm not there seven am Monday he'll give the job to one of the other twenty blokes who applied.'

So young, so grim. It made her sad. 'How's Mel taking the news?' she asked.

Clancy looked away, across the street and above the shops at

124

some distant spot on the horizon. 'Yeah, not good, I suppose, not good. She's pretty cut up about it, really, but she knows we're behind on the rent and stuff, so we got no choice. Plenty of her people here to take care of her with the bub for a bit. Once I'm settled in, I can shift her and the bub up to the property. They got a hut we can stay in, got tank water, so we should be all right. Only a quarter of what we're paying here, too.'

'What about power? Tell me this place has power,' Clementine said, shocked.

'There's a generator. They told me it's enough for hot showers, and there's a kettle there and an electric frypan.'

Clementine felt a rising anger. So much had been taken from this young family. They'd been shoved to the ground, and now the world was kicking them in the guts. She gazed at Clancy, searching for something.

'Lots of us mob have to do it tough. Me and Mel are no different. We'll be all right.'

It was too much. She couldn't bear it. His stoicism made her want to shout at the world, at Gerard and Cranfield and Todd Wakely and those racist dickheads from Earlville and Brose and everyone who had a part in whatever the hell was going on. She counted to three, composed herself.

'Clancy, what really happened at CTS? It just doesn't seem to make sense to me that they fired you, and everyone I've spoken to says the same—nobody can believe it.'

He looked at the pavement, kicked a pebble.

Clementine waited a second. 'We can't believe it, because we all know you're not a thief—are you, Clancy?'

He blinked hard, but said nothing.

'Clance, I might be able to help you. But I need to know what happened.'

He looked away across the street again, crossing his arms across his chest.

'Has someone told you to keep quiet about something? Maybe something you saw, or something someone did that you weren't supposed to know about? Or maybe the Earlville crowd throwing their weight around?'

He looked back at her, angry. 'You can't ask me this stuff.'

'But Clancy—'

'Look, I've got to go. I can't even be seen talking to you.'

'Me? Why am I off limits?' He didn't respond. 'Okay, so there's something you're not supposed to talk about. But I know you're not a thief.'

He stood, motionless, saying nothing, but his body was bursting with words.

'Clancy, who told you not to talk? Was it Frank Cranfield? Maybe I could talk to—'

'No, no, no. Don't even mention names,' he said, his eyes sweeping the street, furtively.

'Okay, okay, it's all right. I won't say anything to Cranfield— don't worry. Maybe I could talk to Gerard Holt, though?'

'Shit, no! Do not fucking talk to Mr Holt.' His hands were behind his ears, gripping his hair.

It started to rain again. Small, gentle drops.

He was on the verge of giving her a name—she knew it. 'Who then? Just tell me where I can start without coming across as nosy. Maybe someone I know well, someone I already chat with regularly?'

'Aw, shit, shit, shit. No, no,' he whimpered, his shoulders crumpling. The rain was coming down heavy now, starting to drive in under the awning.

He took a deep breath, gathered himself up, shook his head. 'No. No,' he said, convincing himself of something, then, turning towards her, 'Just stay out of it, Jonesy. This isn't something you can fix.'

126

He gave her a final glare and took off down the steps and out into the rain, leaving her standing in front of the post office, shivering with cold.

CHAPTER 20

The clock on the dash ticked over to 8.28 pm. It had stopped raining a couple of hours ago and the stately homes of Katinga Heights were dark and quiet. All of them on the high side of the street backed onto bushland. She sat with her hands gripping the steering wheel as she peered into the night, visualising the moves she had planned.

She'd brought two short pieces of wood to prop up against either side of the back fence. They'd give her the extra height she needed to make it over—one on the outside to get into the yard, one on the inside to get back out. Inside the yard, the fence would shield her from the street and the neighbours. Then she must head for the back patio and find the spare keys from under the bricks around the water feature—Gerard had got them from there last time when they'd had a committee meeting at the house and he'd left his keys at the office. She hoped the Holts hadn't changed their hiding place. Once inside, then…she baulked again at the thought of it—creeping around, all in black, beanie and surgical gloves, rummaging through their lives. A wave of disgust rolled over her.

She scanned the street one last time. Clear. She made it through the bush to the back fence in a barrage of barking from the dog two doors up, propped the piece of wood against the fence and used it like a ramp to jump over. No lights came on, and no one appeared to investigate, too used to the dog's frequent alerts to pay attention. She breathed a sigh of relief. That was the most exposed part done, until she had to cross the same empty stretch on her way out.

Finding the keys was like a game of memory. She picked up almost every brick around the water feature, gradually losing hope, until she finally found them. She put on a pair of latex gloves, picked up the keys and made her way past the swimming pool to the back door.

Closing the door behind her, she shone her phone torch around a large and well-equipped entertaining area—lounge suite, gleaming silver bar fridge and floor-to-ceiling wine rack. She tiptoed out into the hallway, pushing open each door as she went. The first was a huge bedroom, a wedding photograph of Bernadette and Gerard hanging on the far wall, a large TV and an open door to an ensuite. Her eyes fell on the bedside table closest to the door. She had a sudden desire to know, justified it by pretending it was part of her search. She approached the table and ran her fingers across the items—a jewellery box, a photograph of a young man, a ceramic dish containing a pair of pearl earrings, a scarf draped across a single hardcover book titled *Beautiful Boy*.

She could feel the Holts' presence. *Good God—what am I doing?* Snooping around their personal things—it sickened her. She backed out of the room.

She tried the next few doors. All bedrooms. She was almost all the way to the front part of the house now, where the hallway opened up into a large open-plan lounge, dining and kitchen area. She pushed on the final door. At last, the office—a large desk, sleek and black, with matching filing cabinet and swivel chair. She brushed past the potted palm near the doorway and tried the filing cabinet. Locked.

She made a start on the desk drawers. Hardly anything in the first one—pens and pencils, paperclips, and a lot of empty space. The next was filled with a neat stack of blank A4 paper. The last drawer was full of what looked like years of warranty cards and manuals, along with a fat wad of receipts held together by a large bulldog clip. She rummaged around underneath until her gloved fingers touched on a set of keys right up the back.

She tried the lock on the filing cabinet—bingo—and began shuffling through the top drawer, checking inside each file. Nothing of interest. She felt around underneath the files and to the back of the drawer. Nothing. She checked her watch. It was just past nine pm. From what Jen had said, the bank function wasn't due to finish until ten pm at the earliest. Plenty of time if the tapes were here in the study, but not a lot if she had to go through the bedrooms or the kitchen to find them. She stepped it up a gear.

No luck with the second drawer.

As she slid open the third drawer she heard a noise—just a car driving up the street. She started checking inside the files. Nothing. She slipped her hands underneath, searching to the back of the drawer. Her gloved fingers fell onto a small cloth bag in the back left corner. She traced her fingertips along it and felt the distinctive shape of two USB sticks.

At that moment she heard footsteps at the front of the house. She stiffened, switching off the torch and standing perfectly still, ears straining, every muscle tensed. A key in the front door. *Oh God.* The front door opening now. She gently shut the drawer, her mind racing. Escaping down the hallway was out of the question—too visible from the front living area. She tiptoed across the carpet to a built-in cupboard on the opposite side of the room, pulled open the double doors. Inside were a row of shelves to the left, and to the right a tall, thin space with a cricket bat, two tennis rackets and an umbrella. She squeezed in, pulling the door shut behind her, barely fitting in the shallow space. The handle of the cricket bat jammed under her left butt cheek.

Had she left the back door open? She couldn't remember. She heard high heels clacking across the tiled floor in the kitchen, a cupboard door opening. Bernadette, home early. She could scarcely breathe. She heard footsteps going past, down the hallway. She remembered her mobile phone. Had she turned it to silent? Yes, she was sure she had.

Bernadette went into one of the rooms off the hall—the main bedroom? Clementine heard a tap running, then the sound of a television. Oh Lord above, the bedrooms were between her and the back door—how was she going to get past? The front door wasn't an option—her chances of scaling the six-foot fence without being noticed were remote and she didn't know how to operate the automatic gates.

She carefully reached for the back pocket of her jeans, adjusting the bat handle out from underneath, and slowly pulled out her mobile phone, her hands sweaty and trembling inside the latex gloves. Yes, it was on silent. She typed in the text: *Help. Trapped inside Holts place. Need u 2 distract Bernadette out front so I can get out back door.*

She waited. Five minutes passed.

A text flashed up onto the screen of her mobile.

On my way. Any ideas?

\|/

It felt like an hour had passed, but the time on her phone showed 9.35 pm. Her shoulders were starting to cramp in the confined space and the air smelt like mouldy tennis balls. She'd heard a toilet flush and then the TV noise had cut out. Was Bernadette asleep perhaps? She wondered if she could risk tiptoeing past the bedroom to the back door. Yes, it might be safer than waiting for backup.

She was just about to send another text telling him not to worry when she heard it—*BOOM!* The whole house shook. It was like a bomb had gone off out the front of the house.

For a moment Clem was rooted to the spot, confused, then she

131

heard the thump of bare feet running up the hallway. She pushed open the cupboard door and cautiously poked her head out into the hallway. The front door was open, and she just caught the top of Bernadette's head bobbing down the porch stairs and out of sight.

Clementine sprinted for the back door, her heart racing. She rushed past the pool toward the back fence, scrambling over using the ramp she'd made with the second piece of wood and landing with a thud on the uneven ground in the bushland behind the yard. Nobody would be looking at the back of the house, not after whatever weapon of mass destruction Torrens had unleashed out front. She picked up the piece of wood she'd left on this side of the fence and ran for the car at the top of the hill.

It wasn't until she arrived back at the cottage that she realised she'd dropped the cloth bag.

CHAPTER 21

It was raining again, loud against the Wombat Cafe's tin roof. The place was empty. Clem bought an apple teacake and sat in the gloomiest corner of the shop. She read the *Valley News* while she waited. All the combatants involved in the brawl at Kenny's service station had been released from hospital, the police investigation continuing.

She rang Jen. Her black dress and pearls had been sensational, she said, but the function had been a bit of a fizzer. Bernadette had left early—apparently she hadn't been feeling well.

By the time Torrens arrived, she'd read the whole paper bar the classifieds and finished her coffee. He lowered his frame onto the spindly-looking aluminium chair, grinning like a Cheshire cat.

'Oh God, I'm so sorry, Torrens, I—' She thought she should begin with an apology, but he swatted it away like a fly.

'What are you going on about? Haven't had that much fun since I was thirteen!' he guffawed and, as she sat there stunned, began to explain the simple joy of a letterbox bomb.

'Couldn't you have just knocked on the front door or something?' she said.

'Nah. That would have looked suss.'

'But your parole?' She felt the rising guilt again.

'Don't sweat it, Jonesy—nobody saw me put it in there, and I used a long fuse. I was long gone before it went up. She was a ripper, though, wasn't she? One of my best.' He grinned.

He hadn't mentioned the fact that she had been the one to seek out his rescue last night—too polite.

The rain ramped up a notch, heavy enough now that they had to lean forward to hear each other speak. Torrens tore off a huge lump of her teacake, shoved all of it in his mouth at once, licking his fingers.

'Listen,' he said, still chewing, 'I don't know exactly what's going on or what you were up to last night, but it seems to me like you care too much about Clancy.'

How did he know this was about Clancy? She hadn't told him anything on that score. It occurred to Clementine that he had prepared for this meeting—his words seemed rehearsed.

'Why do you think it's about Clancy?'

'Oh, come on. Give me some credit. I hear the talk around town. You asking questions, getting yourself neck-deep in trouble. Jesus—other than training you wouldn't be seen in town for weeks! Ever since Clancy quit you're here every other day.'

That obvious, she thought. *And the talk of the town. Good one, Jones.*

'Fact is, this sort of thing goes on all the time. Life's not fair, okay? Clancy has to take it on the chin and move on.' He swallowed the mouthful of teacake, wiped his sausage-sized fingers on a napkin and tossed it onto the table. 'And one thing I'll tell you for free—there's plenty of crims out there just looking for a chance to take people down, and plenty of semi-decent bastards who'll help 'em too if they can make a little for themselves along the way. Too many of 'em for you to handle, coach. This is not a game you can win.' He slapped his hands down on his thighs and leaned back in his chair again, eyeing off the remains of the teacake.

'It's not about Clancy,' she lied.

Torrens shook his head, reached into his back pocket and dumped a small cloth bag on the table. She was astonished.

'Where did you get that?' She reached for it, but he was too quick for her, covering it with his hand.

'Drove up the hill after I set the bomb up, watched you jump the back fence, saw it fall out of your pocket.'

She sighed. 'Look, Torrens, it's a serious situation. Clancy's wife's having a baby, he has no job, and God knows we need him back on the team. Don't you want to win the premiership?'

'Oh yeah. Nothing sweeter. Even if it's just to wipe the smug looks off the faces of those blokes from Earlville and Jeridgalee and all the rest of 'em. And the afterparty! Can you fit the whole town in the Katinga Arms?' He laughed.

'Exactly. So that's why you have to do the right thing and give me that bag.' She kept her eyes on his, unblinking.

'No. No, you don't. I haven't finished yet.' He returned her stare. 'You're damn right I want to win this thing. Me and every other bloke on the team. But you know what? That's not the endgame.' He paused, and the roar of the rain on the tin roof filled the silence.

'You don't know this place, Jonesy, so you don't know what it is you've done for us. You were tough on us boys right from the start, but as long as we were working hard you didn't give a shit about anything else. I couldn't believe it when you let me join the team.' His face seemed older all of a sudden, she could see the years of hard knocks in his eyes. 'My name's poison in this place, let me tell you. People I've known since I was a kid look the other way when they see me on the street. There's friends of my mum's who won't talk to her since I was put away. But you just didn't care. All you saw was a bunch of blokes who wanted the same thing everyone wants: a chance at a bit of success. And for some of us, it was like our past didn't exist—all the loser shit we'd done. You didn't want to know about it, when everyone else in this town could barely stand to look at us. And then, there's a fucking miracle! We started winning! We're doing so bloody good the whole fucking town gets behind us. And you know what I reckon happened? I reckon each of us boys looked under a rock this season and found something there we never even knew existed. Know what that was?'

She shook her head, mute.

'I'll tell you what it was—a shining, sparkly piece of fucking self-respect. Something the counsellor lady in prison told me about. I thought I knew what she meant. I had no idea until I joined this team. Used to be a time I'd dream of finding a packet of weed under my pillow. But no, this is the real thing, the real deal. And for once I fucking didn't have to steal it. No, this time, I worked for it. Self-respect, Jonesy. You taught us that.'

She looked down at her lap, struggling to collect her thoughts.

'You know, I only got that job at the meatworks because of that. Because, for once, I knew I could do it. I finally realised I could do something the right way and succeed. And don't think it's just me. There's other boys on that team that got the same belief in themselves as well.'

She didn't know where to look, what to say, so she said nothing, fidgeting with the napkin, curling its edge up and rolling it flat again.

'So you see, that's what you gotta realise—we've already achieved our endgame. The stash is in the bag and we're counting the money. Don't get me wrong—we're gunna keep fighting, because having that trophy will be the icing on the cake. But don't think that's what it's all about, 'cos it fucking isn't.'

She put the napkin down, placed her hands flat on the table. There was a long silence. The rain beat down.

'Torrens, I get it. I truly do get it. But don't you see? What you're describing is exactly what Clancy's missing out on. He should have that chance as well, the same as you and the rest of the boys, to see it through, keep fighting, play for his teammates, win or lose. God knows he's earned it.'

Torrens slapped his hand down on his leg angrily. She jumped. 'Yeah, but not if it means you breaking into people's houses and shit! Don't you get it? You're the centre of everything that's fucking good about this team. For fuck's sake, there is no fucking team if you're not in the middle of it! What happens if you're caught? Or worse—you run off, trying to give the cops the slip? You were close to running off when you saw them old mates of yours. I bloody put my parole on the line to keep you here. Why d'ya think I did that?' A deep frown had settled on his forehead. 'Wake up, Jonesy, is all I'm asking. Open your eyes. You might just see something bigger than yourself, something worth the sacrifice.' He spoke now as if he'd crossed a line but he didn't care—he would hold nothing back. 'But if you carry on like you have been and something happens, something bad, well I'll tell you what—every man on that team will feel like it's all been a lie, a big fat lie. Work hard? Dig in for your teammates? Fuck no! Do whatever you damn well please, every man for himself. Just another lump of bullshit served large and hot on a big fat spoon and shoved down our throats.'

He looked down at the table. The pounding of the rain on the roof and the sheets of it streaming down the glass door of the cafe felt suffocating. She just wanted the conversation to end, to flee to her cottage in the hills.

When he finally looked up at her again, he spoke calmly. 'That's why you have to quit all that stuff, coach—you've gotta quit it now. And it starts with these,' he said, patting the bag. 'I can't have anything to do with them. The cops have got nothin' on me, but they'll want to find something, so you're going to have to do it. Now, listen, here's what you do. You do not look at whatever's on here. You got that? You don't look at 'em, you just throw 'em in a creek or, if you must return 'em—just chuck the bag over the back fence and walk away.'

He waited for a response. She gave a half-nod. He got up, scraping his chair noisily and walked out, leaving her sitting there alone, like a radioactive piece of shit in the shadows, the last slice of teacake and the cloth bag sitting accusingly on the table in front of her.

CHAPTER 22

She stopped in at the IGA, picked up some groceries and hosed down Mr Nicholls' enthusiasm. They'd won the last home-and-away game on Sunday, finishing second on the ladder. It meant they'd not only made it into the finals, they'd leapfrogged straight into the semis. The whole town was positively buzzing. Clem had kicked herself for not freezing some bread, and now she'd run out of Ryvitas as well.

Mr Nicholls made sure he was at the cash register so he could serve her personally. Yes, she agreed—a great win, history in the making—then reminded him there was a long way to go. He took the opportunity to mention his generous donation for man of the match. Kelsey Flood had won the thousand-dollar cheque last week with his bag of four goals and five contested marks at centre half-forward. It was a shame Clancy wasn't playing—he'd probably have won it and he could certainly use the money, she thought, before Nicholls had pointed out that Kelsey and his dad and younger brother were all still unemployed after the mine had closed.

She pulled out of the car park, stopping at the traffic lights on the corner of Main and Howard streets. Two pedestrians set out from the pavement, one of them Melissa Kennedy.

Melissa's eyes narrowed as she recognised Clementine's car. She drilled Clementine with a look, head tilted back defiantly, jaw thrust out. Then she turned away, keeping her eyes straight ahead as she crossed the street, demonstrating her indifference.

The lights turned green, but Clem didn't notice. Here she was again, on the other side of that great divide.

Clem watched Melissa's black ponytail sway as she crossed the road and heaved her bulk up onto the pavement. She was almost due, perhaps only a week to go. Clem kept watching as she went inside the Salvation Army shop on the other side of the street. A car behind honked its horn. She jumped forward in a panic, stalled, started the engine again and pulled off the road into the first parking space she could find. She sat for a moment but couldn't get her thoughts straight, could not formulate a plan. All she could think was that she had to make an attempt to cross the divide.

She got out of the car and headed for the Salvos shop. The old lady behind the counter smiled at Clem as she came in. Melissa was in the baby clothes section, inspecting a lemon-yellow jumpsuit. Clem made her way toward her, past the men's clothing racks with their mothball smell and the haphazard stacks of second-hand furniture.

'So you decided not to find out if it's a boy or girl?' Clem asked. It was all she could think of.

Melissa turned around and stared at her coldly. She looked tired.

Clem chanced a smile. 'Yellow's safe, they say.'

Melissa turned back to the shelf and picked up a tiny blue jacket. The gap was getting wider, freezing over.

'Hmm, maybe a boy, then?'

Melissa turned her back on Clementine.

'I hear Clancy got a job in Yass.'

Melissa swung around to face her. 'What do you want? Why'd you follow me in here?'

The divide was a glacier, a huge, freezing, impassable expanse between them. Clem scrambled for a credible reason. 'Actually, Melissa, I need your help.'

Melissa looked incredulous. 'What? Are you kidding? What

makes you think I'd want to help you?' She put the little blue jacket back on the shelf, walked towards the manchester section.

Clem stood there for a moment, then followed as Melissa picked up a purple towel with a splash of bleach discolouring one corner and examined the price tag. Clem put her hand on the towel. Melissa looked up, incensed.

'I need your help to understand what's going on, Melissa. I know the Plains mob are unhappy. It's because of me, I know. Maybe the fight was because of me—I don't know—but I want to do something about it, and I don't know how.'

'Fuck off.'

Clementine took a step back, shocked at the venom in her words. Melissa moved off further down the aisle.

'You don't understand. I have to speak at a function up at the school—the Minister for Indigenous Affairs will be there. It's for a good cause—the Indigenous Knowledge Centre.'

Melissa didn't look up from the stack of bedsheets she was surveying, but Clem noticed her blink. Twice.

'You must have heard about it. They're trying to get government funding for it.'

Melissa thumped a hand down on the sheets. 'And what the hell has that got to do with me?'

Clem kept going. 'I thought maybe you could help me with the speech. Maybe some history of the area from an Indigenous perspective or something.'

'Why the hell are you speaking, of all people? Why aren't my mob speaking?'

The response gave Clem hope—at least Melissa was talking. 'Well, I'm pretty sure they are, actually. I think I'm just there to attract a few more of the parents and drum up some more press coverage, apparently.'

Melissa started hunting through the linen again, but Clementine thought she could sense a thaw in the air.

140

'Maybe you could introduce me to your mum or one of the elders? Do you know anyone who might like to help me?'

'Right, you gunna learn all about us in half an hour, yeah?' She stalked off towards the electrical appliances, Clementine trailing closely behind her.

'A bit of background would help,' Clem said. 'Might help me know what not to say, at least.'

Melissa picked up a sad-looking toaster with an eight-dollar price sticker on it. Silence again, but it was definitely there—a swirling of particles in the air, a melting around the edges.

Clementine decided to leave her alone for a bit and made her way back towards the front of the store, stopping to try on a cardigan in the women's clothing section. Her hands shook a little as she struggled with the buttons. It fit well, and she could do with something light for spring. Then she picked out a rug that would be good for Pocket's kennel. Noticing Melissa at the counter, she hurried forward, grabbing the lemon-yellow jumpsuit on the way. She queued behind her with the cardigan, the rug and the jumpsuit.

Melissa was buying two towels. As she handed over the coins, Clem put her things on the counter.

Melissa glanced sideways, saw the jumpsuit, her contempt palpable. 'You can't buy me off, you know, you dirty gubba.'

'It's not for you, shit for brains. I've got a niece in Sydney.'

The retort came quick, like a slap. There was a moment—a horrible, sickening moment, as Clem's words hung suspended between them, the old lady behind the counter looking on in dismay—and then Melissa laughed. A loud, surprised, generous laugh, a laugh that grew wings and soared across the icy divide. Clementine joined in. The lady behind the counter smiled, relieved there wasn't going to be a scene.

They finished paying and walked into the pub next door, carrying their Salvos plastic bags. Melissa had a lemonade, Clem had a wine. They talked about Clancy. The job near Yass had fallen through. Mel didn't want to go anyway, she said, so she was relieved, and Clancy had kept on with his online studies in the meantime. But she was afraid that he wouldn't be able to find another job—not in Katinga, anyway.

Melissa told Clem about the Plains mob—their anguish when Clancy had left the team, their rage when they realised no one from the Plains would be playing in the finals. At first they'd thought that the Earlville gang had intimidated Clementine into getting rid of Clancy and that she'd selected a relative in Richie Jones. But later, Mel said, she'd heard that the Earlville gang had probably threatened Clancy—retribution for his testimony at the bashing trial two years ago. They were used to it, said Mel—more white bullshit. And Clancy not being on the team was just another door slamming in their face, denying them any joy in the Cats' success. Tensions remained high and Mel thought the fight last week was probably just the beginning.

\\/

Nineteen direct hits. How could that be? Thank God she hadn't got into the Facebook thing or had a blog or anything like that.

Clem sat in the front room at the dining table, laptop open in front of her, the wine she'd had with Melissa earlier in the afternoon leaving her slightly fuzzy-headed. She'd received countless slaps on the back in the pub and turned down three offers of a drink. The town was alive with excitement over the Cats' upcoming semifinal, the first in forty years. If they hadn't already heard of her, they knew her now—every man, woman and child in Katinga. She'd become a real live local bloody celebrity.

On the drive home, as she swung the Commodore through the bends up Makepeace Road, one question had consumed her thoughts: how long before one of these people looked her up online? It wouldn't take much to discover her real name, find out about her past. She'd put it off for months, unable to face it—but now, with a mounting sense of panic, she realised she could not delay the task any longer.

She'd been through every one of the hits. Five of them took her to Crozier Dickens' website—old articles she'd written when she worked there. She'd phoned the firm, spoken to Julia, a newly arrived business development manager, who had agreed to take them down or remove Clementine's name so the only attribution would be to her boss, the partner she'd worked for. Julia would have it done within twenty-four hours, she said.

She stared at the screen. Three of the nineteen hits were related to her LinkedIn profile, and she cursed herself for not deleting it. She remembered the day she had attempted to. It was a Sunday. She'd been released on Thursday, bought the Commodore and a new prepaid sim card on Friday, recovered her things from storage on Saturday and she was leaving that Sunday. That was the plan she'd mapped out for herself in those last weeks inside. Going through each step in her mind had been the only way she could get through those final days.

That Sunday morning she'd taken out her iPad at a cafe with free wi-fi, her back to the rear wall. She recalled the shock of seeing the headshot on her profile: the crisp edge of the collar on her cream shirt, the black velvet trim on the lapels of her favourite black suit. Her smile looked so confident, her hair perfectly arranged. She was seeing herself from the other side, a ghost.

But it was the bio that really got to her. The list of qualifications, the string of major files she'd worked on and the endorsements she'd received from big-name partners at the firm. Each word had screamed at her: *FRAUD*. She just wanted to erase it all—her name, her work, her history, everything she'd ever done. She'd tried to delete the LinkedIn profile, but struggled to find the 'delete' option, and with each failed attempt she'd ended up back on the profile page, that perfect smile staring out at her. She'd left her coffee sitting there, jumped in the car and fled. Just drove off and left Sydney forever.

She'd headed west. People hid in the country, didn't they? Hadn't stopped until late. Stayed in a tiny one-pub town, upstairs directly above the public bar. The bed sagged, the window was nailed open, and she had to use a common bathroom down the hall. The next morning she'd showered behind a curtain covered in black mould and brushed her teeth over a yellow-stained enamel basin. The woman she saw in the tiny cracked mirror was not the one in the digital profile. Gone were the expensive blond highlights, the white smiling teeth and lively eyes. In their place—mouse-brown hair, a weariness about her and a mouth set flat across a pale face.

She had kept driving for days, travelling south, staying at cheap hotels overnight and moving on the next day. She used her middle name, Clementine, and no one questioned it. The plan had been pretty simple: drive, be anonymous, don't form any connections. After a week she was sick of driving and didn't know what to do next. Taking a break from the monotony of the car, she'd walked up a mountain and looked down on a little town in a valley below. She drove along a country road, saw a 'For Sale' sign on a tiny, green, run-down cottage tucked in the saddle between two ridges. She'd paid cash, using up most of Gran's inheritance, then hid in the cottage in the hills for another few weeks, venturing into town only to get food and supplies.

That was ten months ago. It felt like years.

Pocket barged his way through the dog door, stood at her knee looking up at her, his tail slapping against the table leg.

'What you been up to, boy?' she said, giving him a pat. His big brown eyes told the story—*having fun in the backyard*. She patted him again and he trotted over to sit at the fireplace, leaving a trail of wet paw-prints on the wooden floor.

She began searching through the settings. Using the laptop instead of a tablet, it had proved easy to delete her LinkedIn account. She moved on to the remaining eleven references, all of them newspaper articles about the accident and her conviction. Although the articles used her first name, it was still dangerous— anyone making a real effort would find her.

A notification flashed up on the screen: incoming email. She clicked it open. It was the same as the previous three:

Thank you for your email. We appreciate your interest in the Daily Herald. We will endeavour to respond to your inquiry within the next twenty-four hours. Your inquiry code is B6254. Please quote this number in all communications about this inquiry.

She got up, went to the kitchen and made herself a cup of tea, her thoughts wandering to the USB sticks still sitting in the glove box of the Commodore. It had been easier than she thought just to close the door and leave them there. And now, after her conversation with Mel, it didn't feel right to keep prying into Clancy's life. He hadn't even told his wife what was going on. Who was she to think she could help?

Her phone rang. Gerard. She let it ring out. He rang back. She would have to take it. They exchanged pleasantries and he moved on to the purpose of the call: 'I hear you're spending time with Torrens, one on one. What's that all about?'

Her stomach clenched tight. 'Extra training sessions. The guy's unfit—he needs to catch up.'

Gerard wasn't impressed. 'Why bother? There's plenty of blokes in the reserves who are fit enough. Christ, Jones, you could have taken one of the boys from the Plains.'

Clementine sighed. 'Because I need his size. You know that, Gerard. He's a huge presence in the ruck and does a power of work up forward when he's resting. We can't do without him. What's this about, anyway? Has there been another complaint?'

He skirted the question. 'You know the Plains community is unhappy. It just seems to me to be one way we could appease a few people.'

'Look, Gerard, you need to deal with the politics, not me. My job is to put the best team on the park each week and hope to God we can keep winning.'

Gerard didn't let go. 'You realise he's not popular around town, Jones. He did a lot of unsavoury things, you know. There's still people hurting.'

'He served his time—I don't see why he shouldn't get a chance, and he's the best man for the job. Footy is giving him a life and some hope.'

'I'm assuming you heard about the incident at my place last week?' Gerard snapped. 'My friends were abused, their vehicle defaced. This week our letterbox was bombed. The police think it was Torrens.'

Her heart sank. She hadn't heard anything more about the investigation since she'd spoken to Torrens.

'You're not his social worker, Jones. Steer clear of him. Steer clear of Clancy as well. Just do your job. Do you understand me?' He rattled off each instruction like gunfire, but it was the final shot that alarmed her most.

'Oh, and by the way, you haven't sent me your resumé yet. I need to have a copy on file. Can you please send it through asap?'

The sun was a gloomy yellow behind the clouds hanging low and heavy on the hills. Morning showers had soaked the already green paddocks and puddles were forming in the yard.

Clem sat herself down at the dining table, turned her laptop on, spooning muesli while she waited for the whirring and beeping to stop. She opened the email account, waited for it to load.

Torrens had reassured her at their Monday training session last night that the police hadn't approached him again. Gerard had formed his own view about Torrens, so it seemed from the telephone conversation she'd had with him yesterday, but it did not appear to be one the police shared. Gerard would probably be there tonight at team training. He'd started turning up to training sessions these last couple of weeks—said he was keen to support the boys through the finals campaign, but she just couldn't shake the feeling that he was continually watching her.

She looked at her inbox. There were replies from two of the five newspapers. She needed them all to wipe the articles—one article was as bad as five or fifteen.

She opened the first one, from the *Daily Post*.

Dear Ms Jones
Thank you for your inquiry. As you can imagine, we are deeply committed to informing our readers and take pride in our contribution as a historical repository of

information. In light of this, our policy is to retain articles
online indefinitely.

   Thank you again for your inquiry.

Shit. She slammed her cereal bowl down, milk sloshing. She should have known. Unless she could show the articles were defamatory, she'd have no chance—and they weren't, of course. They were all true: every line, every detail of the accident, of her conviction. It would all be there forever, hanging over her like a shadow.

A text message beeped on her mobile phone. She went to the bedroom, unplugged it from the charger. From Gerard. *Resumé required today.* She sat on the side of the bed, head in her hands, the rain coming harder, whipped sideways by a rising wind.

Why was he asking for her resumé again so soon? So insistently? Was he on to her? Had he realised she had something to hide? Or was it just her paranoia? All these lies she'd been telling, the appalling things she'd done...of course, it would mess with her head—why wouldn't it? She scrunched her eyes shut, grabbed at her hair. What a fucking mess.

Her thoughts began to come together as she sat there. Whatever the reason for Gerard's sudden interest, she wasn't going to just sit back and wait for an ambush—certainly not from Gerard, not from anyone. She had to be ready. She stood up, paced the room. What she needed was a weapon, something to fight Gerard with if he came after her.

Then it dawned on her—she didn't need a weapon, she needed a shield, her own kind of insurance, something to make him think twice before pursuing her past any further.

She snatched the car keys off the hook in the kitchen and the umbrella by the front door, rushed outside to the Commodore, splashing out through the puddles, the umbrella trying to fold back on itself in the driving wind.

'Fucking bastard!' she screamed. At the umbrella, at the wind and the rain, at Gerard. She opened the car door, the rain splashing onto the front passenger seat, opened the latch to the glove box.

Storming into the cottage, she slammed the door and threw the dripping umbrella on the floor. She slotted the first USB stick into the laptop, her hands wet and trembling. Why couldn't people just leave her alone? Everyone wanting something from her, everyone telling her what to do, from Gerard to Mr Nicholls. Even Torrens.

Torrens. *Well, he can stand on his own two feet, just like I have to*, she thought. *At some stage he has to learn there are no paragons in this world, none.* It was all she could do to hold herself together—being a role model was out of the question. Absurd, anyway, if they only knew who she was, what she'd done.

Her anger brought a rush of clarity. Everything had become ridiculously complicated since Clancy had dropped his bombshell. She had chastised herself for not trying hard enough to keep him in the team, for intruding on Melissa and stirring up tension, but all along she had been second-guessing herself. She needed to back her judgement, keep swimming forward.

It was true—all this drama pursuing Clancy wasn't what she'd planned, and God knows she hadn't come here wanting to be some sort of hero. All she'd wanted was anonymity—to be some place where no one knew her past, so she could breathe despite the suffocating shame. It was a survival strategy. Signing up for the coaching job had been a mistake, but here she was, in the middle of Clancy's pain and the town's dreams. Each step she'd taken had felt like it had to be. And she'd be damned if Gerard and his resumé would be the thing to bring it all crashing down. Fuck him.

The file from the first USB stick appeared on the screen. The sound of the rain pummelling the tin roof was like thunder, the walls of the cottage shuddering in the wind. She selected the video file, pressed play. She could see lines of cars, distorted by the camera's wide-angle lens, through a hazy, morning half-light. She checked the date and time in the bottom-right corner: *8 August*

07:02. About a month ago, just before Clancy quit. The camera, mounted on the warehouse, showed the CTS car park the day after Clancy had quit the team: a bird flitted from the left side of the screen into the stunted wattles at the far edge of the car park, nothing for a moment, and then, at 07:03, a shape appears from beneath the camera. A male, carrying boxes, walking quickly towards the cars, scanning the car park from left to right. He reaches the first row of cars. It's hard to gauge, looking down from above, but he seems tall and solid, a big man.

He keeps walking to the second row, stops at a red hatchback. The same car from the photos Gerard had shown her. Clancy's car.

He opens the back door, throws the boxes onto the back seat, shuts the door hurriedly and turns back to the warehouse—her first glimpse of his face. He's a long way away from the camera, but that hulking frame and thick beard are unmistakable: Frank Cranfield. It was what she'd suspected, but actually seeing it was a shock.

He walks across the car park to the right of the screen, turns and approaches the warehouse from a different direction. The counter at the bottom of the screen is at 07:05 as he walks under the camera and disappears from view.

'Bastard,' she whispered. 'You dirty, lying bastards.' Gerard had needed this tape to stop Cranfield asking for more money, 'insurance' he called it when he spoke to Brose that night: *I want to be able to show him the footage, make him realise how it will look to the police. It's best I have it on hand.*

She felt the cottage tremble again with another huge gust of wind. She sat for a moment, her thoughts racing. So it was confirmed—Clancy had been framed—but she still had no idea why. Why had the company that owned the tattoo parlour paid Cranfield to do it? And why was Gerard involved?

As she removed the USB stick and inserted the other one, the rain eased, fading to soft plops, then nothing. The wind fled with

150

it—one last gust and it was gone. The cottage let out a sigh, settling on its unsteady footings. In the sudden silence, with just the plop of drips from the guttering sploshing into the puddles beneath, she opened another video file and pressed play.

This time the camera was mounted high inside an enormous shed. Not the same shed she had been in to see Wakely, but the same size. An office on the mezzanine level was just visible in the top-right corner of the screen, steel steps descending from it to the warehouse floor below. There was no movement, no workers. She checked the date and time stamp: *31 July 10:50*. A Sunday morning, over five weeks ago.

At first, nothing, just the grey of the concrete and the symmetry of the shelving, then, in the foreground, a forklift, a dark-skinned man at the controls wearing a pale singlet and jeans. He picks up a pallet on the forks and disappears to the back of the warehouse. A minute or two later, the forklift reappears. This time it passes much closer to the camera, and the man's features come into view. It's Clancy.

Movement in the upper right of the screen. Someone coming down the stairs—female legs. The footage is grainy and the woman is wearing some sort of hat, casting a shadow over her face. She stops on the bottom step, calls out to the man. The forklift keeps moving. The woman walks closer, holding her hands up to her mouth like a loudspeaker, shouts at him. The forklift stops and Clancy looks around. The woman is still out of focus, too distant to make out her features, but she's wearing a short skirt, visor, polo top and sandshoes, all in white. Tennis gear?

They seem to be having a conversation, Clancy's face side-on to the camera, the woman walking closer, her face obscured by the visor. He climbs down from the forklift, heads over to a row of lockers, the woman following. He pulls something out of the locker, clothing, a long-sleeved shirt, the top half in fluorescent safety yellow. The woman is standing behind him, very close.

Her back is to the camera. She reaches out, puts one hand on his shoulder. Her touch is like a snakebite—Clancy spins around, pushes her off, backs away. He is speaking—there is an urgency, agitated hand gestures. The woman raises her hands in a shrug, takes a step towards him. He is shaking his head, shutting the locker with his other hand. He turns quickly, walks away, the shirt in one hand, heading for a door on the far wall. There is a sign over the door, just clear enough to make out: *MEN*.

The woman grabs something hanging on the wall. A clipboard. She walks over to him, waving it in the air, still with her back to the camera. He stops, turns around. He is shaking his head again, arms extended, palms up. Pleading? The woman strolls towards him—she's tall, swinging her hips. The footage is grainy and she's still got her back to the camera but a creeping realisation is starting to form in Clem's mind as she watches her walk.

Clancy backs away again, starts turning towards the men's room. The woman's pen hovers over the clipboard. He stops dead in his tracks, his hand on the door, turning his face back to her again, slowly. His shoulders are dropping, his head is lowered—there's a resignation in his stance.

She stands there in front of him, clipboard now dangling by her side. She is waiting for something. Clancy stands straight. Slowly, reluctantly, he removes his singlet. She watches, unmoving. He is bare-chested now, facing the camera, jeans hanging low around his waist. He tries to put the yellow safety shirt on, but the woman takes a small step closer, reaches out towards him. He shuffles a half-step back, towards the door. Her hand brushes his chest, feeling his skin, rests on his waist. He stiffens, rears back.

Clem's heart is pounding. She wants to look away, but she can't—she has to know. Is it who she thinks it is?

The woman leans in, closer still. They are kissing, the woman's hand on his waist. Clancy pulls back, his head turning away from her. She drops her hand, steps towards him, his back is against the door now, her back arches a little as she presses her chest against his. They kiss again, longer this time, their hips together, Clancy's hand around her waist, pulling her closer, her hand on his shoulder now, their heads moving gently. She steps back, takes his hand, loosely, and turns. She is facing the camera now, walking towards it, hips swaying, leading Clancy, his hand in hers.

The visor still obscures her face—but those long legs, that long neck. Could it be? Surely not...

They walk up the steel staircase. Only their legs are visible as they reach the landing. The door to the mezzanine office opens and they go inside. The door closes behind them and the warehouse is still.

Clem sat back in the chair, stunned. After a moment she fumbled for the mouse, rewound the video fifteen seconds, watched them walking towards the camera again.

This time she was sure. It couldn't be anyone else.

Bernadette. The woman was Bernadette Holt.

CHAPTER 24

Clementine sat at the dining table, the white chipboard shelves with the photos of Clancy's wedding day to her left. Clancy sat opposite, arms crossed, jaw set like concrete. It was just after ten am. Clem had slipped and skidded the Commodore down the slushy dirt of Makepeace Road as fast as she could, hoping to catch him at home alone. Melissa was at her mother's place.

'She was gunna report me,' said Clancy. 'Safety breach.'

'The singlet?'

He nodded. 'I already had two breaches and a written warning. They had me all lined up.'

'But why would they target you?'

'There's plenty of blokes don't like seeing a blackfella get on. Like to make it a bit harder for us,' he said through clenched teeth, 'especially an upstart like me.'

He hesitated, as if he'd been through all this in his head so many times, and what was the point? Or maybe it was just who she was. Another white woman.

'You mean payback for testifying in court?' she prompted.

'Yep.' He stood up abruptly and started pacing. 'I slipped up on a safety thing once, sure,' he said bitterly, 'but it was nothin' I hadn't seen others get away with. Some mongrel reported me. Next thing I know, they've dobbed me in for a second one I didn't do. That got me the written warning.'

Clementine grimaced. Safety contraventions were grounds for

154

dismissal. Clancy must have been on the edge of being sacked. 'And so where does Bernadette Holt come in?'

He swung round to face Clementine, eyes blazing. 'After I got the warning, that bitch said she'd help me—said she knew what was going on, was gunna make sure it stopped. I told her I didn't need any help. Well, that wasn't the right answer, was it?' *Smack!* His hand slammed down onto the table. 'She said without her help I wouldn't last five minutes—she'd make sure I got another warning, and I'd be out the door.' He stormed over to the chair again, sat down heavily. 'If I knew I could get another job here I would've told her then and there to shove it. But there's nothin' in Katinga.'

Clem thought back to the clipboard in the video footage, Bernadette had waved it at him. 'She was threatening you with another breach?'

He nodded, dropped his head. 'Oh fuck, fuck, fuck...why did I believe her?' He pushed his chair back, sending the legs squealing over the lino, started pacing again.

'She said it was just a bit of fun, nothing would happen, promised to sort things out'—his words were spitting like oil out of a hot pan—'and now I've ruined everything. I'm gunna lose my Mel. My family won't want to know me. Oh fuck. Oh fuck.' He cupped his face in his hand, squeezing his eyes shut.

'Hey, hey, hey,' Clem said, 'don't get too far ahead of yourself, Clance. Let's talk it through.'

He slumped down in the chair again, staring at the table.

'The way I see it,' said Clem, 'the Holts don't want Melissa to know. They don't want anyone to know. It's damaging for them, for their status, their position, right?'

'What, getting screwed by a black man, you mean?' Clancy snapped.

'No, no, that's not what I meant...I just...well, it just doesn't seem to me like race is the issue.'

'It's always the issue, Jonesy. Colour, race. It's always about fucking race!' There was a long silence.

'Look, all I meant was,' she said gently, 'Bernadette's the general manager, right, the most senior person in the state, and she's gone and coerced a forklift driver half her bloody age into having sex with her while he's trying to mind his own business doing his job. This has scandal written all over it, Clancy. And I don't know if you're aware or not, but Bernadette's after a huge promotion in Sydney. Something like this will end it for her.' She paused—Clancy's eyes were on her. *Good.* 'So, it seems like they just want you out of the way for a bit, out of Katinga, off the footy team, away from anyone who might cotton on, or any situation where you might let it slip accidentally.'

'Damn right they do, but I fucking live here. All Mel's people are here and mine too. And I got...' He gulped. 'I've got my mum, my nan who raised me. They're both buried here.'

It was upsetting, seeing Clancy so torn up, but she needed to get the facts straight. 'So they made you quit the footy team, minimise the risk of it getting out to your mates, I get that, but why did they have you sacked?'

''Cos I wouldn't move to Melbourne and they wanted me outta here. They had a job lined up there for me. I knew Melissa would never go—hell, I didn't want to go either—so I said no. Next thing I know they've loaded my car with gear and I'm out on my arse.'

'Bastards,' she said. 'Guess that's a sign they want you to do what they say.'

'Yep.' He grabbed the back of his neck, his eyes wild and darting. 'I am so fucking screwed.'

'Yes and no. I mean, I would have thought you're in a pretty good position—if it's what you want—to extract some value out of the situation.'

'What the hell are you talking about?'

'A better job, maybe even a cash settlement in return for keeping quiet.'

He groaned. 'You bloody got rocks in your head if you think a black man's got any hope of scoring out of this one, Jonesy.'

She thought for a moment, drumming her fingers on the table. 'So, is that the plan—just play along, keep quiet and it'll all blow over?'

'Pretty much, if you could call it a plan. But, oh God, I don't know how long I can keep lying to Melissa. It's doing my fucking head in, and she so doesn't deserve it.'

He walked to the kitchen window, lifted the curtain to one side and checked the road.

'Well, maybe Bernadette will get the promotion, before you know it the Holts are off to Sydney and you can breathe again. In the meantime, you keep doing what you're doing—going along with it—or at least make it look like you're going along with it.'

'I'm tryin',' he said. 'Not winnin' any Academy Awards, but.'

She looked at the wedding pictures on the shelf. 'This your nan?' she said, pointing.

'Yeah, that's her. Mum died when I was a little tacker. Nan looked after me when Dad was away working up north. She died, but. Little bit after our wedding. When she got sick she told me, "You look after that Mel." Said I was punchin' above my weight.' He smiled, reached across, took the photo from the shelf. 'I can't stop thinking about our baby, wishing Nan could be here to see him.' He sounded choked up now. 'Making sure Mel and I are together when he's born, then who knows...'

Clem couldn't stop the coach inside from bubbling up. 'Hey, stop the bloody self-pity, all right. Man up, for Christ's sake. You're going to be a father soon.'

'Jesus, coach. You sound like my nan,' he chuckled.

'Well, I like her already, in that case.'

She stood up and walked to the kitchen. 'How does a person get a cup of tea around here?'

He got up and followed her to the kitchen. 'No, I told you, Jonesy, you can't stay. I don't want Melissa seeing you here. God, I don't want anyone seeing you here.' He had one hand on the cupboard door, stopping her from opening it. 'Don't want no rumours about you and me, don't want the Holts knowing you've been poking around again. Don't want any more complications—you should go now.'

'Don't sweat, Clancy—I parked around the corner for that very reason.'

She filled the kettle and switched it on, stood silent for a moment.

'How about I talk to Gerard Holt?' she said. 'He can't touch me like he can you. I'll tell him I know he's concealed this evidence about the theft from the warehouse, tell him I know everything. I'll assure him you're not going to say anything, and that if he does anything to you, I'll spoil the party with Bernadette's promotion.'

'No, don't do that.'

'Why not?'

He stood there, shaking his head.

'Clancy Kennedy, don't play bloody silent with me. I know everything now, remember—I've seen it all. There's no secrets anymore. And I'm bloody on your side, so tell me why that won't work.'

Clancy dropped his head, backed away. 'You have no idea.'

'No idea about what?'

'About what I'm dealing with! Who I'm dealing with. Wanna know how I got this?' He pulled up his sleeve angrily. On his forearm was a bright red ring of flesh, a bulging, angry welt, puckered around a blackened centre.

'Oh my God, Clancy. Is that a cigarette burn?'

He nodded.

'Who did this to you?'

'Two guys. They bailed me up outside the pub. One of them told me I had to move out of Katinga, then he stubbed out his fag on my arm.' A desperate look crossed Clancy's face. 'Said something about the bub—as if he'd do the same to him.'

She gasped. Threatening a baby? She struggled to imagine Gerard being behind such a thing. *But then all he has to do is hire the thug. Men like Gerard don't get their hands dirty.*

'Did you get a look at them? Who were they?'

'I dunno, they were wearing masks. I'm pretty sure they're not from Katinga. Saw 'em drive off, but. They were in a Falcon ute.'

She recalled seeing Todd in the blue Falcon ute with his mate Red Flanno.

'What colour ute?' she asked.

'Blue.'

Her mouth went dry. The kettle boiled. She switched it off, got some cups from the cupboard. 'Where do you keep your tea?' she asked, trying to keep her voice steady. Before he could reply, there was the sound of a car coming up the driveway. Clancy peered through a crack in the curtains.

'Shit, it's Tash, Mel's cousin. She can't see you here. You have to hide.' He grabbed her hand, pulling her out of the kitchen, through the dining room and down the hallway. 'Hurry. Under the bed.'

Clancy had been used, threatened and burned. Now was not the time to argue with him. She followed him to the bedroom, scrambled underneath the bed.

He stuck his head under and hissed, 'Stay there until I tell you to move.' He closed the door as he went out.

She looked around. There was a small suitcase down one end of the bed and a single white sock. She could hear voices through the closed door but couldn't make out the words. She recalled the night in the vacant lot, face down in the dirt, hiding. What in the world had her life come to?

She lay there, thinking through what Clancy had told her. He'd insisted she stay out of it, but he didn't understand—threats were one thing, but for Gerard to touch the town's favourite coach was another. Surely she could get him to back off both her and Clancy? She started planning a conversation with Gerard. Or should it be Bernadette?

Bernadette. It was all so hard to believe. Jenny had mentioned tensions in the marriage, and Bernadette herself had suggested it was not much more than 'convenience', but to stoop to this? She'd seemed so urbane, so professional, at the fundraising night. But underneath—a letch, a user of the vulnerable. She had got her moment's gratification and then hung Clancy out to dry. No, she couldn't trust herself to speak to Bernadette—she might not be able to control what came out of her mouth. It had to be Gerard.

The minutes ticked by. Clancy had said Melissa was due back from her check-up at lunchtime. Clementine hoped to God Tash was gone well before then so she could escape. She imagined being there under the bed all day—worse, all night...

A while later she heard footsteps in the hallway. The bedroom door opened then closed again, and Clancy's socks, then his face, appeared in the gap beneath the bed.

'You've gotta get out now, before Mel gets back. I'll open the window—you climb out and jump. It's not far. Jump over the back fence into the neighbours' place and keep walking out the front of the yard. They're not home. Don't let anyone see you.' Clancy's voice was hushed, but he fired off the orders like a sergeant major.

'Okay. Got it.' She grabbed his arm as he went to stand up. 'Clancy?'

'What?'

'You have to stay strong. You can't tell Melissa just yet.'

'Yeah, I know, I know.'

'And I've got some savings, I want to give you some money, help out with rent while you're—'

'No! Just stay away from me. You can't help me. Stay the fuck out of it,' Clancy hissed.

He went to the window and slid it open as she wriggled out from under the bed. She checked the height to the ground, swung her leg over the window and jumped out.

CHAPTER 25

'Ah, Clementine, you've brought your resumé—excellent,' said Gerard, taking a self-satisfied bite from his salad roll and swishing the crumbs off his desk.

Clem could smell the ham and realised she hadn't eaten lunch yet. She sat down in the chair opposite his desk, facing the geese, her back erect, shoulders relaxed. Body language was everything in a negotiation.

'No, I haven't, Gerard. Actually, I think it's time for a different discussion.' Through the vast expanse of windows to her right she could see rolling green paddocks, dairy cattle, heads down in the knee-deep grass, and the midday sun bathing everything in a crisp freshness.

'Oh really?' he said, leaning back into his big leather chair, still chewing.

'I know what Cranfield did,' she said, watching for his reaction. Surprise. A flicker of annoyance? No, more than that—dismay.

He stopped chewing momentarily. 'I have no idea what you're referring to, Jones,' he mumbled through the bread.

'The theft, Gerard. It wasn't Clancy and you know it. In fact you conspired with the perpetrator.' She kept her tone bland, her voice steady, matter-of-fact, as if she were reading from a report.

He sat up straighter, put his roll down on the desk and swallowed the last mouthful, dabbing his face with a napkin.

'Look, Jones,' he said, 'I don't know what you're talking about.

162

I've been open with you, so open that I showed you the file—you saw the images yourself. Not to mention that Clancy confessed.'

'Yes, I've been wondering about that. How exactly did Clancy confess? Did you have him sign a stat dec? Perhaps I could see it?'

'It's part of a confidential deed, Jones—I can't disclose any of the detail.'

'Oh, a deed!' she exclaimed. 'So you sacked him, then made him sign a deed prohibiting him from saying anything about it? I wouldn't have thought a legitimate termination would have required anything of that nature.'

'You know, you speak so well for a former legal clerk, Jones. I really can't wait to read your fascinating CV,' he said, his hands flat on the desk in front of him.

The prick didn't get it. So arrogant. She swallowed hard, lined him up for the next blow.

'I know about Bernadette and Clancy too.'

His face went white, one hand tightening into a fist. The stakes were officially raised.

'I beg your pardon?' His voice squeaked. He cleared his throat. 'You seem to have come by some serious misinformation, Jones. I'm curious who you've been speaking to. If Clancy is spreading any—'

'Let's not play games, Gerard. I'm in possession of information confirming that the accusations against Clancy were false, and I could provide it to the police if I wish.' A lie. She could never risk Torrens' parole. 'I could also send an email to the press and end Bernadette's stellar career with CTS. I suggest you listen to my offer with a little humility.'

'Offer? You think you can get money out of me?' He looked shell-shocked, blinking, lips open.

'Actually, money would be good, now you mention it. Hold that thought while I outline what I have in mind.'

She leaned one elbow on the arm of the chair, a picture of calm, but underneath all systems were on high alert as she strived to maintain her advantage.

'You know I value my privacy, Gerard, in the same way as you do, I'm sure, especially at this delicate time—I mean, Bernadette needs to be without blemish if she's to secure this promotion. And I'm not the only one around here who hopes she gets it, either. I think it would be great for Katinga. So, with that in mind, I'm prepared to do a deal with you.'

His face was a confused mix of relief and discomfort.

'It's very simple,' she said. 'I'll keep quiet about Bernadette's, ah...indiscretion, and about the false accusations against Clancy, in return for which you'll agree to respect my privacy and refrain from asking questions about my past.' She knew he would readily agree to this—she had no way of ensuring that he keep his side of the deal, so it was no skin off his nose. But it was just the first step in the negotiation: ease him in, persuade him into thinking that their interests aligned, that she was, like him, primarily concerned with protecting herself, rather than taking Clancy's side against him.

Gerard searched her face, seeking out hidden traps. He launched forth with typical bluster. 'Well, Jones, let me make this clear: I consider the allegations you've made today to be preposterous, but neither do I have any need to know what secrets you may be protecting from your past. For that reason, and as a mark of my respect for you as a coach, I might be prepared to accommodate your request.'

He was good, she thought, at pretending—making it sound like this was merely a favour he was prepared to grant, a request he would entertain out of the goodness of his heart.

'I'm glad you can see the mutual—'

'But I'm afraid I can't see an arrangement between the two of us as being worthwhile if Clancy is out there spreading lies,' he interjected. 'I mean, if he has some sort of bee in his bonnet about

164

Bernadette'—*Outrageous*, she thought. *Don't react, don't react*—'how do you propose to ensure he doesn't make any allegations public?'

'You seem to be doing a reasonable job of keeping Clancy quiet already,' she said, purposely not mentioning his hired thugs. Clancy had been ordered to keep quiet, so she wanted Gerard to think she'd found out everything independently of Clancy. If Gerard suspected that Clancy had told her anything about the men who'd threatened him, he might order more violence against him.

He carefully picked up his napkin from his lap, placed it on the desk as if it belonged in that precise location. 'I assure you, Jones, I'm not *doing* anything at all. Clancy left here three weeks ago and I haven't seen him since.' She had an image of Pontius Pilate washing his hands of responsibility, leaving cigarette burns and such matters to the chief priests. But this was exactly what she'd wanted—Gerard initiating a component of the deal, something that she would duly concede to, giving him that winning feeling.

'Fair point,' she said. 'And given I'm not here to play games, I'm prepared to ensure Clancy remains silent about these matters, provided you, and all of your associates, stay away from him.' That was as close as she would hazard in referring to his brutal thugs.

She could see Gerard was mulling it over, sizing up her ability to hold up her side of the bargain, this component vitally important to him.

'And as part of this deal,' she continued, 'you and your associates will stop harassing him into leaving town. He's here for the birth of his child, otherwise the deal's off and I'm on my way to the police and the media.'

Gerard squirmed in the big leather chair. He couldn't give his express agreement to this without implying he had indeed been involved in harassing Clancy to leave, but he gave her a shrug, which was enough.

165

'Excellent, so it's settled then. Any questions?'

'No, I think the arrangement is clear enough.'

She reached across, extending her hand. He did the same and they shook on it, fake smiles all around.

With nothing much left to say, she became aware again of the smell of ham wafting across the desk. She stood up, leaned across and picked up his salad roll, took a bite from the other end, placed it back on the napkin and walked out.

\\/

Clementine turned off the highway and onto Makepeace Road. Despite the rain, two dozen supporters had turned up at training to watch the team splash through their drills. They were at the school sports field, so as not to further damage the oval before the finals. But the team had been flat. Having made it into the finals, it was almost as if the job was done. And having the bye didn't help—she almost wished they'd had to play an elimination final. She'd spent a good deal of time trying to get them to refocus, get them excited about the semi-final to come.

Gerard had been there, which had surprised her. She'd thought he might steer clear of her after their conversation at lunchtime. An element of doubt had crept in. Had he agreed too quickly? Was there something she had missed?

As she pulled up at the top of her driveway the sun had set behind the ridge, splaying great smears of pink. The little green cottage was quiet in the still evening air. Something missing. The usual frenzied welcome from Pocket. The lazy bugger—probably curled up on his mat, couldn't be arsed to greet her.

The pebbles along the pathway crunched under her feet. She noticed the tap dripping around the garden hose near the water tank. *A job for Rowan?* she thought, as she selected the front door key from the ring. Key raised, she stopped. Was the door open already? She couldn't tell in the dark. She pushed it gently, caught her breath as it swung open. She always locked it. Maybe she'd just forgotten?

She realised with a shudder how isolated she was out here.

Without opening the door further, she reached in and flipped the light switch just inside the door. The front hall lit up and she saw glass shattered on the mat. She caught her breath. Now that the light was on she could see one corner of the thick pane in the top part of the door was gone, a jagged edge framing where it had been.

Her mind moved rapidly, adrenaline pinging through her limbs. Pocket? Not a sound from him. *Oh God. They could still be here. Get back in the car, ring the police.* No, they would take half an hour to get here. Jim. She'd call Jim from next door.

Possibilities flashed through her head as she took out her phone: the cigarette-burn thugs, or just a drugged-up teenager with a hammer?

God, where is Pocket?

She took one step inside, holding the phone to her ear as she yelled, 'Is anyone here? I'm calling the police now. If you're here, take whatever it is you came for and go out the back door. I don't want any trouble.'

She waited a second. The house was silent. The phone kept ringing. *Pick up, Jim!* 'Pocket!' she cried. Nothing.

She switched the outside porch light on and looked back out into the front yard. Just the car and the wattle trees along the fence line. If they were here, they were likely to be inside or in the backyard, where there was more cover.

She yelled again, 'If you're here, make your way out the back. I won't chase you. I don't want any trouble.'

Jim's number rang out. *Shit.* She started talking to an imaginary triple-zero operator as she stepped across the threshold. 'Police... Lot 22, Makepeace Road, Katinga...There's been a break-in...'

Her bedroom was the first room on the right. She turned on the light switch. A mess. Clothes on the floor, hanging out of open drawers, wardrobe doors open, the bedside lamp upended and the painting above the bed ripped down the centre, its frame mangled. The doona was in a pile in the corner and the mattress half off the bed frame. Then she smelt it. *Oh my God, someone has taken a dump on the sheets.* She stumbled back out into the hallway. 'Pocket!' Still silence.

She shouted again, 'Pocket? Come here, boy.' Nothing. She reached the front room, flicking on the lights as she went. Bureau drawers were open, papers flung across the room, chairs overturned, and a huge dark stain on the mat under the table. Her eyes were drawn to the dining table: a tomahawk was lodged deep in the middle of it.

She called Jim's number again, her hands trembling. 'Pocket? Come here, boy,' she shouted, sobbing now, stumbling through to the kitchen. Still no Pocket. Every cupboard open, drawers hanging out or upside down on the floor, utensils and pots scattered across the lino, crockery smashed into hundreds of pieces, strawberry jam oozing bright red from a broken glass jar on the bench, an upturned milk carton dripping into a slippery puddle on the floor. She picked her way across the debris. A glob of mucous stared up at her from the sink like a vile, green eye.

She grabbed a torch from the laundry. As she opened the back door she heard a whimper and rushed outside. Where had it come from?

'Pocket?' she called, sweeping the torch across the yard, searching for eyes, for shapes in the ring of bushes around the edge—canine or human. The whimper again. Very near, behind her.

She ducked down, shone the torch under the house. Pocket was lying about a metre in, not moving, his leg extended at a sickening angle and the fur around his face covered in blood.

The torch hit the ground with a clunk as she dropped to her

belly and wriggled towards him, pushing through the cobwebs. She slipped her hands underneath his shivering body and slid him out slowly, Pocket crying in pain, tears streaming down her face. She got him into the car, ran inside for a blanket and a bottle of water. It was then that she found it—a plain envelope, propped upright on the top shelf of the fridge. She grabbed the water and ran, opening the envelope as she sprinted to the car.

This is just a bit of Fun we've got more much more Coming your way BITCH!!! Stay away from Clancy!!!

    PS We know your Hiding something.

CHAPTER 26

Clementine spread one blanket on the floor in the back of the station wagon. The after-hours vet in Earlville had given her three. She lay down on top, fully clothed, Pocket's blood smeared down the front of her jumper, and pulled the other two up around her shoulders. The shivering, she realised, was not from the cold. It was residual shock.

The vet had said that Pocket needed a night at the animal hospital on painkillers but, all going well, should be strong enough to go home tomorrow with a round of antibiotics for the gash in his head. She said the leg fracture was blunt-force trauma, and that it could have been a blow with the back of the tomahawk. Clementine had cried, loud exhausted sobs, there in the surgery, the vet's hand on her shoulder and Pocket asleep on his mat in a cage.

It was after eleven o'clock. She looked out through the rear window. A half-moon emerged from behind a thick cloud, lighting up the gumnuts hanging from a scraggly tree on the nature strip. She was in the northern suburbs of Earlville, parked right across from the vet, on a street lined with old fibro homes. Now, alone in the silence, she felt it would have been better to park in front of the police station.

No, she thought. Whoever it was had achieved their end, scaring her senseless. They would not be pursuing her now.

It was hard to think—there was a throb above her eyes, and her shoulders were already starting to ache from the cold, hard floor beneath her—but the question of who wanted to frighten her badly enough to hurt Pocket and smash up her house would not go away. She thought back to her conversation with Melissa. The Plains community were sure Clancy's departure from the team had been the result of a threat from the Earlville gang—payback for his testimony in court. Perhaps someone had seen her with Clancy at the post office or with Mel at the pub and it had got back to the thugs at Earlville. They might have been angry that she was befriending the couple in some way, interfering in their grand scheme to make Clancy suffer.

Or what about Gerard? His thugs had burned Clancy—they wouldn't think twice about hurting a dog. Gerard had agreed only hours before to leave her alone, but what if the break-in had already been planned and he hadn't had time to call it off? Perhaps they'd gone in immediately after she'd left home, before the deal was done. That might account for Gerard's overly agreeable response—he knew the deed had already been done, whether he agreed or not. Or maybe Gerard had agreed just to shut her up and had no intention of leaving her in peace.

But surely Gerard wouldn't hire people so evil as to break a dog's leg? All this for his wife's promotion?

She lay on her back, staring up at the sky through the back window of the wagon. The moon had slipped behind a large cloud, thick enough to dim its light to almost nothing. The throbbing above her eyes had become a sharp pain, spreading towards the back of her head.

She thought back to the first of the violent acts. It had been completed by her own hands, the night she'd sprayed those revolting lies on Andrew's car and slashed his tyres. Maybe this was how he and Rosemary had felt. Maybe it was karma.

\\//

It must have been at least an hour later when she woke, as the clouds had cleared completely and the moon was nowhere in sight. There had been a loud noise, and she could hear yelling. There it was again, a rock on a corrugated-iron roof. She sat up in the back of the wagon, looked around. The shouts were coming from the corner, further up the street. Lights came on inside the nearby houses, illuminating a crowd of young men on the street, a few of them with shaven heads. Something cold crept over her skin, and the hairs on the back of her neck stood up.

She threw off the blankets and clambered over the back seat, slid down into the driver's seat. She was breathing fast, fumbling for her keys. The shouting was getting closer—the crowd had moved onto the street where she was parked.

She turned the key. The starter motor chugged, but nothing fired. She tried again, and it took hold briefly, then stalled. She waited a moment, telling herself the appearance of the angry throng was a coincidence, nothing to do with her.

She turned the key again and checked her side mirror, gasping as she recognised a bald head reflecting the streetlight—Red Flanno. He was screaming abuse at a house on the corner. A projectile flew from somewhere in the crowd—a brick silhouetted in the streetlight, soaring through the air. She heard the crash of shattering glass.

She turned the key again, pumping the accelerator. The engine fired and she planted her foot, her eyes fixed on the rear-view mirror as she pulled away from the curb.

The sound of sirens in the distance, the crowd running, scattering in all directions. Then, from deeper in the pack, a fiery bottle came sailing through the air, trailing two feet of flames behind it, crashing through a window of a tiny, run-down house at the end of the street. She gasped, looked again to the spot where the bottle had come from.

There—towards the back, head shaved, running with the rest of them—was Todd Wakely.

CHAPTER 27

The last training session before the semi-final was back at the Cats' home ground in Katinga, which was a good thing. They hadn't played there for over two weeks, and she wanted them to reacquaint themselves with the idiosyncrasies of the ground. She'd been surprised at how the turf had held up. Only a few days of sunshine and, apart from the roped-off areas in front of the goals and in the middle, it was reasonably solid. Every little positive was important at this end of the season, and as she'd walked through the cheering crowd of Katinga supporters who'd turned up to watch the Cats train, she'd stopped at the council groundskeeper, shook his hand and congratulated him. The crowd gave him a cheer, surging around him to slap him on the back as she strode off onto the field.

Among the supporters she recognised a few: Mrs Lemmon in her long woollen coat and matching hand-knitted red beanie buttoned up under her chin; John Wakely; Gerard; the Flood family (all six of them); Mr Nicholls and his wife from the IGA; and Rowan hovering at the back of the crowd with a couple of men who'd offered to shout her a drink at the pub the other day.

Jenny and Trev were there too, beaming at her. They'd arrived early, waving at her as she'd got out of the car. She felt a rush of gratitude towards them both. She wished she could speak to Jen about the break-in. The simple comfort of friendship...a hug from a mate...so much she had surrendered for her exile in the hills.

A noisy band of players appeared from the sheds, making their way onto the ground. There seemed to be more than the usual amount of laughter—or was it actually jeering? As she looked across she saw Todd Wakely in the centre of the group, his shorn head shining snow-white beneath the floodlights, like a skullcap where his tousled mop of hair had been. The boys were giving him a fair dinkum ribbing.

Good, she thought, but as she watched, the taunts seemed to be getting aggressive. She saw Maggot Maloney and Conti shove Wakely, sending him staggering into a couple of others, who shoved him back again.

She decided to call them into a huddle before the usual warm-up laps. 'Hey, over here!' she called, beckoning.

They gathered around, Clementine in the centre, the men towering over her.

'Right. Everybody settle down,' she said.

Those who'd been jogging on the spot, the ones who were still elbowing Todd Wakely, all stood still now—twenty-five men, expectant, wanting something, whatever it was she had to give.

'Thank you. Now, listen up. I may be mistaken, but you blokes seem to have forgotten something.' She looked around the men huddled in close. 'Anyone remember we're in a semi-final on Saturday? Huh, anyone?' Silence. 'Let me remind you, then. The Katinga Cats are in their first semi-final in forty years. Am I right?'

They nodded, mumbling their assent, a handful of the more vocal ones shouting: 'Yeah!'

'Too bloody right! And look around you. Look over at the sidelines there.' Clem nodded towards the cluster of supporters. Twenty-five heads swivelled. 'The good people of Katinga have come out here tonight in the cold and the dark just to support you blokes.'

Beasley, standing on the inside of the circle close to Clem, turned back to look at her. His pimply face was full of surprise

174

when, inches from his nose, she yelled, 'I said *look*, Beasley! Don't take your eyes off them! These people are counting on you! Take it in—take a moment to take it all in.' She paused, surveying the team. Every one of the players now had his eyes trained on the little knot of supporters under the glow of the floodlights. Some fans were chatting, the back row laughing at something, others stamping their feet for warmth, puffs of vapour coming from their mouths, and all of them full of pride, full of hope for their team.

'Look harder. There's mums and dads, sisters and brothers, your boss, your co-worker, even little old ladies out here in the cold.' She paused again. 'All right, eyes on me, men.' Bodies turned in unison back towards her. She waited a second until they were still. 'Now, what I want to know is, how did you get to this point? How on earth did you come from the wooden spoon last year to make it to the finals? What was the secret ingredient?'

'Teamwork!' yelled Sellingham.

'That's right, teamwork. So no matter what your differences, no matter who you are, what you do for a crust or how you cut your hair, you're a band of brothers, right?'

'Yeah,' they chorused.

'Bloody hell,' Clem said, indignant. 'Say it like you mean it.'

A thunderous shout of 'Yeah!' then the supporters joining in, cheering from the sidelines, until the sound rang in Clementine's ears.

Now that she had them thinking as one, she moved on to the common enemy. 'Okay, this Saturday we're playing the Digby Dingoes.' She scanned the pack of heads around her, every face alive with the prospect of combat now. 'They're a bloody good team. They run hard and fast, and they deserve to be in the semi-final. But you know what? Those Digby Dingbats have no idea what you've been through, not a frigging clue. They haven't had to endure thirty-four years of struggle. They don't know what it is to build from nothing to be the best team in the comp.' Another

175

group shout of 'Yeah!' and a round of cheers. 'They've got no bloody idea what teamwork is. And you're going to run right over the top of them like a steamroller on Saturday.'

The players' hoots and bellows were deafening. They thumped each other on the back, whooped and shouted. The excitement was contagious, the supporters joining in with a lusty round of cheering from the sidelines.

'Off you go then, men—two laps, first one easy, second one medium, back here for stretches. We'll do some light drills with the ball and then talk tactics.'

The players headed off, moving as one unit, bobbing heads, bare arms and thighs flashing under the lights, the stampede of boots fading to a dull rumble as they reached the far side of the oval.

As the men jogged around the perimeter she stood in the middle of the field, writing notes on her clipboard. The oval's lights lit up the insects buzzing in the radiance, ravenous and swarming after so much rain. Above the artificial glow was the Milky Way—a rash of brilliant white flickering, surrounded by sapphire haloes.

She took a few deep breaths. She'd been on edge since the break-in, spent all yesterday cleaning up, alone in the cottage and, for the first time, feeling lonely up there. Pocket was still in a lot of pain and needed more care, so she'd left him at the vet and would pick him up tomorrow. She hadn't realised how much she relied on the little fella's company.

She had also reported the break-in to the police yesterday. Constable Miller had taken all the details over the phone. She left out the threatening note and made it all sound like drug addicts pissed off at finding nothing worth stealing—she couldn't mention anything about Clancy. Miller sounded busy, so Clem had told him not to rush over. The damage was done in any event and all cleaned up now. He'd promised to drop in the next day and asked her for the latest on the team, whether the boys were in good shape for the semi-final on Saturday.

An hour later and the team had finished the session. They trickled past her on their way to the sheds. She clapped and yelled congratulations, praising them for their hard work. As Wakely passed her, she tapped him on the arm.

'Hold on a minute,' she said. 'I want a word with you.'

He pulled up, sweat pouring down his face, arms glistening.

'What's going on, Todd?'

'What? You mean my new hairdo?' He grinned.

'No,' she said, a worried look on her face. 'Look, I saw you, Todd. The other night, at the riot.'

'Nah, not me, Jonesy. I was home.'

'I was there at the vet in Earlville. I saw you running and I saw you somewhere near that Molotov cocktail.' The ground was silent now, all of the players in the sheds, most of the supporters gone home, just the deep, mellow *boobook* of a mopoke in the darkness.

He looked at her, shifting his weight from one foot to the other.

'Those blokes you're with, they're thugs, common thugs,' she said. 'You'll end up with a conviction and a criminal record, and then you'll be screwed, simple as that.'

He bristled, crossed his arms across his chest. 'Didn't do nothin'. No crime in running. Just a bit of extra training.'

'They're bad people, Todd—you should stay away from them. They're only going to get you into trouble. You're young, and you have a future—don't let them ruin your life.'

'No, you're wrong there, Jonesy. They're good blokes.'

'I'm worried for you, Todd. It's a bad scene, and you're not just hurting other people—you're going to get hurt yourself.'

He looked away, shuffling his feet. 'I'm all right. It's all good.'

'So who's the guy I saw you with the other day, coming back from Earlville? Blue ute, the skinhead at the wheel.'

'You mean Cleggy?' he asked.

'Who's Cleggy?'

'Jase. Jason Clegg. He's a good guy. He's been helping me train at the gym.'

So Red Flanno has a name, she thought, *and he hangs around in gyms.*

'He's not giving you any gear, is he?'

'Nah, I can't afford it...I mean, no, he doesn't do that stuff anyway.'

'Yeah, well, stay away from it, right. It's totally not on. We're going to win this thing fair and square, and you don't need it anyway—look at you, you're a bloody superstar these days.'

He puffed out his chest, smiled.

'Is there anything else we need to speak about, Todd? You're not going to be out throwing any more bricks, are you? Because I don't want you in the lock-up for the semi-final.'

That seemed to shock him, the reality of being arrested, the fear of missing out. He blinked and shook his head.

'Good,' she said and started walking back to the sideline.

'Umm, well, actually, I do need to let you know something...' he mumbled.

She stopped, turned. 'Yes?'

'Well, ah. Well, see, it's something you need to know.'

'Out with it, Wakely.'

'Well, it's...You...Well, you just need to stay out of it.'

'Stay out of what?'

'The Clancy thing,' he whispered.

Heat rose in her neck and fanned out like a flame across her cheeks.

'What do you mean, *the Clancy thing*?'

'You know, him leaving the team and stuff. You shouldn't be talking to him or trying to get him back.'

'I'll talk to whoever I damn well please, Wakely—no racist shitheads are going to tell me what to do, and you can take that back to your friends and tell 'em to shove it where the sun don't shine.'

'Aw, Jonesy, don't be like that…There's talk, you know, about what he said in the court case a few years back. It's just not safe for you to be around him.'

'Did you and your thug mates break into my house?' she said, eyes blazing.

'What? What are you talking about?'

He looked genuinely confused. Wakely may not have been involved, she thought—he would have been exhausted after training and then he'd have had to drive all the way to Earlville later to participate in the riot—but maybe his associates were responsible.

'Somebody broke into my house, roughed up my dog. Was it you?'

'No, Jonesy, never—I'd never do that.'

'Was it your mates, then? Jason Clegg?' Her anger was tumbling out, unfiltered.

He said nothing, shaking his head, fear in his eyes.

'This is where it leads, this nonsense. This is where it all ends up!' She was breathing heavily, glaring at his downcast face. She counted to five. 'Todd, you're bigger than all this. You know that. You don't belong in that crowd. Your team is here, right here. It's us that's on your side, not these brutes who throw bricks at people's roofs and set houses alight, for Christ's sake.'

He swallowed, started fidgeting with the hem of his guernsey.

She let it rest, hoping it was enough, hoping she'd broken through. 'All right, then, I believe you, but I don't trust your mates, not for one second. Now go get changed.' He started walking away, relieved. 'Oh, and look after yourself, okay?' she called after him. 'I don't want you getting any injuries before the game—in fact give the gym a miss. I'd wrap you in cottonwool if I could.'

He turned, smiled, trotted off to the sheds.

She walked over to the car park, feeling weary with the weight of these young men and their futures. Rowan was over by his van, looking thoughtful. Wakely Senior was standing nearby on his own, an anxious look on his face. He'd been watching her with Todd. She went over, asked him for his thoughts on the training session, any pointers. He had little comment to make—the man was like a wound-up spring.

'Just had a chat with young Todd. Bit of a worry, that new hairdo,' she said, smiling.

Wakely looked relieved that she'd brought it up.

'Oh, it's horrible. I don't know what to do with the boy,' he said, his eyes darting around the car park at the remaining supporters and the players now beginning to emerge from the sheds. 'I'm sick with worry about him. His mother would turn in her grave if she saw his head looking like that'—he leaned in close, lowering his voice—'and the company he's keeping. It's no good, it's no good at all.' He cast another nervous look across the car park.

She said it was probably just a phase, something he had to go through before he woke up to the fact it was all bollocks. Then she gave Wakely something to do: 'Get some good food into him this week, John, and plenty of sleep. I've told him not to go to the gym because I don't want any injuries, so if you could keep him occupied at night, that would be good—maybe watch some replays of the AFL finals from last year with him? I've got copies— I'll drop them in to you. Anything to keep him home.'

He grabbed at the idea like a lifeline.

As he drove off, she walked over to her car, parked next to Rowan's van. Rowan was there, leaning against it, waiting for her still. He wore his usual khaki jacket, which emphasised his broad shoulders, dirty jeans, wide brown belt hugging narrow hips. She caught herself—the fact that she was even noticing these things was a problem. She needed to get back behind the wall, fortify the ramparts. She took a deep breath of icy air.

'Bloody hell, eh. The Cats,' he grinned, as she approached.

She smiled. 'Yep. Who would've believed it?'

He stood up straight, his thumb hooked over the top of his front jeans pocket. 'Up for a meal at the pub before you head for the hills?'

She felt both a flash of desire and a rush of anxiety. 'Thanks, but I have a casserole I need to finish up at home,' she lied, wondering whether she'd remembered to top up the cans of soup in the pantry.

'Ha, you're like me. Nothin' better than your own company, right?'

'Pretty much.'

'Well, what about the pub Friday night? They do a good chicken parma special.'

His smile was framed by an un-sculpted three-day growth and his eyes had an optimistic sparkle. *This has to stop*, she thought. 'I'm having a quiet one, sorry—gotta study up on the game plan,' she said as she opened the rear door and threw her bag in, hoping the stab of regret she was feeling wasn't obvious.

He gave her another smile, walked to the driver's side of his van. 'No worries. See you at the game.' He was still smiling as he opened the front door of the van. 'Semi-final, bloody hell...' He shook his head, grunted, as if he never thought he'd see the day.

As she was pulling out of the car park, she noticed Torrens coming out of the sheds. He jogged over, waving. She stopped and wound down the window.

'Have you heard anything from the cops?' he asked, leaning down to speak to her.

'No, not since that first house call. You?'

'They dropped the whole Audi thing after they saw the lump on my head—very authentic,' he laughed. 'They're all over me like a rash for the letterbox, but. Threatening me with me parole and stuff.'

Guilt slithered through her like a snake. It was the same feeling, always. Was Torrens' life the next one she would destroy?

'God, I'm so sorry I got you involved that night, Torrens.'

'Nah, don't worry about it,' he said. 'They've got nothin' on me—they'll lose interest and it'll be over in a day or so.'

'Maybe I should talk to Sergeant Phillips, tell him how well you're doing.'

'Shit no, don't do that. That'll make the old git even more suspicious. Just keep quiet and it'll all blow over.'

She wasn't so sure, but there didn't seem to be anything she could do. 'All right, well, let me know if anything happens. Maybe I can help. God knows you've done so much for me.'

'Yeah, well, like I said, just keep behaving yourself—stay out of other people's houses unless you've got an invitation,' he laughed.

'How's the job going?' she asked.

'Bloody brilliant,' he boomed. 'I'm a champion boner now, Jonesy, the best one they've got—employee of the week this week. Me big mug's up on the noticeboard and all!' They giggled like schoolkids.

She'd needed a good laugh, she thought as she drove away. Win, lose or draw, God bless Torrens.

CHAPTER 28

She gently scooped Pocket up from the back of the wagon. He whimpered as she carried him in and carefully set him down, his sad little cast sticking out to one side and his head ensconced in a huge plastic cone. His face had been shaved and a row of stitches, bulging and raw, ran from his right eye up to his ear.

At around four-forty, her mobile rang. Torrens.

'Are you sitting down, coach?'

Oh my God, he's been charged, she thought. 'No. Should I be?'

'Yes,' he said gravely.

'What is it?' she said, bracing herself.

'Clancy's missing.'

She stood there, staring out the kitchen window at Jim's paddocks, momentarily paralysed, her mind reeling.

Torrens told the story. Clancy had been drinking at the pub last night. He'd had a few too many, staggered out and hadn't been seen since. At first the police said the most likely thing was he'd be sleeping it off somewhere and would turn up soon. But someone found his phone around three pm, its screen smashed, and with the fight last week and the riot, the police commenced a search straightaway, covering the main routes from the pub to Clancy's place and expanding out from there. Torrens had heard the story from a mate, Pete Jameson, who'd been at the pub and had been speaking with Clancy before he left. Apparently Clancy had been worked up about something, Torrens didn't know what. She pressed him until he reluctantly gave up his mate's phone number.

'Leave it alone, Jonesy. Not your job to go after this one—leave it to the coppers to investigate and come join the search. I'm off there now myself.'

Clementine told herself not to panic as she rang Jameson's number. It rang out. She dialled Gerard's number. What did he know? He had to be involved. Had he broken their bargain? It went straight to voicemail. Probably just as well—she needed to calm down before she took him on.

She topped up Pocket's water bowl and left him with some treats in reach, threw on a jacket, jumped in the Commodore and roared down the driveway. The shadows across the paddocks were long and foreboding as she sped past, the cattle beginning to make their way to the milking shed.

Her phone rang as she sped along Makepeace Road. It was Torrens' mate Pete Jameson.

'Is that the lady footy coach?' He spoke with a slow country drawl.

'Yes, that's me. Thanks for calling me back, Peter,' Clem said. 'Apparently you were one of the last people to see Clancy before he left the pub?'

'Yeah. Turns out I was the last to speak with him.'

'Torrens said he was worked up about something,' she said.

'Yeah, he was well and truly under the weather. Looked like he'd been on it all afternoon. He was saying how everything was ruined, repeating it over and over, seemed to be blaming himself for something. I tried to calm him down for a bit, but he was pretty upset.'

'Did he say what was ruined?'

'Nah, nothing I could make out. He was slurring so much I could hardly understand a word. He was going on about some woman, I think, but that's about as much as I could pick up.'

Clementine reached the end of the straight stretch, braking

heavily for the first of the sharp bends down the hill.

'Did he talk to anyone else?'

'Nah, not while I was there. He was sitting at the bar on his own. People were giving him a wide berth.'

'Did anyone overhear him talking to you?'

'Well, maybe. Not sure. There were a few people in the bar.'

'Who?' Jameson's slow country plod was driving her crazy.

'A couple of locals. They were up the other end of the bar from Clancy, but.'

'Anyone else?'

'There were these two German chicks at the table closest to that end of the bar. I think they might have been backpackers—all right to look at, but their English wasn't real good. Only other table close enough was two blokes from out of town,' Jameson said.

'Know their names?' She was throwing the Commodore around the bends, spraying gravel into the thick undergrowth and fighting the urge to hurry Jameson along.

'Nah. Never seen 'em before.'

'Can you describe them?'

'One of them was a skinhead, and he was bloody huge—gym junkie, I reckon. The other guy was shorter. He had his back to me, wore a baseball cap.'

'Do you know when they left? Was it at the same time as Clancy?' She turned onto the main road and took the Commodore up to 150 kilometres an hour.

'Geez, I dunno. They might have done, but I wasn't paying attention. I did see Clancy leave, but. I was pretty pleased to see him go by then, bloody miserable bastard. I don't bloody know him from a bar of soap—I just happened to be the one who copped it. Anyway, dunno what the fuss is all about. He's probably sleeping it off in a gutter somewhere.'

She was turning onto the main road to Katinga now, tyres screeching.

Clementine pressed the button at the front gate and waited impatiently, glaring at the impeccably trimmed edges on the front lawn. There was a buzzing sound and a click. She pushed open the gate and marched through the garden and up the steps to the porch.

The front door opened. Bernadette stood there in the doorway. Clem had only ever seen her perfectly made up, but now she looked spotty and pale. Had she been crying perhaps? Clem really hoped she was suffering.

Bernadette forced a smile. 'Clementine. Hello.'

'Hello. Is Gerard in?' she said, not even attempting to return the smile. She was still unsure if she could contain herself as far as Bernadette was concerned. Besides, she didn't know how much Gerard had told Bernadette about their deal or what was going on with Clancy. He might be keeping his wife at a distance so she could deny knowledge if anything came to light, keeping her shiny reputation intact for the big job. Best to speak to Gerard on his own.

'Yes, yes, of course. Come in,' she said, stepping aside and ushering her in.

Clementine had been in the house twice, once for the committee meeting and once to steal the tapes—she'd never entered by the front door before. An imposing abstract painting and a few framed photographs hung on the wall in the spacious tiled foyer. She noticed one of Gerard and Bernadette in ski gear and another of a young man with Bernadette's features. Their son?

Bernadette showed her into the living area. Gerard was seated in a wingback chair in the space between a luxurious L-shaped lounge and a huge polished teak dining table, reading the paper. He looked up as she came in.

'Gerard, I might let you and Clementine talk, if you don't mind,' said Bernadette. 'I'm expecting a call from head office.'

'Yes, of course,' he said, folding the paper and placing it on the coffee table in front of him.

Bernadette turned to Clementine. 'But do tell me, Clementine—has there been any word? We've been so worried.'

Clementine was taken aback. Bernadette sounded genuinely shaken. Was she feeling remorse? Maybe she could be another source, an angle, or even a wedge against Gerard.

'I've heard nothing more since I got the call half an hour ago.'

Bernadette nodded, said, 'Oh. I'm…I'm sorry,' before hurriedly turning towards the hallway. Clementine wondered what it was she was sorry for—the abuse of power, the predatory lust, the ruining of young lives? She needed to be sorry for all of it, from beginning to end.

'Please, take a seat, Clementine,' said Gerard.

She remained standing. 'What's going on, Gerard?' she said. 'I thought we had a deal.'

His face dropped as she spoke, as if affronted. 'Well, yes, Jones, we do. I don't know what you think—'

'Cut the crap, Gerard. What have you done with him?'

'Why on earth would you assume I've got anything to do with it? Perhaps you haven't heard the details, but Clancy got *himself* drunk and wandered off from the pub. It's got nothing to do with me.'

'Don't take me for a fool, Gerard,' she snapped.

'Oh, come on, Jones. It's been a terrible day for all of us. Please, sit down. Let me get you a drink.'

He was a picture of charm, gesturing to a chair, smiling at her in his carefully pressed chinos. She wanted to squeeze the information out of him with her own bare hands, but she needed to hold it together, let Gerard relax a bit, then make her play. She bit her tongue, walked slowly to the chair, sat down.

'Now, can I get you a drink?' he said.

'No,' she said a little too aggressively. 'I mean, no, I'm fine, thank you.' *Calm down, get him talking,* she thought, gripping the arms of the chair. 'Bernadette seems shaken. How is she taking all this?'

'Oh, very badly, as you can imagine. She feels responsible for all the staff, especially since we so recently terminated Clancy's employment. Nonsense, of course. Workplace safety can never be compromised.'

Unbelievable. He was still denying what Bernadette had done. She dug her nails in under the thick piping along the edge of the armrest.

'Anyway, Clancy's probably passed out somewhere.' He flourished a hand in the air. 'Perhaps he's hurt his leg or something. They'll find him, fix him up and this whole episode will all look a little melodramatic.' He crossed one leg over the other, leaned on the armrest, affecting a relaxed pose.

She kept her voice civil, measured. 'I admire your optimism, Gerard, but I'm afraid I didn't come here for empty reassurances. I'm on my way to see the police for an update on the search. I'm trying to decide before I see Sergeant Phillips if there's anything I know about Clancy—anything about possible enemies, for instance—that he might be interested in finding out.' She saw him squirm. *Good.*

'I don't care for your insinuations, Jones. Yes, we have a deal and nothing has happened to change that, nothing at all. I've continued to act in accordance with my undertaking to you, I've not looked any further into your past and I assure you I'm just as surprised by the turn of events as you are. To be honest, it's my fear that perhaps *you* have not stuck to your side of the bargain, which, as you would recall, included keeping Clancy quiet.'

'So they were your men, then?' she said.

'What are you talking about?'

'You had two of your boys in the pub last night, didn't you? They were worried Clancy was drunk and about to say something.

Why else would you be worried about Clancy keeping his mouth shut?'

'Boys? What boys? I'm sorry, but I have no idea what you're talking about, Jones.'

'Who were they, Gerard? Where do you find these people?'

He sighed, stood up and moved towards the drinks cabinet. 'Scotch?' he asked, with his back to her.

'No thank you.'

'Suit yourself.' He poured himself a nip, replaced the top on the crystal decanter, rocked back on his heels with one hand in his pocket.

He's making me wait, punishing me for impertinence, she thought.

'Jones, I do not have "boys". I'm a businessman. I deal with other businessmen. And I think you're being paranoid.' He sat down again, relaxing into his chair and resting his Scotch glass on the arm.

Was she being paranoid? She went through Gerard's connection to everything that stunk in the Clancy affair. He'd been speaking with a man called Brose that night when he mentioned the CCTV footage—his 'insurance', as he'd put it. Brose—who drove a motorbike, and was short and stocky, just like Clancy's description of the man who burned his arm—had promised to 'take care' of something for him. Brose, Ambrose Macpherson, had showed up on the ASIC register as a director of BT Regional, the company that had paid Cranfield to frame Clancy. And yet none of this was conclusive, all of it vague, shadowy. And what about the Earlville gang? One of the leaders, Red Flanno—Jason Clegg—was also short and stocky, and drove a blue Flacon ute similar to the one identified by Clancy. But that feud had been running for years, unrelated to CTS and the Holts. It was impossible to reconcile the few facts she had. She needed more information and she wasn't leaving this house until she got it.

'Clancy's missing, Gerard, just tell me—'

'This is simple, Jones,' he interrupted. 'We did a deal and I expect you to honour your side of the bargain. Don't go pursuing Clancy, don't pursue any of this business, don't go searching for names, don't do anything but coach the team and keep your nose clean—that's all you have to do.'

His condescending manner tipped her over the edge. 'Gerard, I know about Brose. I know he's involved,' she hissed, her head perfectly steady.

A darkness fell across his face. 'I have no idea who you're referring to.' The words were delivered ice-cool, with a touch of indignation, but everything about his body screamed there was something else. She searched his eyes. Nothing.

'He drives a motorbike and owns the tattoo parlour, doesn't he, your Brose? Takes care of things for you.'

'You're not talking any sense. I think you'd better leave,' he said, setting his glass on the table with a clunk, scowling as he stood up.

'You've reneged, haven't you, Gerard? Your thugs rang you from the pub, didn't they? You got nervous and you let them off the leash. What have they done to Clancy?' The words came out in a rush—she couldn't hold her fury in a moment longer.

'You're leaving now. I want you out.' He pointed at the door.

She stood up, they were a metre apart. She could feel the heat flaming in her face. 'Are you sure you know what these people are capable of? You'd better stop them before this goes too far, Gerard.'

'Oh, I know exactly their capabilities.' His voice was a slow-burning fire now, she'd finally broken through the ice wall. 'Let me tell *you* something, Jones'—he pointed his finger at her—'and then I want you out of this house. The best leaders are the best recruiters. They get the right people around them, the right people for the job,' he snarled. 'I hired you, didn't I? The best coach Katinga has ever seen. So you see, Jones, I am a very good recruiter. You'll find that the people I work with—"these people", as you call them—get things done, whatever it takes.'

It was a threat, a confirmation, everything. She was shocked. He went ahead of her, opened the front door. As she walked past him, he gripped her forearm, leaned down and spoke in her ear. 'How's your dog, by the way?'

\/

The front door shut behind her. She walked down the front steps towards the gate, her skin prickling, a mix of rage and fear boiling in her stomach. Gerard was involved—it was 'his people' who had trashed her house, attacked Pocket. They 'got things done', that's for damn sure.

She was still struggling to take in the new information when she realised Bernadette was standing by the front gate, partially concealed behind the hedge that ran along the path. Bernadette reached out, touched her arm as she approached the front gate.

'Clementine, I know what you must think of me,' she said, 'but please, you have to believe me, I never meant for any of this to happen.'

'Which part?' snapped Clementine. 'The bit where you coerced Clancy into having sex, or the cover-up afterwards?'

A puff of breeze fluttered through the leaves in the hedge. 'Have you never done anything you regret?' she said.

Clementine flinched—it was like a cold bucket of water in her face.

Bernadette looked away, towards the far side of the yard. 'I've wished a thousand times I could take it back,' she whispered. 'What possessed me...why would I...'

The words were so familiar to Clementine. They were her words, her story. It took her breath away.

'I don't expect you to believe anything I say at this point,

191

Clementine, but I really must tell you something—something you need to know. I'm sure you guessed at it the other night at the fundraiser. You see, I have a chance at a role in head office. It's a significant step up. It's more than that, it's—' Bernadette caught herself, stopping short of saying something.

'What? Tell me. There has to be more to it than a promotion. Surely.'

Bernadette shook her head. 'Believe me—it's very important for both of us, more than you can imagine. If you do as Gerard asks and we can just get through this bad patch, things will be okay. I'll make sure of it.'

'I don't understand. You're putting Clancy through this because you want a promotion?'

'I can't tell you everything, Clementine—I can't. Please, you have to trust me.'

'You're going to get a big salary increase and share options, I get that, but—'

'Please, I can't tell you everything that's going on, Clementine— I just can't. All I can tell you is that I do intend to make it up to Clancy—it's just that I can't do it now. But it won't be long. A few weeks, maybe a month, that's all.'

Clementine was beside herself, but it seemed Bernadette was not going to divulge anything further. 'Well, then, at least tell me, where is Clancy? Is he safe? What do you know?'

'I don't know anything, really, I don't. I only know that he's missing, and that is of immense concern to me, more than you can imagine, especially knowing the state he must be in.'

Clementine knew this must be deliberate ignorance, that Bernadette had made sure she didn't know—keeping her hands clean, at least when it came to the cover-up.

'So let me get this straight, Bernadette—once you've got the promotion, Clancy will suddenly reappear, yes? But what if you don't get the job? What if Gerard's "boys" take it too far?

How can you guarantee Clancy's return?'

Bernadette just shook her head and looked away, as if she refused to allow any of those thoughts.

'Bernadette, I need to know—I need your help.'

'No, no, that's not what you need. You don't need to do anything. It will all be okay—just give it time, give me time. I won't let you or Clancy down.'

'Bernadette, there might not be a Clancy. Do you have any idea what these men are like?'

Bernadette winced. 'Please, just do what Gerard asks. You simply must.' She shivered. 'If you don't, the consequences for you, for Clancy...well, they don't bear thinking about.'

\\/

She waited to speak with Sergeant Phillips at the police station. He was noncommittal. No trace of Clancy yet but no sign of any foul play either. He was flat out coordinating the search and she left him to do his job.

The sunset struck an orange warning over the mountains as Clementine pulled out of Katinga, and by the time she reached the cottage it was dark. Pocket cried when he saw her. He got up, whimpering as he hobbled to the door on three legs. She let him out for a bit, fed him his antibiotics, made sure he ate, filled his water bowl, got him comfortable again.

She was about to go back to town to join the search when her phone rang. Torrens. They'd found Clancy's shoe, soaked in blood, but no Clancy.

\\/

She felt sick, staggered to the chest of drawers in the bedroom, rifling through the bills and junk mail until she found the document

193

she was looking for. She grabbed her backpack and locked the door on the way out and for the second time that day she was hurtling down the driveway, the Commodore bouncing and shuddering over the rain-carved ruts.

On the seat next to her were the company searches she'd printed out, listing all the directors and their home addresses, including the one for Ambrose Macpherson, Director, BT Holdings. She just hoped she wouldn't be too late.

CHAPTER 29

Clementine woke to the smell of Pocket's blood on the passenger's seat. She'd washed the seat cover and scrubbed the seat, but it was still there—faint, accusing.

She rubbed her eyes and checked the clock. How long had she dozed off for? An hour. It was six-thirty, and the sun was on its way up, spreading a soft dawn light over a misty Earlville. She checked the house. No lights in the windows, or in the shed to the side of the house. She checked her phone for new messages. Nothing.

She had driven to Ambrose Macpherson's address at Speyside Street—the second house from the corner—stopping only for fuel and supplies (a couple of day-old corned beef sandwiches, an iced coffee, a bottle of water and a packet of Tim Tams). She'd gone the back way, and pulled up in the street that adjoined his. Two flowering wattle trees made a wall of foliage on the corner. She parked close enough so she could just see Brose's house and hoped to God her beaten-up old Commodore wouldn't attract any attention.

It must have been about nine last night when she'd seen a short, stocky man in jeans and a jumper come out of the front of the house. He had opened the roller door on the shed halfway and then made a call on his mobile from the driveway. He looked like he was waiting for something. Just after he'd pocketed his phone, a vehicle approached from the other end of Speyside Street. A blue ute. *The* blue ute.

The man checked up and down the street, opened the roller door to its full height, moving swiftly. The ute rolled in and he walked in behind it, quickly sliding the roller door closed. The driver wore a beanie and had the bulk of a body builder. Not enough light to make out his features.

She'd tried to stay awake by eating and drinking the supplies she'd bought at the fuel station, but she'd dozed off two or three times.

Smears of orange and pink preceded the sun still hidden behind the ridge. Around her the front lawns were covered in a fine dusting of frost. It looked like it would be a cold, clear day. Semi-final day. She went through the starting eighteen in her head, then the match-ups she'd worked out for the Digby Dingoes' key players, pulling the blanket around her more tightly and checking her phone again. No new texts. The last one yesterday afternoon had been from Torrens, telling her he'd been out searching for Clancy but had gone home after dark when the search was suspended for the night. Hundreds of people had turned up, he said, combing the creek, searching the grassy ditches either side of the main road to the north and the dense bush to the west of Katinga.

She went over and over her conversations with the Holts, searching for any clue about where Clancy might be. Bernadette's promotion depended on keeping her skeleton in the closet quiet. But to go to these lengths?

Clem ran through the details of a few recent corporate sex scandals in her head. All men in positions of power—executives, representatives of their organisations, of whom a higher standard was expected. Was it their gender or their power that made it scandalous? Either way, Bernadette was right to fear the publicity. Unless she had friends in very high places, she would almost certainly find herself shuffled out the door of CTS. There was significant wealth on offer for any senior executive in a company about to list on the ASX. She thought of Clancy and Melissa's housing commission home. The contrast disgusted her.

Now here she was and Clancy abducted. *Abducted*. The word stuck in her head. A word she'd never thought she'd have need of. Abducted by violent men. Men who would smash a dog's leg with a tomahawk, stub a cigarette out on a man's arm, make threats against unborn babies.

It dawned on her—*God, Clementine, you think you can do this on your own?* Maybe she should tell the police. She fought with the idea. Yesterday she hadn't wanted to distract them from the search, and today, in the cold light of dawn, the fear of dropping Torrens in it loomed large. She would be laying a trail for them, taking them back to the Audi job, the clean-up afterwards when she'd overheard Gerard and Brose, the burglary, the theft of the USB sticks and the letterbox bomb. All of it leading them to Torrens, like an arrow to a bullseye—and what an easy target he would be for them with his history.

Another life she would ruin.

And all because of a hunch—for that was all it was at this stage, a hunch that perhaps Ambrose Macpherson had kidnapped Clancy.

At that moment she saw movement at the house, the front door opening, Brose walking over to the shed in jeans and a black leather jacket, a backpack slung over his shoulder. He turned the key in the side door of the shed, checking the street before he entered. She saw a light come on inside, shining through the cracks in the door. The other man, the ute driver, emerged from the house. He wore Doc Martens boots, jeans and a hoodie covering his head. She slunk lower in the seat as he looked up and down the street on his way towards the shed.

The roller door began crawling its way up. She threw off the blanket, checked the Commodore was in neutral. She could see the second man's boots and calves and the back of the ute. A silver Harley appeared, its exhaust blurting and puffing. Brose with his

197

hands high on the hooped handlebars, boots forward on the pegs, rolling casually onto the street. No sign of Clancy.

She turned the key in the ignition. The Commodore spluttered and stalled in the cold. *Oh bloody hell, come on. Start, you mongrel.* She turned the key again, this time pumping the accelerator. The engine kicked in just as the motorbike swung right out of the driveway, away from her and towards the hill at the other end of the street.

She inched the Commodore forward, waiting for the second man to emerge. He was still inside the shed as the roller door started to rattle its way down. Then the side door opened and he stepped out of the darkness into the morning light, hood pushed back, head shaven. Red Flanno. Jason Clegg. The Earlville gang, connected to Ambrose. Her heart was pounding, and she fought off a sudden desire to turn around and head straight home to Katinga.

Clegg went back into the house. Creeping forward to the corner, she swung left and rolled past number 12 at a casual pace, watching for movement. The windows were heavily curtained. She increased her speed, then pressed down hard on the accelerator as she hit the base of the hill.

Approaching the crest, she saw the motorbike taking a right turn three blocks away. Down the hill and the Commodore was up to 110, then heavy on the brakes and down the gears, before taking the same right turn.

She caught a glimpse of the bike as it leaned over left, disappearing up a side street. Brose was in a hurry or just enjoying his Harley. She planted her foot down hard, hit the brakes as late as she dared, tyres screeching as she swung left into the corner, thankful that under his helmet and with the sound of the Harley, he wouldn't hear a thing.

The road ahead stretched straight to a T-junction in the distance. The bike was moving very fast, half a kilometre away now, slowing for the intersection. Brose took a right, leaning into the corner.

She moved through the gears, revving hard between each change, the Commodore leaping forward as she released the clutch. Approaching the intersection, she saw the sign pointing right to the Earlville airport. Right hand down, tyres screaming, the wagon skidded across the asphalt, flicking momentarily into the gravel on the shoulder. She straightened, powered forward, a cloud of dust behind her and a faint odour of burning rubber wafting through the cabin. Adrenaline tingled through her hands as she gripped the wheel.

She had the old Commodore up to 170 now. It really seemed to come alive, flying over the potholes as if they weren't there.

She caught a glimpse of the motorbike flashing in the low rays of the rising sun as Brose rounded a bend up ahead and slipped behind a row of trees. She started counting. Twenty seconds before she reached the same bend. The turn pulled out into a long straight stretch. She got a good view of the motorbike up ahead—Brose was enjoying his early-morning ride, gunning down the empty highway.

She took the Commodore back up to 170, foot flat to the boards.

He took the next curve to the right and disappeared behind a strip of bushland that marked the start of the hills around the north of Earlville. She started counting again, arrived at the bend twenty-four seconds later.

They were winding through the hills now. She ignored the 50-kilometre speed sign and the single white line down the middle of the road, hugging each curve tight on the wrong side of the road, holding her breath for that moment of blindness, breathing out again as she saw the empty road slithering on ahead to the next bend. The Commodore swung wildly as it rounded each turn, then bounded forward as she pushed down on the accelerator.

For the next five kilometres, she saw nothing of the motorbike on the winding road. Pulling out of the final bend and pointing the Commodore down the hill, she peered ahead anxiously up the straight. Nothing. Shit. The road was straight for at least a kilometre before it twisted left behind a large shearing shed.

She dashed to the first crossroad and slowed, scanning left and right. Nothing. She slammed her foot down again, passed the airport sign.

She slowed again, checking left down the airport road. Away in the distance something flashed silver, like a mirror in the sunlight. She wrenched the steering wheel down, feeling the rear wheels slide into the dirt as the arse slid out. She relaxed into the slide, allowing the car to slow a little before straightening and pushing the pedal as hard as she could.

She hit the sixty-kilometre zone at ninety and followed the road that ran around the northern end of the airport car park before easing into the long curve that would take her towards the terminal building.

She looked across the car park. It was long and narrow, faded white lines dividing each bay, about two-thirds empty. No motorbikes in the first section. She slowed and drew close to the rear of a white Volvo moving at a leisurely pace up the road, a Panama hat and a tartan rug on the rear dash. She kept slowing, slowed some more, ground her teeth. *Come on, Grandpa.*

As the Volvo inched towards the turn into the drop-off road at the front of the terminal, she caught sight of a motorbike in the middle of the car park. Sports bike. Bright red fuel tank.

The Volvo paused to give way to some imaginary traffic and then crept forward, Clementine following close behind. She scanned the length of the road. No Harley. The terminal stretched low and narrow to her left. A young couple in baggy clothes with lots of pockets and huge backpacks ambled along the footpath to her right.

Grandpa came to a stop at the pedestrian crossing. She drummed the steering wheel with her thumb impatiently, eyes crawling over the car park as far as she could see. An older woman wearing a puffed blue parka and hauling a large case behind her began struggling over the crossing.

No motorbikes in the middle section of the car park. She started on the last section. An old Landcruiser was reversing out of a space in the furthest corner. As it rolled away, she could see the space behind it—and the Harley, with its big looping handlebars and silver tank. Her heart started thumping, she blinked, checked— definitely Brose's Harley. She scoured the car park between the bike and the crossing. A figure appeared from behind the middle row of cars. Short, stocky, bald head, black leather jacket. He was metres from the crossing, metres from seeing her.

The old lady in the parka had reached the other side of the crossing and was hauling her case up the ramp onto the footpath. There were no more pedestrians in sight. *Oh God, Grandpa, stay where you are, stay where you are.* She saw the wispy white hair on his head swing to the right, towards the car park. Brose was three strides from the crossing. With the courtesy of another era, Grandpa waited. Brose gave him a nod as he stepped purposefully onto the road.

She pretended to reach for something on the passenger-side floor of the car, stayed down and counted to ten, then peeked up over the dashboard. Brose was through the automatic doors of the terminal and dear old Grandpa had started to roll forward across the crossing.

\I/

Clementine entered the terminal from the door farthest from the check-in area. There were a handful of people at the counters, a larger group sitting at the two departure gates and a queue at the hole-in-the-wall cafe just opposite the gates. Brose was third in line, his back to her.

She checked the flight monitor. There was the 8.10 am to Goorinda, arriving 9.05 am, and an 11.30 am to Sydney, then nothing until 3 pm. She googled Goorinda on her phone. A regional town east of central New South Wales, just under five hours' drive away according to Google Maps.

Had to be the early flight he was taking. No other reason to get up at the crack of dawn. She stood there, staring at the screen. It was 7.13 am. Just under fifty minutes before departure and less than seven hours until the siren started the semi-final. She checked online for flights out of Goorinda airport. Nothing until four o'clock in the afternoon. Her head dropped. Her whole body felt hollow.

She went outdoors and took a deep lungful of the chill air, hurrying away from the activity at the front of the terminal, circumnavigating a family with four daughters, all with blond, plaited pigtails and identical Barbie suitcases. At the end of the building was a low bench hard up against the concrete wall of the terminal facing a gravelled yard, cigarette butts strewn around it. She dropped her bag, sat down, staring at her feet.

She had staked out Brose's house hoping to find some sign of Clancy or something that might link Brose with Clancy's disappearance at least. She'd thought Brose had to be involved. And she still thought that, but nothing last night or this morning had brought her any closer to confirming it. She'd hoped, when he'd turned off at the airport road, that perhaps he was picking someone or something up, pushed the thought of him actually flying somewhere out of her head. And now, here she was, still no closer to knowing whether he was going on a holiday to visit his mother or on his way to wherever they'd taken Clancy.

She went through all the things that had happened that suggested Brose was involved. She could not shake the feeling that this was the man who would lead her to Clancy.

Her throat felt dry. Thirty-four years without a final, fifty years without a premiership. All the nights in front of the computer planning, strategising, all the cold, wet training sessions, the sweat, the bruises, the knocks, the elation, the disappointment.

She leaned back against the wall and closed her eyes. The cold seeped through her jumper and crept into her bones. She stayed there, wanting the cold to hurt her, burn her. She imagined the players, the looks on their faces. She hadn't missed a single training session, let alone a game. She pressed her back harder against the wall, her hair catching and pulling in the tiny cracks in the concrete blocks.

It wasn't just the players—it was the whole town, and their big, patient hearts. Mrs Lemmon, Wakely, the Floods, all of them. The years of drought and of plenty, of drought again, then rain, and then the mine closing.

Maybe they'll be okay without me, thought Clementine. *It's not impossible.* They'd had a win without Clancy last week; they could win without her. *Sellingham knows the patterns, he's captain, he can be leader for the day.* She could ring him, take him through the match-ups and her game plan in detail.

She opened her eyes. The sun had lifted clear of the hills on the horizon. It burned gold against the early blue of the sky and pushed a pink blush up through the thin strands of cloud above.

She thought through the possibilities. Following Brose was the only thing she could think of that might lead her to Clancy. But it could be nothing—he could be going on a business trip, a holiday, visiting family for all she knew. Hardly convincing for the police unless she told them about Brose's conversation with Gerard and the CCTV footage.

She thought of Melissa, her baby due any day now. She imagined her in a hospital bed, cradling a beautiful newborn with Clancy's big brown eyes, swaddled in cotton blankets. She saw Melissa surrounded by family—her mum, sisters, brothers, cousin Tash, the aunties. Everyone but Clancy.

The gravel at her feet was dry and cold, the edge of each pebble clear and crisp in the fresh morning light. A magpie landed on the fence at the end of the yard, looked left, looked right, threw his head back and warbled.

She knew what she had to do.

She walked into the terminal, through the automatic doors, and passed her credit card and driver's licence across the counter. 'I need a seat on the Goorinda flight, please, as far away from my boss as possible. I spend all week with him and I don't want to ruin my weekend.'

'Of course. His name?' asked the smiling woman at the check-in counter.

'Mr Ambrose Macpherson.'

\\/

She waited outside on the bench seat in the gravelled yard, eating the last of the Tim Tams. First she texted Gerard: *Sick. Can't make it. Have briefed Sello.*

Then she rang Sellingham. He was shocked, distraught at first, but she told him to grow up, took him through the game plan, the match-ups.

Then her phone rang. Rowan. He was at the cottage. He'd dropped by to check on the shed roof after the wind the night before, make sure it was solid. Wanted to wish her well for the semi-final.

'Want me to sort out the glass in the front door?' he asked.

'Can you do glass?'

'Yeah. Piece of piss,' he said. He'd come next week on Wednesday to fit it. 'So where are you, anyway?' he asked.

She cast around for an excuse. 'Already in town. Having breakfast at the Wombat Cafe, going over the game plan.'

'Ngh,' he grunted, 'that's my local. Didn't see you there.

Recommend the teacake.' He hung up.

Rowan would be at the game. He would know she'd lied. But he wasn't one to disclose secrets, thank goodness.

She texted Torrens next: *Sick. Can't make it. Sello's in charge. Help him out—keep the boys together.* She felt her insides tear apart, had a sudden urge to scream.

She had left Jenny till last. *Can't make it. Told everyone I'm sick. Will explain later. Can you check in on Pocket? He has one antibiotic twice a day. They're in the fridge. Key's under the flowerpot, front door.*

She thought about Pocket, felt a wave of loneliness closely followed by fear. She was on her own, pursuing a man who, as far as she knew, was a brutal criminal, and no one, not a soul, knew where she was.

She picked up the phone again, dialled Rowan's number.

'I lied. I'm not at the cafe. I'm at the Earlville airport. I'm booked on the 8.10 flight to Goorinda.'

'What the hell?'

'I can't explain, but I won't be at the game and I've told everyone I'm sick. I just wanted someone to know where I actually was.'

'Why are you going to Goorinda? It's the semi-final, for Christ's sake.'

She wanted to tell him, to unload the whole story on him in one big torrent, just to have one person in the world know what she was carrying around, but she said nothing.

'Come on,' Rowan said. 'What's going on? You can tell me.'

She heard the concern in his voice, knew that he sensed her fear—in her words, her silence, everything she did and didn't say.

She hung up.

CHAPTER 30

The young flight attendant was standing at the top of the stairs, just outside the cabin at the front of the plane, checking Brose's boarding pass. As Clementine walked across the tarmac behind the family with the girls and the Barbie suitcases, she counted the plane's windows. Eleven. She checked her boarding pass. Seat number 11A—the last row.

She kept her face lowered as she handed her boarding pass to the attendant. Brose was squeezing past a man sitting in the aisle seat of the third row, to her left. She followed closely behind the mother and the girls as she sidled down the aisle, keeping her face right the whole time.

\\\/

Boarding was delayed and then they sat on the tarmac for half an hour. By the time they landed in Goorinda, it was just after ten am. She waited in her seat, watched Brose disembark in the first flush of passengers, then followed a dozen or so others between them. In the terminal, he walked straight out the glass doors to the pick-up area. She watched from inside as he lit up a cigarette.

Down the far end of the road to the right in front of the terminal, was a single taxi, waiting for a fare. *Good*—she didn't have a plan B for ground transport other than that. Of the remaining passengers, half a dozen or so dragged suitcases across the pedestrian crossing

206

to the car park. She kept one eye on Brose and another on the cab. Nobody was heading towards it, but there was a man standing halfway between the passengers waiting for pick-up and the taxi rank. He wore navy work trousers and a crisply ironed camel-coloured shirt and was smoking like there was no tomorrow.

She waited. Ambrose sucked on his cigarette in deep draughts, exhaling hurriedly and then sucking at it again. *Not much time to enjoy it*, she thought. *His pick-up will be here soon.* The family of Barbie girls with their Barbie suitcases had been welcomed by an elderly couple. They all trotted past her and outside, the flock parting and streaming around Brose, reforming again as they crossed the road towards the car park. She looked to her right. The man in the navy trousers checked his watch, took another drag on his cigarette and sauntered towards a garbage bin over by the terminal about twenty metres from the cab. *Shit, hurry up, Brose.*

She saw Brose hitch his backpack over his shoulder as a late-model black van with smoked-glass windows slowed and pulled up in the pick-up lane next to him. She ventured through the glass doors outside, keeping her head down, and headed for the taxi rank. Brose opened the door of the van, took one last drag, stubbed out his cigarette on the pavement and swung himself up into the passenger's seat. As the van rolled away, she started running towards the cab.

At that moment, the man in the navy trousers ground out his cigarette against the top of the garbage bin and began ambling towards the cab, towing his suitcase behind. He arrived before her, bending down as he passed the front of the taxi, catching the eye of the driver and pointing at the boot. The driver nodded, opened his door. As she rushed to get there, the man was approaching the boot, the cab driver with one foot out the door. She grabbed the handle, flung open the door, yelling, 'Emergency! Hospital! Quick!' and threw herself inside. The driver hesitated, but the man in the navy trousers waved him on. He drew his foot back inside the car, shut his door. She wound her window down and gave the man a wave of thanks as they pulled away from the curb.

The young cab driver looked at her confused as they cruised down the pick-up lane and out onto the road.

'Ma'am, we have no hospital in Goorinda. Do you want me to take you to Quindalga? They have one there.'

'No, no, it's okay. I just want to follow that black van, please.'

He shook his head, tutted.

\\\/

Her back was sweating against the vinyl seat. The driver turned up the air conditioning. They passed by farms with glossy-flanked cattle and row after row of knee-high leafy vegetables, green and vigorous in the gently sloping fields. The black van was about a kilometre ahead on the straight road out of the airport, with just two cars between them.

She asked the driver to close the gap on the car in front, then remembered her phone was still in flight mode. She switched it back on. Three texts and three missed calls. All the missed calls and one text were from Gerard: *Call me.* The two other texts were from Rowan:

You don't sound good. call me

I'm on my way to Goorinda.

The surprise came first, then the relief—she was a long way from anywhere, she knew no one...Then the guilt: she could be leading him into danger. She hesitated a moment, typed in a message, deleted it, typed in another message—*It's all good, I'm OK. Please turn back*—then bit her lip, her finger hovering over the send button. She closed her eyes and pressed send.

They were entering an industrial area on the outskirts of town, big sheds, tall chain-link fences, yards arrayed with trucks and heavy equipment. They passed a sign, *Goorinda—Population*

1237, then a shed with a sign covering an entire wall: *Clearham Technology & Services*. She craned her neck as they went past.

They were only a few hundred metres behind the van when they entered the town's sixty zone. The convoy of cars coming from the airport concertinaed together as they made their way past a succession of side streets lined with nondescript weatherboard houses shaded by gum trees, their roots bulging under the bitumen.

They crossed a bridge spanned with wrought-iron trusses and approached the town centre. She kept her eyes peeled for police stations but saw none. A man was sweeping the red-brick pavement in front of a low-slung weatherboard pub with wide verandahs and a green tin roof, its cream walls smudged with dust. The Royal Hotel commanded almost a whole block, the small end of its L-shape jutting around the corner into the side street.

The black van slowed up ahead. It swung sharp right across the road and into a car space directly in front of the pub.

'Keep driving, please,' said Clem. They passed it going the other way, a Mitsubishi Delica, the windows so dark she couldn't see the driver or Brose. 'Okay, do a U-turn, please, and head back up the main street,' she said once they were out of sight.

She stopped him outside the hotel, about ten spaces away from the van. Brose and his driver were just outside the pub's main entrance on the corner. The driver was tall and thin, wearing brown square-pointed cowboy boots, skinny jeans and a blue checked shirt. Brose had taken his leather jacket off and was sporting a red long-sleeved shirt, unbuttoned and flapping open. He looked up the street towards the cab, and she sank lower in the seat. Under his red shirt he wore a white T-shirt, his stomach protruding over the top of his belt. He pulled a grey baseball cap on over his bald head and walked indoors.

'How much if I ask you to wait?' she asked the cab driver.

'Two dollars fifty a minute, ma'am.'

She searched for her credit card. It wasn't in her bag. It wasn't in her pocket. *Shit*. She must have lost it at the terminal or left it on the plane. The cab driver drove her around the block to an ATM. She used her mobile phone to withdraw as much cash as the machine would allow, two thousand dollars, and they drove back around to the pub. The black van was still there. She paid the fare and handed him an extra eighty dollars, told him to wait for half an hour and that if she didn't come out, he was free to go.

She checked her phone—10.35 am—and got out of the cab. The man had finished sweeping out the front of the hotel and disappeared inside through a second, smaller entrance, about fifteen metres away from the corner where Brose had entered.

She peered through the second entrance cautiously, her heartbeat quickening. A few high tables with padded stools stood here and there on the faded green carpet; behind them was a long timber bar. A row of framed sporting memorabilia, mostly signed rugby league jerseys, adorned the wall above the bar. It was empty, except for the barman, who had his back to her, stacking bottles in the fridge. She could hear the sounds of a poker machine to her left, and distant voices to her right, beyond the bar, out of sight.

She stepped inside, her eyes adjusting to the dim light and made her way right, looked around the corner. More high tables with stools, and at the other end of the bar area was a door with a sign above it that said *Bistro*.

She jumped as she heard the main door directly behind her swing open. Two old men in crumpled akubra hats sauntered in, greeting the barman like an old mate. While they ordered, she slipped outside again and turned down the side street, sticking close to the wall. Peeping through the window, she saw two figures at a table near the back of the bistro, Brose and the skinny guy, two glasses of beer in front of them. She ducked out of sight, walked back up to the main street. The cabbie was still parked out the front, reading the paper.

Stepping inside through the door she'd originally come in,

she headed left, passing a cluster of indoor plants that formed something of a screen. Inside the gaming room she saw a boy playing the machines—*barely drinking age, surely*—pasty white face, baby cheeks and a pink pillow of flesh spilling out over the top of his jeans. He pushed a button. Lights flashed, pictures whirred around and a garish tune chimed. He stared and pressed the button again.

Behind the squadron of poker machines were the toilets. She came back into the bar and sat on a high stool behind the indoor plants at the table in the corner furthest from the window. From there she had a good view of both entrances to the pub—she could see Brose if he came this way and would have time to slip into the poker machine room and hide behind the wall of machines or in the toilets.

Ten minutes passed. No one had come in or gone out since the two old men, who were now sitting at the bar, beers in hand. She needed to go to the toilet, but she was afraid Brose might leave before she could make it back. She leaned forward on her stool to peer through the leafy screen in front of her, pulled back quickly when she saw a figure approaching the bar at the other end of the room. Brose. He ordered, waited, then walked back to the bistro with a packet of chips.

She sat for another ten minutes keeping her eyes on the doors, checking the window every now and then for the cab. It was still there. The barman came over, asked if she'd like a drink. She ordered a soda water and some peanuts so as not to draw attention to herself. A group of men sauntered in and then a bunch of women in polo shirts and visors. Golf or tennis group finished for the morning? She watched them laughing, sipping their gin and tonics.

She could not put off the toilet any longer. Passing the boy at the machines, she went into the ladies. On the way out, she opened the door a crack, peeked out into the poker room. No one but the boy.

She decided to check the bistro again from the street outside, make sure they hadn't left while she was in the toilets. Peering through the window, she saw Brose's driver sitting at their table, staring at his phone. There were two half-glasses of beer in front of him, but Brose was nowhere to be seen. A moment of panic, her eyes darting to the front door as she imagined Brose having left on his own in the van, just moments ago, and Clancy lost forever. She walked back around to the main street. The van was still there, and so was the cabbie, overstaying his half-hour, still reading the paper.

Brose might be in the gents or he might have gone to play the pokies. She almost ran to the screened area, snaked her head inside the pokie machine room. Just Poker Boy. *Good, Brose must be in the gents'.*

She started over to the wall of machines at the back of the room to hide before he came out. From the corner of her eye she saw movement, a door opening. A man emerged from the toilet, directly opposite her. Short, stocky, red shirt, white T-shirt, baseball cap. Brose. He looked up.

Clementine turned away, hurried for the ladies' toilet behind the pokies. She pushed through the heavy door, forcing it closed to speed it up, slipped into a cubicle, slid the lock across and slumped onto the toilet seat.

Had he recognised her? Gerard would have told him about her, sent him a photo for sure. She'd been on the front page of the *Valley News*. But maybe he hadn't even noticed her? Had she looked startled or had she managed to act casual?

She sat on the toilet seat, head in her hands. *Fuck. Fuck. Fuck.* She checked her phone. Eleven am. Nothing from Jen, a single text from Rowan: *ETA 1 pm.* He'd ignored her text.

She tried his number. No answer.

She tried to focus. *Okay,* she thought, *assume the worst. Ambrose has recognised you. He's not leaving the pub without you, no matter how long you sit in the toilets. Rowan's still*

212

hours away. You're on your own. Nothing untoward has actually happened and there's been no sign of any connection with Clancy, so the cops won't take you seriously. She thought of the cigarette burn and Pocket's mangled leg. No matter which way she sliced it, she needed help. She needed Rowan, and she needed him to know where she was. If her hunch turned out to be correct, he was her best chance, maybe her only chance.

She pulled her phone out again, sent him a text to say she was at the Royal Hotel. It wasn't enough, though. She needed him to know where they took her if she was captured.

Think, Jones, think. She stared at the floor. She could feel the cold blast of the air-conditioning vent directly above, chilling her neck. She stared unseeing at the blank screen of her phone, searching for some sort of a plan. It came to her suddenly.

She reached for the toilet roll, tore off a couple of sheets, scrabbled in her bag for a pen. Then she scrolled through the contacts list on the phone, copying numbers onto the toilet paper. When she was done, she folded the paper and tucked it into her sock. She tapped a few more commands into the phone and then left the cubicle, stopping to wash her hands and splash water on her face at the tiny sink in the corner.

She pushed the door open a crack and peeked out into the poker machine room. No Brose in sight. The boy-man was still there, pressing buttons and feeding coins into the machine. She hurried over to him, spoke urgently: 'I'd like to buy your phone.'

He looked at her blankly. 'What?'

'I'll give you a thousand for your phone, but I need it now.' She hoped his phone was nothing fancy and this would be enough, but she had another grand to play with if she needed to haggle.

'Eh?'

'One. Thousand. Dollars. Cash. For your phone.'

'A thousand? What the...Who are you?'

'Listen, I don't have much time. I really need a phone. You could take your Facebook off it, whatever—I'm not interested in your personal stuff. I just really need a phone, urgently.' She pulled out her wallet, glanced over her shoulder at the main bar, turned back and began counting out the cash.

'Yeah? You for real?' His eyes were following the notes as she riffled through them.

'Yes, yes, a thousand.' She was glaring at him, her eyes wide with impatience. She noticed his acne. God, he *was* just a kid.

'Deal?' It was more a command than a question. She glanced over her shoulder at the bar again. It was starting to fill with men in fluoro gear—smoko or early lunch. No Brose in sight.

'Hell yeah.' He reached for his back pocket, slid out his phone. An old model Samsung with a cracked screen. *Could have offered less*, she thought.

'Do you have a password?' asked Clementine.

'Yes, 3232,' he said as he started tapping. 'I'm just deleting Facebook and Instagram. There's nothing much on here anyone would want anyway.' She could hear excitement in his voice now as he started to believe his good luck.

'You on prepaid?' she said.

'Yeah. Just topped it up on Thursday. Fifty bucks. You gunna give me extra for that?'

'Fuck off. I'm giving you everything I've got,' she lied. 'What's the number?' He told her the number and she typed it into her own phone.

'Here you go.' She passed him the cash and he gave her the phone, taking the money with a wide grin.

Clementine locked the screen, then tested the password. Bingo. She checked over her shoulder again and hurried to the toilets, ducking behind poker machines along the way. The door to the bistro was obscured by the growing crowd in the bar.

She locked herself in the same cubicle again, took out her phone and used it to call the boy's phone. When it rang, she hung up, then turned both phones to mute. Then she downloaded an app on the boy's phone and sent texts to Rowan and Jenny: *This is my new phone number in case you can't get me on the old one.* To Rowan she added: *I've been spotted. There's a chance I'm about to be kidnapped and taken to wherever Clancy is. Two guys. I'm sending you a link to a phone tracking app. Download it and add this number so you can find me. Hurry.*

She lifted up her shirt, shoved the phone inside her bra above the underwire and beneath her left breast.

Standing at the basin, she washed her hands again. In the mirror her face was pale, her hair still messy from a night sleeping in the car. She took a step back from the mirror and inspected herself. The phone in her bra was uncomfortable but invisible, no protruding corners to give her away.

She hurriedly dried her hands on a paper towel, opened the door a crack, checked the poker machine room and crept out towards the bank of machines she'd chosen as a hiding place. She crossed the no-man's land between the toilet door and the machines, Poker Boy in the other corner, turned into the aisle between the two rows of machines. And there he was. Red shirt, white T-shirt, baseball cap, legs spread wide and a newspaper resting over his right hand.

Brose nodded, as if he'd been expecting her, his eyes dark and unsmiling. He moved quickly and assuredly, stepping behind her, his right hand behind her back. She felt the cold metal muzzle of a gun against her spine. 'You're coming with us, Ms Jones,' he whispered in her ear. His breath smelt of beer as it brushed the back of her neck. 'No drama, just walk out casually and I won't hurt you.'

As Brose nudged her forward, Clementine glanced at the boy playing the poker machine. He hardly even looked up.

\\//

Out on the pavement, Brose opened the sliding side door of the van and gave her another nudge. She climbed in and sat facing the rear. He climbed in after her and sat facing the front.

'Okay, my little lady, first things first then, eh,' said Brose. 'I'm going to have to ask you to hand over your phone. We can't have you texting all your friends about the grand old time you're having up here on holiday, can we?' He sniggered, enjoying himself.

She pulled her old phone from her back pocket and handed it to him. The van pulled away from the kerb and as her body rocked back into the seat she felt a pinch under her breast as the boy's phone wedged itself up against the underwire.

CHAPTER 31

The blindfold was tied tight, a nip of pain in her scalp where the knot tugged at her hair. The crunch and crackle of the tyres told her they had turned onto a dirt road; she guessed they'd been driving for about forty minutes. The phone chafed under her breast and she could smell Brose, beery, salty.

She lurched sideways as they took another right. Were they speeding, or was it just her inability to anticipate the corner?

She decided to try her luck with a question. 'Where's Clancy?'

'Did I say you could speak?' Ambrose snapped. They sat in silence again for a moment. Then he sneered, enjoying the power or just bored, and said, 'You'll see him soon enough. We're bringing you two together for a brief reunion...brief but poignant.'

'What have you done to him?'

'Ha, I wouldn't touch a hair on his pretty little black head. No, no, that's a job I'm saving for you. A new experience for you, I should think.'

She flinched, her tongue wedged tight against her throat. 'What are you talking about?'

'Oh, never mind, never mind, just enjoy the ride, princess.'

They hit a pothole with a fierce jolt.

'Jesus Christ, Hardy,' Brose yelled, 'are you blind? I could see that crater a mile off.'

'Yeah, yeah, keep your pants on, Grandma,' came the voice from the driver's seat. 'Why don't you have a little nanna nap?'

Brose swore under his breath. 'All around me, fucking every-where, useless fuckwits.'

She stared ahead into the blackness of her blindfold, clutched the seat as they rounded another bend.

They'd spent over half an hour parked near a shopping centre, Hardy getting some sort of supplies. Brose had sat there with her in the van the whole time, and the windows were such a dark tint that nobody could have seen in without pressing their face against the glass.

When Hardy had returned they'd driven through the town and taken a series of turns until she had no idea if she was facing north, south, east or west. She'd felt the car straighten, speed up—a highway. Then a right-hand turn onto the dirt road they were on now. She wondered if Rowan could see her? A blip on his phone screen?

She imagined the gun in Brose's lap, his hand resting on the grip. It had sent a shiver across her neck. She was glad she couldn't see. She knew nothing about violent men. Was there a line between cigarette burns and murder? A line that even a man like Brose wouldn't cross? She wanted it to be so and her mind grabbed hold of the idea, but with every bend in the road a cold blast of fear would usher in the opposite proposition—that Brose was simply a cold-blooded killer.

She tried to concentrate, memorising important details, about the car, the two men. She tried to calculate Rowan's progress, how far he'd have travelled by now, how far away he was still. He must be at least forty-five minutes behind them, she thought. She heard a click from the dashboard in front, then music—unexpectedly gentle. John Denver. The singing seemed distant at first, as she went over and over the maths, then it slowly crept into her consciousness—a soft, honeyed voice. Brose, singing 'Sweet Surrender'.

It was like listening to the devil.

Hardy turned the music off. They had started into another windy stretch and he was throwing the van around the bends again.

'Hey, could we slow down?' said Clem. 'I think I'm going to be sick.'

She was starting to feel queasy, but she also wanted to buy time, give Rowan a chance to catch up.

'Cool it, Hardy. You don't want to be cleaning up last night's carrots,' Brose said.

After a while she tried another question. 'Can you tell me what this is about?' She could feel his eyes on her face. 'Why would Gerard be doing this? All of this over a promotion?'

He snorted. 'So much you don't understand, princess. I'll tell you one thing, though…I finally got the boss to agree with me. The stupid cow can't save him now.'

'Who? Bernadette, you mean? Is Gerard the boss?'

Brose laughed. 'Oh, now that's fucking hilarious.'

'Explain it to me,' she demanded.

'Well, I could, I suppose. It must be killing you. But I'm afraid it's a rule of mine not to get ahead of myself. I'm very good at what I do, princess.' There was a long pause. She heard rocks crunching and flying up from under the tyres, a blustery wind buffeting the car.

Then she felt his hot breath on her face as he leaned forward. 'Maybe I'll tell you when you've dug a big hole for you and your black boyfriend to lay down in. That would be a good time, I think. I'd like to see you satisfied'—he breathed another breath on her face—'completely *in the know* before Hardy shovels the dirt over you.'

As they started to climb, the van slowed. It had taken her a while to stop shaking, but the one thought she clung to was that Clancy was still alive. She counted the bends as they wound up a hill. Nine so far, tight, some of them hairpins. A waft of cigarette smoke made its way into the back.

'Oh, for fuck's sake, Hardy, no smoking in the vehicles. How many times do I have to tell you?'

'Come on, Macca, just a quick puff. I noticed you snuck one in back there at the terminal.'

'I said put it out, Hardy.'

'Aw, come on, Grandma. Here, I'll put the window down.'

Clem heard the squeal of the leather seat as Brose jumped forward out of his seat, his shoulder brushing hers as he shouted into Hardy's ear, inches from her own, 'Put the fucking thing out now!'

'Righto, boss, keep your shirt on.' She heard Hardy suck in one more breath, then a blast of outside air as he opened his window. It was cool and moist and it whipped around the cabin in a frenzy. Brose sat back in his seat and Hardy put the window back up.

They drove in silence. Where were they? Was Rowan tracking her? Even if he was, he was a long way behind. She tried doing the sums in her head again. He seemed to be speeding based on his last update. Thirty minutes behind, forty perhaps? She was no longer confident in the maths, racked her brain for ways to stall. The more time she could burn up, the closer he'd come to catching up. *Think, girl, think.* She couldn't come up with anything better—it would have to do.

She mulled it over for another minute, then cleared her throat. 'Excuse me, but I need to go to the toilet,' she said, her voice faltering.

'Ah, princess, I'm sorry, but you're just going to have to hold it in. We'll be there in twenty minutes,' said Brose.

She crossed her legs, jiggled her foot. The road had straightened and flattened out. They were no longer driving uphill. She could hear bellbirds and parrots. Forest. Elevated, in a mountain area on a dirt road.

She waited for a couple of minutes. 'I'm very sorry, but I don't think I can wait.'

'Oh, bloody hell. Typical woman. Hardy, pull over when you can—princess needs to go behind a bush,' said Brose.

Oh, shit, she thought, *that won't do.* 'Ah, no, sorry—I'm afraid I need an actual toilet.'

'We won't look, princess, I promise,' said Brose.

'No, no, it's not that…it's, ah…it's that time of the month,' she lied. 'Things are going to get messy.'

'Oh, for Christ's sake, that's disgusting,' said Brose. She heard Hardy let out a groan in the front seat.

'When's the next servo, Hardy?' said Brose.

'Not far. Maybe five kays.'

They rattled on in silence, then she heard the tick of the indicator, felt the van slow, a small bump—the lip of a driveway.

'Toilet's over there,' said Brose. 'Pull up in front of it so's you can't see anything from the shop.' The van slowed, came to a stop. 'Go and get the key, Hardy.' She heard the driver's door open. 'And leave the engine running—it's cold out there.'

A township in the mountains with a service station. That's got to be reasonably rare.

They waited. *The shop must be some distance away*, she thought. The sliding door rolled open.

'All clear?' asked Brose.

'Yep. Van's blocking his view and he's trying to fix the fridge anyway,' said Hardy.

'Okay, princess, I'm going to help you out, and you are going to do exactly, and I mean exactly, what I tell you, right?'

She nodded.

'In and out, do what you have to do and back in the van. No

221

talking, no yelling, no screaming—not a sound, or you won't be seeing your black boyfriend again. You got that, princess?'

She nodded again.

She heard Brose get out of his seat, felt his hand on hers. 'Out you come, easy does it.' She shuffled forward, letting him guide her. His fingers were rough but surprisingly gentle. She imagined him a surgical killer, his honeyed voice singing John Denver as he sliced. It sent a tremor through her body.

He grabbed her other hand. 'Big step now.'

She took a step down, onto the running board.

'Another one.'

She took another step down, onto the ground. The fresh mountain air filled her lungs. The wind was blowing strong, flapping at her jeans. She heard it whine, heard the clatter and rattle of branches and leaves, the swoosh of something softer—fern fronds, perhaps. Were they in a rainforest?

She heard the click of a key in a lock and the squeak of a heavy door, smelled the overpowering odour of one of those old-fashioned deodorant blocks. Brose untied the blindfold, whipped it away and pushed her forward. She looked over her shoulder, catching a brief glimpse of thick bush on a steep slope behind him as he pulled the door shut after her.

There she was standing in the cubicle, on her own, the wind drowning out the quiet sob of relief that collapsed from her mouth.

She slid the bolt across.

'Hey, keep the door unlocked,' Brose shouted.

She stood there, groping under her bra for the phone.

'I said, unlock the door.'

With the heavy door between them and the blindfold gone, Clem felt a surge of defiance. 'The door won't stay shut without the bolt,' she yelled. 'And I assure you, Brose, you do not want to see this.' Using his name out loud gave her a sudden thrill of power.

The phone peeled away from her left breast, leaving a stinging

222

strip of raw skin. Time 12.35 pm. No calls or texts. Rowan must have known it would be dangerous to contact her.

She pulled out the folded piece of toilet paper with the phone numbers from her sock, her heart thumping. The wind was howling like a banshee now, branches bashing and scraping against the corrugated iron of the toilet roof. She hoped it was enough to cover the sound of her voice. She rang Rowan's number.

He picked up straightaway. 'Clem?'

'Shhhh,' she whispered.

'Are you okay?' he asked.

'Yes, for now. I'm in a black Mitsubishi Delica van, tinted windows, two men—Ambrose Macpherson from the Earlville tattoo parlour and a bloke called Hardy. Brose has a gun. I'm in the toilet at a servo. They're taking me to Clancy. Can you see where I am?'

'You're a blip on the screen and it's jumping all over the shop. Must be poor mobile range. Right now you're showing up at Dunberry. It's up in the ranges near the Arkuna National Park. I'm about twenty minutes behind you.'

Her breath came out in a rush. She was not alone. She wanted to cry.

'Clem, this app only works while your phone's on. How much charge do you have?'

Oh God, she hadn't even thought of that. She took the phone from her ear, checked the indicator in the corner.

Her voice was trembling now. 'One bar, flashing amber. Shit, Rowan, please hurry.'

'I'm right behind you, Clem. I've got you covered.'

'They're killers, Rowan,' she whispered.

'Hang in there—don't do anything crazy. Just do whatever they say. I'm calling the police, they'll be on their way, hang on.'

A fist pounded on the door. 'Hurry up in there! We haven't got all day.'

She clicked the phone off and tucked it back into her bra, under her right breast this time, her hands shaking, fumbling with the buttons on her shirt. Then she sat there, silent, breathing as steadily as she could. She needed to play for more time, give Rowan the chance to catch up.

'Okay, princess, I'm officially all out of patience. Bring the angle grinder, Hardy.'

She sat back down and began counting off the seconds in her head, trying to keep track of how much time she could soak up. There was a patch of damp on the pockmarked concrete floor and the heavy wooden door hung crooked from its rusted hinges, weighted down by decades of graffiti. She read the initials framed by love hearts—some barely scratched through the flaking paint, others carved deep into the timber—then the curses and insults and phone numbers scrawled in thick black felt-tip pen.

She briefly considered running to the service station attendant when the door opened, but it didn't serve her purpose—she needed Brose to take her to Clancy. A rescue mid-journey would not assist. Besides, she now fully expected that, if the attendant asked any questions, they would just kill him as well. Although her mind tried to push the thought away, it appeared they must be travelling somewhere remote where Brose felt it was safe to dispose of bodies.

She tried not to think about it, focused on the seconds ticking by, each one a priceless gift. Her battery might die, there might be no mobile reception, Rowan might trace the phone but arrive too late. *Stall, Jones. Stall.*

She'd been sitting in silence about three minutes, perhaps a little longer, when she heard Brose swear.

'Hurry up, Hardy,' Brose called out. 'What's taking you so long?'

'Fuckin' thing's underneath the friggin' spare tyre,' yelled Hardy from the van.

'Come on, princess, you're just wasting our time now. Out you come,' said Brose.

She stalled some more, counting off the seconds, made it to three and a half minutes, heard the rear door of the van slam shut, footsteps.

'Gunna make a bit of noise, boss. Think old mate might hear?'

'Give it to me. Go and tell him we're cutting a bit of pipe in the van or something,' said Brose.

She heard Hardy's footsteps fade. Should she come out before Brose started the machine? She didn't want the service station attendant rushing out and putting himself in danger. She waited a moment longer.

'Right, bitch. Here it comes. Get your fingers ready—I'm gunna take one of them too when I'm finished on the door,' said Brose.

'Okay, okay, I'm coming out,' she cried.

'You fuckin' little tease. I've had just about enough of you. Get out. Now!'

She checked the phone under her breast, pulled the chain to flush the toilet, slid the bolt back and pushed open the door.

Brose was waiting, grabbed her wrists, crossed them behind her back and slipped a cable tie around. She winced as he pulled it tight. They'd parked the Delica as a barrier between the shop and the toilet. The service station attendant wouldn't have seen a thing.

'That's what bad girls get for being a bloody nuisance,' Brose snarled as he tied the blindfold. He spun her around, nudged the gun into her spine again and pushed her forward three steps, then up into the van. Then he slammed her ankles together, bound them in cable ties too.

She had only saved a grand total of about five minutes all up. Hardy arrived back and the van took off abruptly. She nearly toppled off the seat. The cable ties around her wrists and ankles dug in as she lurched forward. She was tied up like a mud crab waiting for the pot, and with the blindfold back on, all the strength and defiance of her brief minutes of freedom drained away.

She couldn't give up, though—she had to buy more time. An

idea entered her head. There was no time to think it through, but she had to give it a shot. Suddenly, she allowed her whole body to go limp, pretending to faint, slumping forward and pushing off with one foot—it only took the slightest touch to propel her body down and towards the sliding door. She rolled her shoulders and then braced for the impact. Her head slammed against the door with a hollow thud then speared down into the foot well.

'Holy shit! Stop the car, Hardy,' Brose yelled. 'She's bloody fainted or something. Fuck.' She felt his hands trying to haul her up. 'Come round and open the door, she's bloody stuck upside down here,' he said to Hardy. She felt the doorhandle engage and the sliding door open with a rush. She made sure she tumbled down onto the concrete headfirst, hitting the ground with a crack, pain shooting through her skull.

'Shit a brick, Hardy, I said slow!' Brose was out in a moment, positioning himself between Clementine and the service station shop. 'Oh, you fucking moron, Hardy, you absolute fucking moron.'

She felt his hands rolling her over. The blindfold had slipped, but she kept her eyes closed. Something warm on her wrist? Blood from the twist and cut of the cable ties.

'Quick, get the blindfold off before the guy in there sees anything,' said Brose. 'Hurry up, he's coming out.' She felt his hands on her wrists, then a cold metal blade, and suddenly her hands were free. She felt the blade against her ankles, the cable tie ping open, and let her feet fall away, limp.

'Are you right there?' The voice came from about ten metres away. She allowed her eyes to flutter open and then roll sideways in a daze.

'Yeah, mate. I reckon she just fainted, that's all.' Brose was kneeling in front of her. 'Are you okay, sweetheart?' he asked with sickening concern. She desperately wanted to scream out to the attendant and rush into his arms. She couldn't put him in danger, couldn't abandon Clancy. She stayed silent, her head throbbing so hard it felt like a hammer inside.

'Where am I?' she said, rolling her eyes back the other way and staring blankly. The guy was tall and scrawny, somewhere around thirty or forty.

'You're at the Caltex servo in Dunberry, love,' he said, helpfully.

Dunberry. The app was working! *Rowan's on his way. Stall, Jones, stall.*

'Maybe I should get her something to drink,' the attendant suggested.

Before Brose could intervene, she groaned, 'Oh, yes, please—could you?'

'No worries,' said the attendant. 'You boys want anything?'

'No, all good—thanks, mate. Much appreciated,' said Brose.

The attendant turned and headed back to the shop.

When he was out of earshot, Brose leaned in close. 'You fucking bitch. You're going to pay for that.' His face was an inch from hers, his eyes flashing. 'You say a word to this bloke and I'll slit your throat and his before you can blink.' He brought the point of his knife up to her face. She gulped, her mouth dry.

'We should go, Macca, before this joker comes back out.'

'Then he'll definitely know something's up, you fucking dipshit. Just chill.'

Hardy leaned up against the van as Brose wiped the blood from Clementine's wrist with the sleeve of his jacket. 'You see this, princess? This blood? There'll be a lot more of it, my girl, a lot more when I'm finished with you—and the more you fuck me around, the longer I'll draw it out. Oh yes, darlin', I'm an expert in making things last, and not just pain, either.' He was leering, mouth open, a string of saliva spanning the gap between his teeth. She felt a wave of dread. Sheer dread like she'd never felt before.

'Now, get the fuck back in the van and keep your mouth shut until the guy gets back.'

She pushed herself up slowly and got back in the van. Brose stood with his legs wide apart and his hands on his hips, eyes toward the shop, Hardy watching her closely.

They waited, perhaps two minutes. 'What the fuck is this bloke doing, making cocktails or something?' said Brose. 'Go in and see what's going on,' he told Hardy. 'And make sure he's not making any phone calls.'

The sun was high and the wind was beginning to drop. She closed her eyes for a moment, preparing herself for whatever came next. The smell of petrol and eucalyptus wafted into the van. As the minutes passed, she imagined Rowan racing towards her. More than ten minutes saved overall, she estimated, maybe fifteen. *Oh God, please come quick.*

Hardy appeared in the shop doorway, holding the door open for the attendant. They came to the van.

'Here you go, love,' said the attendant. 'A coffee and some chocolate, and two more coffees for you fellas. Sorry for the wait. Bloody fridge's been on the blink. Milk was off. All of it! Had to go up to the house for another bottle. Oh, and Mum told me you should drink this first, love.' He thrust a plastic mug at her. 'Hot apple cider vinegar and honey—supposed to be good for fainting.'

'Tell your mum thanks,' Clem croaked.

She looked straight at the attendant as she reached out for the cup, making sure the red welt on her wrist was visible, drawing his eyes to hers, then widening them, twice, like flashing headlights. She saw him cock his head slightly. He glanced across at Brose, then back to her. She was sure he had registered her signal. Fear, danger. She was sure he had seen it.

'Thanks, mate,' said Brose, leaning forward across Clementine. 'Here take some money for this lot,' and he held out two twenty-dollar notes.

'Nah, no charge, buddy,' said the attendant, a hint of nervousness in his voice.

Hardy slammed the sliding door shut behind Brose and went around to the driver's seat. The van rolled forward to the exit. She could see the attendant watching the car leave. She'd hoped he'd seen enough. *Ring the police, man. Tell them which way we went. Please, God.*

\\/

They drove another fifteen minutes. She wondered if the battery on her phone had died. Her thoughts drifted to the semi-final. It would be only an hour or so before the opening siren. She imagined Sellingham gathering the team in a pre-match huddle, firing them up, the crowd shifting in anticipation, the umpire blowing his whistle, striding forward and slamming the ball into the turf for the first bounce. Torrens would be muscling up in the ruck, eyes up, body on body, leveraging his bulk like she'd shown him when she realised he couldn't jump to save himself.

She closed her eyes behind the blindfold, sent up a little prayer. *Good luck to each of you, all my guys.* Her heart was heavy like a stone.

Her hands felt swollen, the blood pooling beyond the edges of the electrical tape. Brose had been furious with Hardy for not bringing more cable ties. Humiliated, Hardy had bound the tape tighter and tighter around her wrists.

The van was slowing, stopping. Hardy's door opened; she heard his footsteps crunching, then the squeak of a gate swinging open. That was when she felt it, the vibration beneath her breast, and then, an instant later, the unmistakable sound of a ringtone. Poker Boy's ringtone.

Her mouth dropped. The volume switch must have been nudged during the scuffle, or maybe when she fell out of the van. Maybe she'd inadvertently pressed it on in the toilet cubicle.

'What the fuck?' Brose bellowed. 'Is that a phone? Oh, for fuck's

229

sake.' She felt his hands shoving her down on the seat, patting her sides, groping her crotch, lifting her jumper. 'You stupid fucking bitch,' he snarled, ripping the phone out from under her breast and cracking her across the face with the back of his hand, knuckles crashing into her jaw, throwing her sideways onto the seat.

CHAPTER 32

Pain was pulsing through her jaw and the salty taste of blood filled her mouth. Hardy opened the side door and the mountain air rushed in. The blindfold had loosened a little and she could see underneath it. 'What's the code, bitch?' Brose said as he stepped out of the van. Clem mumbled the number and he began flicking through Poker Boy's phone. She could see the ground—patches of grass and dirt—and the bottom half of an open gate with a 'Private Property' sign hanging from it. The intermittent crack of whipbirds pierced the air.

'So, let's see,' Brose said, scowling. 'You sent a text at eleven—from the pub, I'd guess—and made a call to the same number at twelve-twenty. That would have been about the time of the Dunberry toilet stop.' His voice was calm, calculating.

'Fucking bitch,' said Hardy.

'Now, who did you call, princess? Not the same person who just rang you just now, by the looks of it. Maybe the police? It's a mobile number, though, so not likely.'

She was silent, keeping her eyes fixed on Brose's legs from under the blindfold.

Hardy was looking over Brose's shoulder. 'The phone's still in range, Macca,' he said.

'I can see that, Hardy, you dickhead.'

'Whoever she called might have called the cops. They'll be tracking the phone now.'

'No shit, Sherlock. But the closest police station is Safton, right—we're closer to there than Goorinda from here. They're probably an hour away yet. Time enough for us to get the job done and out of here. What we need to do, though, is have our princess here call her knight in shining armour—find out how far away he is.'

She could have told Rowan to go back. Instead she'd sat in the cubicle, pleaded with him to follow. It was as if she'd drawn a target on his forehead. She felt sick.

'Sit up,' said Brose as he climbed inside the van. 'No funny business now, princess, otherwise we'll have to punish you. There's worse things than dying, you know.' He gave her a vicious smirk.

He held the phone to the side of her head. 'Just tell whoever it is that you're safe and ask him how far away he is. Nothing more.'

He'd put the phone on speaker. She heard it ringing, then Rowan's voice.

'Clem?'

She could hear Rowan's van rattling and roaring in the background, speeding towards her. 'Rowan, it's me. I'm okay.'

'Good on you, Clem. I can see you, you're about—'

'No!' she yelled. 'Don't say it!'

Brose snatched the phone away. 'Listen, mate, I have your bitch here and we're about to do something very unpleasant to her if you don't tell me where you are.'

'No! No, don't hurt her—just tell me what's going on.'

'No stalling, fuckwit. How far away are you?'

'Tell me what's going on first.'

'You tell me where you are now, mate, before my associate here slices off a piece of her.'

'No, no, wait, man, I'm nowhere, I'm—'

'Lying fuck! Bozo, cut the top of her ear off,' he yelled. Hardy moved quickly, grabbing her head, the blindfold slipping off. She screamed as he tugged at her ear, then she felt the burning. A flash of pink passed the corner of her eye to her right. She turned, saw a small semicircle of pink, bloody flesh on the floor. She shrieked.

Rowan's voice was desperate. 'Stop! Stop! Please! Stop! I'm about forty minutes away. What do you want me to do?'

Brose looked at his watch. 'Turn around and go back, and we'll look after your girlfriend here.'

'Right, got it. Anything you say. Don't hurt her. I'm doing a U-turn now.'

Clementine sobbed, warm blood streaming down her neck, the raw flesh throbbing in the chill air. Red and black shapes swam before her eyes, clashing and colliding, bile rising and swirling in her stomach.

\\/

The van raced down the narrow dirt track, branches and shrubs crowding in on either side. Hardy *yee-hah*'d over every bump, like it was some sort of thrill ride, every jolt sending a burst of pain through her head. The blindfold lay around her neck, wet with blood. They hadn't bothered to retie it. No need, she guessed— they were sure of accomplishing their mission now, and dead women tell no tales.

It was hard to focus, impossible to think, but she had to try. Rowan had said he was forty minutes away, but she knew he must be closer by now—much closer. Maybe less than five minutes, given this latest delay. But he was turning back, and Brose had said the police were an hour away—too late. It would be just her and Clancy. Clancy might even be dead already, and she would die now too. But at least Rowan would be safe.

The bush thickened, ferns and dense undergrowth crowding around enormous trunks, the track darker under a dense rainforest canopy. They bumped and jolted their way down a gentle slope, then Hardy gunned the accelerator, taking them up and over a steep rise and plunging down the other side before pulling up sharply in a sunny clearing next to a small aluminium shed. One side glared in the sun's reflection, the other walls were shaded by the rainforest looming high above, the roof covered in leaves.

The clearing was wide enough for a broad turning circle, with thigh-high bracken and grass fringing the perimeter. The grass in the centre was shorter, as if worn down by vehicles.

Brose reached forward and sliced through the electrical tape around her feet and opened the side door, shoving her towards it. She felt woozy, stumbled. Hardy was waiting and caught her as she was about to fall down the steps.

'Fuck's sake, woman!' he yelled, stumbling with her weight. 'You can bloody well stand on your own and carry the shovel, bitch.' He drew his bloodied knife and sawed through the tape around her wrists.

'Don't give her a weapon, you fool!' Brose shouted as he stepped out of the van.

Hardy scowled, spat on the ground fiercely, then grabbed Clem's arm and started marching her away. She tried to resist, digging her heels into the ground. If there was a one in a million chance that Rowan or the police might arrive in time, she had to keep stalling.

'Hold your horses, Hardy. I'm fuckin' choosing the spot. That's why I'm in charge, remember?' said Brose, shaking his head and glaring at Hardy. 'Farkenhell! You're just as likely to put 'em somewhere they'll wash away in the rain!' He stomped away to the back of the van.

Hardy pulled up, still locked onto her arm, waiting. She heard a noise from inside the shed. 'Clancy!' she yelled.

'Jonesy!' The cry came from the shed. 'Jonesy, is that you? I'm in here!' The relief in his voice was like a song. Just to hear it gave her hope.

Brose was still at the back of the van. She could hear him rummaging around. He made no attempt to quiet them. Nothing mattered now. They would both be dead in minutes. This forest would be their hidden grave, out in the middle of nowhere.

'Hang tough, Clance. These two fuckers are armed. We have to work together now,' she yelled.

Clancy moaned; she thought she heard him swear, too, as he realised she wasn't alone, but when he spoke his voice was loud and steady. 'No worries. We can take 'em out, Jonesy.'

'Shut the fuck up, you two,' said Hardy. He sheathed his knife and pulled a gun from the waistband of his jeans.

Another yell from the shed: 'Has Mel had the baby yet?'

'No. She's waiting for you to come back.' Her whole head throbbed, the pain almost blinding, but she felt a strange elation. She'd found Clancy, still alive—the game wasn't over yet.

'Baby's gunna have no daddy,' Brose shouted. He shut the van door and strode past towards the shed, his red shirt flapping up behind, revealing the gun shoved down the back of his pants and his knife in a small brown holster at his side. He held a shovel in one hand.

She could hear the clink of chains inside the shed, feet shuffling forward, and then Clancy emerged from the shadows, Brose clutching his elbow, propelling him forward. Clancy was missing a shoe and his leg was covered in blood from his bare foot up to the knee of his jeans. He had a huge swelling above one eye, and his hands were bound together. She choked back a sob at the condition he was in but gave him the most confident smile she could muster.

'Great to see you, Jonesy. You don't look too good, but,' he said in a croaky voice, smiling back.

Before she could respond, she heard a noise in the distance. They all heard it. A vehicle, getting closer. Hardy swivelled to face the track. In that split second Clem saw her chance, shoving Hardy in the chest with all her weight, yelling, 'RUN!' at Clancy at the same time. Caught off balance, Hardy stumbled, dropping his gun, and fell heavily to the ground with a loud yelp as his shoulder buckled awkwardly underneath him.

Turning to the shed, she saw Brose had dropped the shovel and had his arms locked around Clancy in a bear hug. Clancy twisted and writhed, trying to escape his grasp.

She ran full pelt, throwing herself at Brose as she heard an engine revving—screaming almost—a vehicle roaring up the steep rise just before the clearing. She hit Brose's back with a thwack, the impact enough to send all three of them to the ground. Rolling onto the grass, she saw something white from the corner of her eye, turned just in time to see Dempsey's Handyman Van, front wheels airborne, come crashing down onto the track, hurtling towards them.

It all happened in an instant—Rowan shouting from his open window; Hardy groaning, staggering to his knees, crawling towards his gun, his left arm limp by his side; Brose reaching for the pistol in the back of his pants; her own voice yelling, 'GUN!'; Clancy slamming his bound arms down on Brose's hand, pinning it to the ground. Clem was scrambling to her feet as she saw Hardy, side-on to the track, swinging his gun towards the van over his left shoulder. A shot rang out, the van skidded sideways, then a sickening thud as it rammed into Hardy's flank, sending him flying through the air. He hit the side of the shed with a loud crash and slid to the ground, facedown, motionless.

Brose managed to pull out his knife, Clancy struggling to get out of the way. She lunged for the shovel just as Brose slashed the blade across Clancy's arm, a burst of crimson appearing on his sleeve. She swung the shovel but Brose ducked and rolled, the shovel slamming into the ground where his head had been. He made for his gun, which had fallen from his trousers a few metres away. Clancy was staggering to his feet, wincing with pain.

The van had spun around, Rowan was shouting, 'RUN!' as he veered away from the shed and headed straight for Brose.

She pulled Clancy up and away, stumbled towards the bush, looking over her shoulder to see Brose, with the gun now, swinging it around towards the van. Through the front windscreen she saw Rowan fling himself flat across the front seats. A shot rang out, just as the driver-side door flung open, slamming into Brose.

She screamed, started running back to the clearing, back to Rowan. She saw him leap out of the van towards Brose into the long grass at the perimeter of the clearing. She couldn't see, just the top of the grass moving, a loud grunt, then another shot.

'ROWAN!' she screamed, and then, as if in slow motion, she saw a bald head emerging from the grass, alone.

Clancy finally had his chance, drew his bound hands high over his head, pulled them down sharply against his abdomen, snapping the cable tie. He grabbed hold of her and ran, dragging her into the bush. Brose was on his feet, running towards them, limping, blood streaming from his nose.

\|/

She ran, deeper and deeper into the bush, Clancy a few steps ahead of her, crashing through the forest. The arm of his shirt was wet with blood. Her mind was racing, and her breath came in heavy sobs. *What if Rowan's dead? I killed him. I lured him here. What if he's still alive and we've left him there bleeding?*

'Clancy, we have to go back,' she cried.

'We can't help him if we're dead.' He didn't stop, kept running.

They were weaving between tree trunks, ducking around fern fronds, pushing through bushy shrubs. She swiped wildly at branches, trying to clear a path, vines flicking into her face, scratching and tearing. She tripped, stumbled onto the spongy leaves and debris on the forest floor. Clancy hauled her up and they kept running.

It was dark and damp and shadowy under the canopy, a

shaft of sunlight speared through a gap, spotlighting a pocket of undergrowth. They were cutting across a steep slope on a mountain. She struggled to keep up. Clancy slowed, beckoned— 'Come on! Come on!'—then he turned and kept running.

A vine whipped across her face, thorns tearing tiny plugs of flesh, scraping the raw and bleeding nothingness on her ear. Breathing hard, she turned to look over her shoulder. In the distance, between the ferns and leaves and giant trunks she saw a flash of red, then a metallic glint. Brose, fifty metres or so behind them.

They pressed on. She felt the ground becoming harder under her feet; there was more light; the ferns were thinning. They must have come around to the northern side of the mountain—different terrain, more sun, less forest.

'Clancy, he'll see us, get a shot in,' she said, puffing.

'There's rocks up ahead. We'll split up there. You run down the slope, make a noise, distract him—I'll take him from behind the rocks.'

They ran on. She could see a rocky outcrop looming ahead, took another look back over her shoulder, caught the glint of Brose's bald head reflecting a shaft of light.

Clancy pulled ahead, weaving through the trees, sparse and scattered now, the land sloping away sharply to his left. He had just reached the edge of a rocky plateau when she saw him stumble and go down. Terror sent a fresh burst of adrenaline pumping through her, and she sprinted towards him, squatted by his side.

'Are you okay?' she asked, keeping her voice low.

'Yes,' he said, but his face contorted in pain, his ankle twisted beneath him, trapped in a crevice in the rock.

He tried to get up, couldn't, held out his hand and she pulled him up. He started hobbling towards the wall of rock up ahead. A steep ravine fell away to their left, almost vertical. She couldn't see how far it dropped from where she was standing. 'Go now,' he whispered fiercely, nodding his head towards the bush, back where they'd come from. 'Run down the slope, make sure he hears you.'

'You can't take him on your own, not like this,' she protested.

Clancy turned back to look at her, one hand against the craggy rock behind him, eyes flashing. 'Jonesy—you gotta run. It's our only chance.'

'Oh God, Clancy.' She swallowed, hesitated, Clancy nodded, then she took off down towards the denser bush behind, plunging back into the forest and hurtling down the slope, making as much noise as she could, crying out whenever a branch scratched her arms or slashed her face.

She looked back. Brose emerged into the rocky clearing, just in front of the outcrop where Clancy lay in wait. He looked down in her direction. He saw her, saw her scramble for cover, and immediately took a shot, the bullet hitting the huge tree behind her with a thud, just above her head, as the crack of the gunshot echoed through the valley. She dived behind the tree, sheltering behind its girth, peered out cautiously, her heart pounding in her chest. Then she saw Brose turn away, as if responding to something behind him, sweeping his gun before him in an arc. Clancy appeared above, on top of the rocky outcrop. He took an almighty leap high into the air, arms spread like a sugar glider. He hit Brose hard and they both fell out of sight. She heard grunting, a thud, imagined them wrestling on the ground, started running back up the slope, grabbing at trees and vines to pull herself up.

Looking up, she could see them now, wrestling on the rocky ledge, locked together, Brose's hand on Clancy's throat, Clancy struggling to pull it away, his other hand on Brose's wrist, forcing the gun to the side and away. She saw them lunge and stagger, dangerously close to the edge of the ravine. She called out—'CLANCY, THE CLIFF!' Clancy had his back to the ravine. He was forcing Brose's gun hand down, twisting it, bringing the muzzle towards Brose's body. Brose resisted, thrusting back, they shuffled another step closer to the ravine. Clancy let out a loud grunt, wrenching at Brose's gun hand. A shot rang out. She screamed. There was a blur of movement, and Brose fell back out of sight, as Clancy tipped backwards, arms circling in windmills in vacant air, tumbling over the edge with a bloodcurdling scream.

CHAPTER 33

She didn't hear him land. *Oh God*. She didn't hear him land.

She started moving, pushing across towards the ravine to her left, stumbling in her haste, desperate. The slope was getting steeper as she got closer to the ravine. She lost her footing, started crabbing sideways, grabbing on to tree roots and branches. She took another tentative step, clutching at a sapling, the dirt crumbling around it, the roots lifting and sending her sliding down the slope, snatching at ferns and roots until her shoe lodged against a rock a couple of metres below.

She stood there, gasping, looked down. After a second or two, she tried another couple of steps, crab-like to her left, but it was no good—the slope was too steep, she could go no further. She leaned into the face of the slope, a tree root in each hand, her right foot balancing on a rock, her left scraping uselessly at the slope.

She looked down again, following the length of the slope until it disappeared into the thick foliage below. Her leg began to shake. Across to her left, through the forest, she could see the ravine—a cleft in the rock, maybe ten metres wide, falling away vertically.

Clancy could be at the base of the precipice. She didn't know how far down—it was a drop beyond seeing. There were no jutting ledges, no shelves, just a sheer, relentless cliff. She tried to slow her breathing, straining her ears, listening for a cry, a groan. Nothing. A parrot squawked overhead. Silence again.

Could anyone survive such a fall? And what if Clancy had been shot? He may even have been dead before he landed. Tears fogged her vision.

What if he isn't dead, though? He could be lying at the bottom of the ravine, injured, bleeding. Until he could be found, the possibility remained, however remote. She could yell out, find out where he was. Then what? She'd need paramedics, a helicopter maybe. And it would give her position away to Brose.

She heard movement, looked up and saw a pebble bouncing down from above and to her left, watched it clatter down the ravine. It had come from the rocky ledge where the struggle had taken place, from where Clancy had fallen.

She couldn't move, numb with fear.

Brose was alive.

She forced herself to go through her choices. She couldn't get across to the ravine, couldn't get to Clancy if he was lying on a shelf somewhere halfway down. She could go down the slope and search at the bottom. She could go across to the right, where the slope was gentler, and then up to try to deal with Brose. If she was lucky, he'd be injured, might even have lost his gun. Or she could hide. Or simply try to find her way back to the shed in the clearing, praying that the police had turned up. She thought of Rowan, lying in the long grass, wondered again if he was alive or dead, and for a moment let fear and grief overwhelm her.

She took a deep breath, trying to calm herself. Whichever option she took, she couldn't remain where she was, stuck on this steep slope, barely able to move, a sitting duck if Brose were to find her. She started easing her way back to her right, where the slope was less severe, stopping along the way behind a tree to check above, towards the ledge from where the pebble had come. Nothing moved, not that she could see, but Brose might have retreated to the forest and be making his way towards her now through the trees.

She considered her options again, finally admitting to herself that there was little point going down to the bottom of the ravine—she would surely be searching for Clancy's body. She was shaking against the rough bark of the tree, tears flowing down her face. She brushed them away with filthy hands, tried to focus on the other two options.

Brose was either seriously injured and no longer a threat or already coming after her. She tried to estimate the time that had passed since they left the gate at the top of the driveway. Brose had said then that the police were at least an hour away, assuming Rowan had alerted them when she contacted him from the service station in Dunberry. Perhaps thirty or forty minutes had passed since then. So if Rowan had called them, they were around half an hour away.

If she made for the clearing she would have to assume Brose was in pursuit or lying in wait for her. She'd have to stay well clear of him, head across at this level on the slope before cutting upwards to the trail she and Clancy had hacked.

The irony was that her best chance at survival might be meeting up with Brose at some point over half an hour from now, when the police should be within earshot—Brose firing his weapon would bring them to her rescue.

The alternative was to find a big tree on the flatter ground, hide until she heard a helicopter or a search party. She could make a dash for higher ground if it was a chopper, start waving her arms around like mad. But what if Brose saw her? If he was conscious when she approached, she was more than likely dead.

Maybe she should just hide and wait for help to come to her? She took a moment, visualising herself huddled inside a hollow tree. The hairs on the back of her neck stood up and she shuddered.

She looked up at the ledge. There was no sound or movement. She stood up in a half-crouch, started out, towards the clearing but following a wide loop, stepping slowly, her feet light and careful on the forest floor.

It was just not an option, hiding in a hole, waiting for Ambrose Macpherson to reach around with his blade and slit her throat.

\I/

She kept moving, trying to estimate time, knowing that each minute she survived could bring her closer to rescue. It felt like she'd been going for at least thirty minutes when she heard a noise. She snuck behind a giant myrtle, stood there listening, her back pressed against the damp of its trunk. There it was again, the sound of bushes being swept aside and springing back, faint, distant. She had been careful—treading lightly, using a walking stick to steady herself, stooping low under the branches, picking a path around the ferns—but this was the noise of someone taking no care at all.

The noise continued. She held her breath.

Could it be a search party? No yelling, no shouted names, noise enough only for one. Her skin prickled. He was here, somewhere above her on the trail.

Heart thudding, she willed herself to push away from the tree, turn and crouch at its base, peering around the trunk. Nothing but a tangled mess of vines and ferns and leaves, winking in the columns of light. Then she saw it—amid the crowded shadows, the dense green—a flash of red.

She swung her head back behind the tree, shivered, her fingernails digging into the mossy bark. If he found her...She caught her breath, the knife flashed in her head, the silvery length of its blade. She forced herself to look out from behind the tree again. He was closer now, swishing branches aside, the pistol in his hand.

She had kept her course across the mountain slope and slightly downwards to be conservative, trying to put distance between her and Brose, but she'd grown more and more anxious the longer she stayed away from the trail, fearing she'd get lost in the never-ending bush, and had eventually begun veering uphill again.

He was about twenty metres away, higher up the slope but behind her, further back towards the rocky outcrop. She had come dangerously close. She could hear the crunch of leaves now, moving closer. If Brose stuck to the trail, he would pass by only a few metres from her. She hauled herself upright, her back against the tree. Brose was still moving towards her on the trail. Then her ears pricked: a voice, a long way away, faint, very faint. It was a shout, someone calling.

The crunch of the leaves and the swish of the branches above her stopped. He had heard the shout too. Silence. She and Brose were both there, only metres away from each other now, deep in the forest, listening. She could hear him, the sound of his breathing, and kept her own breath shallow, quiet. The seconds passed, then the same voice again, calling out, but fainter this time—she could barely hear it. *A search party, it had to be, but oh God, they're moving away.* She closed her eyes, willed the thought of Brose's knife out of her mind, threw her head back and yelled, 'Over here! I'm over here! Help!'

She heard his footsteps and the swoosh of bushes, faster this time, getting closer. She shuffled to her left as he approached, keeping the tree between them, holding her breath now, willing him past, shuffling right again as she heard him go by. Craning her head to the left, she saw his red shirt, bald head, moving down the rough trail about five metres away. She was behind him now. He was sweeping the ferns aside with his gun in his left hand, his right hand cradling his stomach, stopping to lean on a tree then taking a few more steps. He was ten metres away now. Her eyes widened as she noticed the large dark patch on the back of his shirt. Blood?

He stopped, listened, his back still towards her, then began turning. She pulled her head behind the tree. All she could hear was his raspy breathing. She had not heard any reply from the search party. *They hadn't heard her, they'd moved on, and she'd given away her position to Brose.* She held her breath. She heard his steps coming back towards her along the trail. She was on her own and he was coming for her.

Slowly, silently, she swapped her walking stick around, heavy end down. She heard him stop, his breath laboured. She tightened her grip on the walking stick, now a club. He took a few more steps, haltingly, as if he might be staggering. She waited, willing him to turn away, to keep moving, so she would be behind him again. But he stopped, maybe two or three metres away. A gurgling sound. He spat. It was weak, lacking force, more like a dribble. Injured. He had to be injured.

She closed her eyes for a moment, took a deep breath and leapt out from the shelter of the myrtle, lunging through the undergrowth towards him. He was leaning on a young tree, looked up, shock on his face as she came charging at him. She was swinging the club, throwing her whole weight into it, as he was raising his gun hand up and towards her. She smashed the club hard into his forearm with a sickening crunch, the momentum sending her toppling to her knees as she heard the shot, saw the gun fly from his grasp. The bullet cracked against the trunk of a tree close by.

She scrambled to get back on her feet. Brose had already pulled his knife from its holster, the deathly curve of the blade glinting in the light as he struggled to his knees.

'I'll skin you alive, you bitch,' he growled.

She launched towards him, roaring, springing out of a half-crouch, collecting him in the midriff with the club and sending him to the ground with a thud. He lay there, not moving. She took a step back into the scrub, panting with the effort. The gun lay in the shadows on the forest floor. She snatched it up, pointed it at him.

He was lying on his back, looking straight up at the canopy, groaning. His red shirt was torn and his white T-shirt had ridden up, exposing a crescent of belly. Dark hair, soft pink skin and a small, black hole, surrounded by dark, dried blood. Fresh crimson blood was oozing out of the hole by the teaspoonful, covering the brown leaves on the ground.

Clementine yelled again as loud as she could, 'Help. Over here! Help!' Surely they had heard the gunshot. She kept her eyes on Brose. His face was white, beads of sweat across his lip.

'You shot Clancy,' she murmured. 'You killed him.'

His eyes rolled towards her, glazed and staring. He mouthed the word *no*. She shouted to the searchers again, thought she heard the faintest of answering cries. She crept forward a few small steps, her hand quivering as she kept the gun trained on him, her nose filled with the metallic scent of his blood.

'Shot myself,' he wheezed through blue lips.

Blood was forming a pool beneath him. She tried to make sense of what he'd just said. Clancy hadn't been shot? For a moment she rejoiced, thinking he was still alive. But she'd seen him go over the cliff. How could he survive that? She yelled out again to the searchers. Was that a response? She could not be sure.

Brose's breath was coming in faint puffs, and he groaned again.

'Looks like you're going to die here, arsehole,' she said.

He managed a half-grin and a slight nod. It shocked her, that he could acknowledge his own death like that. Perhaps men like Brose anticipated their own violent death, embraced it.

In the distance, a long way off, she heard a shout. She yelled again and heard another shout, a little closer, in return. The sound sent a rush of adrenaline through her.

She should at least try to keep Brose alive, staunch the blood flow, she thought. But the thought of taking one step closer filled her with terror. She could no more approach Ambrose Macpherson than pet a funnel-web.

'I can stop the bleeding,' she said. 'I can help you, if you tell me what the hell's going on, why you went after Clancy.'

'Doesn't end here,' he croaked.

'What are you talking about?'

His lips moved again and she just caught the words: 'They won't stop...until debt's...paid.'

'Who won't stop? What debt?' She didn't understand any of it. 'You killed Clancy, you fucking bastard.' She felt the rage welling up, threatening to overwhelm her.

The slightest shake of his head. 'Saw him move.' He gasped another breath. 'After he fell.'

She let out a whimper. Could she believe him?

The voices of the searchers were closer—she could now hear them moving through the undergrowth—and she yelled out again. There was a swift shout in reply.

Brose swallowed, his breath a rapid, shallow panting, his face white and his eyes sinking even as she watched. 'Holt,' he said, his voice barely a whisper. 'Let Holt die...he deserves it.' He groaned softly, eyes closing.

'Holt? Gerard Holt? Is the debt his? Brose, you have to tell me.' She crouched down, closer. 'Brose. Ambrose. What debt?'

No answer. No breath. His head lolled to one side, cushioned by the moist mulch of the forest floor.

She sat, her back against the tree, staring at his lifeless form. She had done this before, of course—seen a person die. At least in this case she did not cause Ambrose Macpherson's death. She was ashamed to draw the distinction. Her chin dropped to her chest and she breathed in the sweet smell of the leaves and the rotting wood and the damp earth, waiting to be found.

CHAPTER 34

The door opened. The hefty bulk of Sergeant Johnson re-entered the room, holding a folder this time. The fluorescent lights were beginning to hurt her eyes. Exhausted after the day's events, Clementine could barely sit up straight. She had spent some time at the Safton Hospital—a couple of stitches in her face, her ear dressed and bandaged, and been given a referral to a specialist for possible reconstructive surgery. The rest would heal itself.

The Safton police had nothing but suspicion for her—mostly disguised with a well-practised civility, but suspicion nonetheless. She realised now that while Phillips and Miller had been professional in their dealings with her in Katinga, there had been a kind of warmth in the way they went about their job. Here she was a complete stranger, someone without reputation, surfacing in the middle of an evil sequence of violence.

A young constable sat opposite her, drumming her pen on the table between them. Clementine had been through the facts—those she was willing to share—several times with both of them: the chase, the kidnapping, Rowan's arrival and everything that followed...but it was not enough—they were not satisfied.

Her body was weak, her mind drained, but she must remain alert. She knew she didn't have to say anything. She knew everything she said could be used as evidence—of course she knew all that.

Her thoughts drifted back to the moment when the message came through, over the radios of the two young SES officers who had escorted her through the forest back to the clearing, a helicopter rescue crew reporting in clipped, crackling static: male, early twenties, multiple fractures, suspected head and internal injuries, serious but stable condition. She had dropped to her knees, there in the bush, her head in her hands, a rescuer wrapping his arms around her shoulders. And then the second message, moments later, confirming that Rowan was being treated for a gunshot wound to the leg, non-life-threatening. She had wept quietly for a long time.

'Well, Ms Jones,' the sergeant said, closing the door behind him, 'you've been most helpful so far. Thank you. We're almost done.' He sat down, placed the folder in front of him and poured Clem some water from the jug on the table, pushing the small plastic cup across to her. They already had her DNA from her first conviction. She picked up the cup, drank a small sip.

Everything was just like the first time. It could almost have been the same police station, any police station across the globe, really, where the earliest signs of a person's guilt or innocence are divined in that first moment, the justice system's first awakenings, before the whole awful, magnificent machine cranks and grinds into action.

The sergeant watched Clementine put the cup back on the table, the room silent for a moment. He nodded at the constable, who reached forward, switched on the recorder and said: 'Interview resumed at 16.05.'

Sergeant Johnson opened the folder in front of him, carefully turned through the pages—forms, typed notes, all upside down from where Clem sat. She couldn't make out what they were. Page after page, just the sound of paper sliding against paper. Then a page with a picture, a photograph. Clem looked from her side of the table, her breath catching in her throat as she recognised the two crumpled cars.

Johnson glanced at her, flipped another page—a closer shot of the driver's side door, caved inward violently. Then an even closer shot, a view of the interior, darkness within, and just the shadowy form of a person inside.

No, no, don't turn the page.

He reached for the corner of the page, started to turn it. She closed her eyes, but the image was there, in her head, so vivid, so lifelike...Sue Markham's head, her neck broken, slumped at that hideous angle on the steering wheel, the blood in her hair, on her blouse, eyes wide and staring. Staring.

Clementine looked away from the table, breathing hard and slow.

'Are you okay, Ms Jones? Do you need a break?'

No. She just wanted this interview to end. She wanted the peaceful homeliness of her cottage, the mountain gums and Pocket. She turned her head towards the sergeant, making sure not to look down at the folder, shook her head.

'Subject has indicated she does not want a break,' he said. He waited a moment, closed the file.

Was that it? No questions? He just wanted to unsettle her? Humiliate her? It made her angry. Yes, Sue Markham was dead. She would always be dead, and it was Clementine who had killed her. But Clancy Kennedy was so very alive. Alive but still in danger— the threat to Clancy's life had not ended with Brose's death. He had said as much. She could do nothing for Sue Markham, no matter how many pictures Sergeant Johnson showed her. But Clancy, Melissa—she could do something for them. And the only thing she wanted now was to make sure she got out of this room without incriminating Torrens. Johnson's ploy had backfired, seriously. Clementine's focus was bullet-like.

'Mr Macpherson died of a single gunshot wound to the stomach,' said Johnson. 'You were the only one there when he died. You told us you held his gun and pointed it at him.'

She sat, defiant, waiting for the question.

'Ms Jones, did you shoot Ambrose Macpherson?'

She shook her head.

'For the recording, please, Ms Jones.'

'No, I did not,' she said.

'Well, then, perhaps you'd like to tell us how you knew to follow Ambrose Macpherson?'

She began, slow and deliberate, making sure to repeat the same answers she'd already given as closely as possible. 'I got this tattoo, a couple of weeks ago. I was nervous about hygiene and infections, it was my first one. I wanted to know the tattooists had a good record, complied with health law, you know, run by reputable people'—the constable scribbled a note—'so I researched the company, checked them out online, did a company search. Ambrose Macpherson was a director of various companies in the corporate group that owned the tattoo parlour.'

'You did a company search to check for hygiene?' The constable was sceptical.

'Of course. Financial health of the company, the quality of the directors...it all tells you if the business can afford the right gear, the best people, that sort of thing.' Factually accurate, but none of it relevant.

The constable raised her eyebrows, nodded, like she might use that approach herself next time.

'Go on,' said the sergeant.

'Well, he was in the tattoo shop when I went there'—her first outright lie—'and I heard the tattooist refer to him as Ambrose.'

The sergeant held her gaze as the constable scribbled another note.

She told them about her conversation with Clancy at the post office, the cigarette burn, the threat to his family, and the description he had given of one of the men.

'Clancy's description—it just sounded like this bloke, Macpherson,' she said.

Johnson looked unimpressed. 'Why had he threatened Clancy?'

'I don't know, Clancy refused to tell me.'

'So you'd seen Macpherson just the once, in the tattoo parlour. Must have been a good description Clancy gave you.'

She recalled that night, scrubbing blood off the rocks in the vacant block next door to the Holts' place, Brose's face...*Stop thinking, Jones. He can see it in your face.*

She shrugged, nodded. 'Reasonably good.'

'And that's it? Sounds like a slim lead,' he said.

She sat as still as she could, nodded, agreeing with him, 'Yes, it was. Not much more than a hunch, really.'

'Why didn't you tell the police about all this when Clancy went missing? You knew they were out searching, the SES as well, they'd found a bloodied shoe, it was very serious and yet you went off on your own.'

'Like you said, it was a slim lead, a hunch, sergeant, nothing more. It seemed ridiculous—I thought the police would just laugh at me and I didn't want to interrupt the search effort. For all I knew they were close to finding Clancy.'

'You didn't think to report the assault on Clancy, the cigarette burn, after he'd gone missing?'

'Oh, I wanted to, but Clancy had begged me not to. He was adamant. Said it would make matters worse for him and his family.'

She took another sip of water, wondering whether drinking the water was one of those indicators they teach cops to look out for when a suspect may be lying.

'Ms Jones, we know you must have had a difficult time in prison—lawyers don't fare well inside. Perhaps you knew Mr Macpherson through someone you met there?'

'No,' she said.

'Many good people get mixed up in trouble, often innocently,' said the sergeant. 'You might have needed protection inside, for survival. Nothing wrong with that. But perhaps you owe someone something now?'

'No, I don't.'

'Perhaps you had a task you had to fulfil? A job for someone?'

'No.'

He paused a moment. 'You see, Macpherson was a known member of a well-organised criminal gang. All sorts of things in his repertoire—guns, drugs, you name it. I just thought you might have got roped into something?'

'No,' she said.

'So you claim you attacked him in self-defence?'

'Like I said, he was going to shoot me. I hit him with a stick, knocking the gun from his hand, then he came at me with a knife.' She was matter-of-fact, careful to repeat each step exactly as she had recounted it to them the first time. 'I hit him again with the stick, and then I picked up the gun in case he came at me again. He was lying there, he said he'd shot himself in the fight with Clancy, and then he died. That was it. I did not fire any shots.'

There was a long pause, the three of them sitting there, Johnson searching her face. Clem felt the pressure building.

They know. They know I am a killer and that I'm living a lie.

Sergeant Johnson stood up, scooping up the file he'd brought.

Then the words everything inside her was screaming for: 'Interview ended 16.35. You're free to go, Ms Jones.'

\\/

The flight to Earlville landed at nine that night. She walked beside Rowan as he hobbled on his crutches from the tarmac into the terminal, then went to get the Commodore and bring it around. She helped him into the back seat, his leg up and his back leaning up against the door.

She'd tried to make the journey home to his place as smooth

as possible, avoiding potholes and slowing for the bends, and she'd also tried, as best she could, to thank him, choking up at the thought of what would have happened to her and Clancy had he not arrived.

He shrugged it off, said he wouldn't have done it for just anyone.

Her voice had cracked again when she mentioned the moment he'd been shot and the agony of having to leave him behind there, concealed in the long grass, injured, possibly dead.

'Shit yeah,' he said. 'My hay fever was playing up something shocking.'

They laughed and she snuck a glance in the rear-view mirror to catch a look at his smile.

Rowan's house was a run-down weatherboard Californian bungalow on the outskirts of Katinga. A porch light came on as they approached. The lawn was patchy, long spindly weeds spiking up at the base of the walls, but the exterior was gleaming with a fresh coat of paint. She helped him out of the car, carried his bag of medication. The front verandah floorboards sloped down at one end. There was parsley and mint growing in a pot at the front door.

The rooms inside were sparse, vast expanses of cold floorboards with little furniture to speak of, her footsteps echoing so loudly she felt it best to tiptoe. Rowan decided he'd sleep in the living room, where there was a fire and the TV.

She got him comfortable on the lonely-looking old couch, set the fire and made them both a cup of tea.

'Thanks,' he said.

She brought the single wooden chair from the kitchen into the living room for herself, so she could sit there with him. They drank the tea in silence, too tired to speak, the fire cracking and spitting. Afterwards, she found a set of old-fashioned nesting tables in the spare room, carried one out to the lounge and set it down next to him. Next she found a jug and a glass in the half-empty cupboard above the sink, filled them both with water and arranged them on the little table, within easy reach.

As she was bending over the table, he said softly, 'It's been a while since anyone's done anything for me.'

'It's the least I could do after everything you did for me,' she said. He shrugged it off, looked away.

His mobile phone beeped: a low battery warning. Her hand came up to her collar as she recalled the moment in the service station toilet at Dunberry.

'Never good to let your phone battery drop too low,' he said, chuckling.

'Yeah, yeah. Thanks for the tip. Where can I find your charger?' she asked.

'Bedroom. Down the hall, second door on your left.'

On the bedside table, there was a single photo in a frame. Rowan, younger, clean-shaven and smiling. In front, with her back nestled into him, was a tiny woman with short blond hair and a mischievous smile. His arms were wrapped around her, his head bent down to rest on hers.

Clem came back to the living room, plugged the charger in.

'I nursed Kate here, you know. In this house,' he said.

Clem looked over at him, nodded.

'For months. She slipped away before my eyes, right here in this house. I couldn't stop it.'

Clem sat down on the kitchen chair. 'You gave her all the help you could.'

'Yeah. I did. Then she needed more than I could give her,' he said, 'so I carried her out to the car, took her to the hospital in Earlville. She was always small, my Kate, but she was like…like a tiny bird—nothing left of her by then.'

His grief filled the room.

'She looked pretty. In the photo in your room.'

He cleared his throat. 'Yes, she was. Way too good for me.'

Clem sat down next to him on the wooden chair again.

'I locked up the house after that, shot through for a couple of years,' he said. 'Couldn't bear to be here. Only been back six months or so.' He paused, searching the walls, 'Hard to make the place feel like home again.'

She smiled and looked around the emptiness. 'Just a tip, Rowan, for what it's worth—maybe a few more sticks of furniture might help?'

He laughed. It was a relief, and the room felt lighter.

She remembered the medications, got the bag from the kitchen and read the labels, handing him two large red capsules from the first box and a small white pill from the second.

As he swigged them down with the water, she picked up her coat from the back of the kitchen chair, slung it over her arm and took the chair back to the kitchen. A wave of tiredness washed over her.

When she came back to the living room he beckoned her over to the couch. She hesitated for a moment, then took a few steps towards him, thinking he had more to tell her about Kate. He held out his hand, took the tips of her fingers and pulled her closer. She knelt down on the bare floorboards next to the couch. She felt the warmth of the fire on her back as he smoothed her dishevelled hair away from her eyes, the touch of his rough fingers foreign, making her scalp tingle.

She knew she should leave, but after everything that had happened she could not find the will to resist. Her head was a fog, all her usual defences powerless against a sudden longing to feel the touch of another human being.

He gently pulled her head towards his. She could smell his earthiness. The brush of his lips on hers lingered only briefly but reached deep within her being. She let him kiss her again, kissing him back this time, eyes closed, feeling the fullness of him. An indescribable flood of relief rushed over her. She opened her eyes, smiled and stood up to leave without a word.

At the cottage she paused under the mountain gum, looking up at the pitch-black sky and the moon. The Milky Way was out in all its brilliance again. She put her hand on the trunk and felt the earth under her feet, asked whether the kiss was a mistake. She felt a puff of breeze across her cheeks, heard the shush of the leaves, and there was no more answer than that.

CHAPTER 35

She sat at the table reading the news on her laptop, glancing at the clock every now and then. Mercifully, she had slept in, but it was still too early to ring anyone.

The wind was charging about outside, ushering clouds across the sky, and the morning chill had lost its winter bite. She felt hopeful about what the spring would bring.

She got up to make a coffee. Her head was swimming with an interminable replay of last night with Rowan. And when that subsided, the police interview would resume its loop. She sat back down at the dining table with the straw-weave mat still covering the split in the middle.

Her mobile buzzed. A text message from Rowan: *Thanks for your help*.

It was her fault he was injured.

Pocket pushed his head through the dog door and limped across the lino floor. He was able to put more weight on his leg now and showed little sign of pain anymore. He flopped down at her feet, put his head on his paws. The fur had started growing around his face again. She sat on the floor, tickled him on his belly. His tail thumped and his rear leg started an involuntary running motion.

She needed more information on the Holts' debt. She knew who to ask. But first she rang Melissa, at the hospital. Clancy was still in intensive care, she said, but he'd had a good night. The doctor said the head injury was not as serious as they thought and the broken bones would heal, a full recovery expected. Mel was buoyant with the news and Clem felt a great knot of tension in her neck unwind.

Melissa was thanking her again, passing the phone to her mum to thank her as well, wanting her to speak to cousin Tash, who'd driven all night to be there with them. It sat uncomfortably with Clem. They didn't know who she was, what she'd done that could never be repaired.

She changed the subject to the baby.

'Yep, he's due today,' said Mel, 'and with all this drama I don't reckon he'll keep us waiting.' She laughed. 'Least I'm in the right place, eh.'

'Mel, before you go, can you tell me if Clancy said anything?'

'About what?'

'Well, anything. I mean anything that might give us a hint as to why all this happened.'

'He hasn't said anything to me. There was that stuff at the pub the cops told me about. Something about a woman. I'll fuckin' kill him if he's been shopping it around, I'll fuckin' break every other bone in his body.'

She wondered if Clancy would tell Melissa now. Secrecy had become a habit for Clem, but it had burned a hole inside Clancy, and with the looseness of alcohol it had come spilling out at the bar the night he'd been abducted. *Yes, Clancy will tell Mel*, she was sure of it—the truth would out now.

And, when the time was right, she must give Melissa the gift of the rest of Clancy's story, how Clancy had wrestled with his situation, grieved for what might come between them, his devastated remorse, his courage despite such powerful forces, such formidable enemies arrayed against him. This was the whole story, so much more than a momentary lapse.

She felt the irony, that it would be her—Clementine Jones, who had hidden her own name, lied about so much of herself—

who would bring the truth to Melissa.

The sun emerged from behind the cloud, spreading a shaft of golden light across the room. She fanned out her fingers, feeling her hand's warmth on the table, found her voice again. 'Yeah, well don't do anything rash, hey? And let me know if he says anything, anything at all, okay?'

Next she rang Jenny's mobile.

'Oh, Clem, it's so good to hear your voice. Are you okay?'

'Yes, all good, Jen. A few scratches and bumps but not much else.' She didn't mention the ear.

'So what the hell happened? You have to tell me everything. All I know is that Clancy fell down a cliff and that bloke with the handyman business—what's his name, Dempsey? Yeah, Dempsey—got shot in the leg. Someone said one of the crooks was killed.'

'Jen, all of that sounds about right, and I promise I'll tell you every detail, but I need your help first.'

'Oh God,' Jen groaned, 'I can't help you like last time, Clem, you know that.'

'No, no, nothing like that. I just want to know about the Holts. Have they got any significant debt or money problems you know about?'

'The Holts? Have they got something to do with this?' Jen sounded bewildered.

'I don't know,' she lied, 'but if you could just fill me in on their money problems, it might help.'

There was a pause.

'Look, Clem. I've warned you before about the Holts. They're powerful people. You shouldn't be messing with them.'

'Yes, I know, Jen, and I wouldn't be asking if it wasn't important, I swear. Was there some sort of debt?'

Jen sighed loudly.

'You know Clancy was almost killed, Jen. This could help. You never know.'

'Well, I don't know why you can't just bloody leave it to the police, but I'll tell you what I know, and then you can tell them, okay? You're not going crusading around the countryside again on your own. You tell the police or I will, right?'

'Absolutely, Jen.'

'Yes, they have had money problems. It's all to do with their son,' she said reluctantly.

The son. Of course.

'Nathan Holt was a drug addict, still is for all I know, probably getting more of it in prison than he is outside.' Jen sniffed. 'His parents spent a small fortune on him for a couple of years there. I know because they bank with us, but it was all around town too, of course—you can imagine the gossip was running hot. Anyway, they spent a terrible lot of money on rehab at those expensive clinics for a while, and then they even tried to set him up somewhere in the South Pacific, some place where they hoped there weren't so many drugs around, Fiji, I think.' She took a breath. 'Yes, that sounds right, there were all these foreign exchange transactions, transfers to Fiji...and mind you, that's confidential, you can't repeat that,' she warned, 'but if you tell the cops you think it's about money and Nathan, they can look at the records and they'll find out on their own, no need for people like you to stick your nose in.'

'Yes, that's a good point, Jen.'

'Well, they bought a business over there, and a house, but it didn't last. Nathan must have stuffed up the business, probably drinking kava or something if he couldn't get the drugs. They ended up just closing the business down. It was loaded with debt, though, and even when they sold the house they'd bought him, there was still a lot left owing. Gerard was in and out of the bank for months, sorting out the money, poor bugger, had to put a second mortgage over their place in Katinga Heights. He can be a pompous arse sometimes, but he really tried his best for that boy. They wouldn't have come close to clearing that second mortgage yet, not even on the money they make.'

The debt had to be repaid, Ambrose had said. Was this the debt?

'Clem, are you still there?'

'Yes, sorry, Jen, must be a bad connection. Look, thanks so much for that. I don't know whether it's got anything to do with anything, but you just never know.'

'Well, make sure you tell the cops when you see them, right?'

Clem heard a beeping noise on her phone.

'Yes, will do, Jen. Gotta go, I have another call coming...'

'By the way, dinner tomorrow night at our place. No excuses.'

'I'll let you know. Gotta go.' She hung up, took the next call. It was Torrens.

'Jonesy, you fuckin' legend!' he yelled.

She ran her hand across the back of her neck, feeling like a fraud. He pushed her for details, wanting to know what type of gun, whether she'd shot the dead guy, how she managed to escape. She changed the subject.

'I heard about the game—so what the hell happened?' she asked.

'Yeah, bloody terrible, we were. I blame you, of course. You're off saving the world, and we're going down the toilet!' He was shouting like she was in the next paddock. 'Fuckin' prelim final now, coach! Sudden death against the Lions. You better be at training on Tuesday...'

Warm-up, conditioning, a few drills, warm-down—the easy pattern was like music. She craved the routine, the comforting completeness of it.

'...half the town'll be there, I reckon.'

She shook her head, took up the mantle again. 'Yeah, well, we need to focus now, not get distracted by the town fan club. You're not celebrities yet, you know.' The clouds had almost completely disappeared and the sun was filling the room. Pocket looked up at her, yawned and stretched his good leg.

'Ha! That's it, Jonesy, come and give us a good kick up the arse, please, I beg you!' He laughed so hard it made him snort.

They spoke about the game for a bit, what had gone wrong, what had gone well. Then she asked him.

'Listen, Torrens, I have a question…did you ever know Nathan Holt?'

'Shit, yeah. Bloody little rich kid junkie owed money every other week. One of my regulars.'

'So did he pay up?'

'Let's just say I was good at my job.' He sniggered. 'At least until I got caught and went inside.'

'He's at Loddon, I hear. Do you know what for?'

'I dunno exactly, but it was something to do with dealing. He was in a world of trouble.'

'What do you mean?'

'He'd sold a fuckin' shitload of gear and kept the cash is what I heard, the stupid dickhead. Got roughed up really bad not long after he arrived inside.'

'So what happened? Did he pay up?'

'God knows. I got out pretty soon after that, but I can tell you this, that poor bugger wasn't doing anything much for a very long time after the bashing he copped. I heard he was in solitary after he got out of hospital, for his own protection. That's about the time I got out.'

'You reckon it was a lot of money?'

'I heard it was hundreds of thousands. He was a fucking idiot, eh. But that's junkies for ya.'

Clem got up, walked outside to get some air. The debt Torrens knew of was probably additional to the losses in Fiji. The Holts' house in Katinga Heights must be worth close to a million, and mortgaged to the max.

'Whaddya wanna know for anyway? What's he got to do with anything?'

'Oh, nothing really, just that Gerard seemed upset the other day.'

'I'm not surprised. If Nathan gets out alive, he's dead meat anyway if Mummy and Daddy don't pay up for him.'

She stiffened. The sun had disappeared again, and the wind nipped at her face and whipped her hair across the bandage on her ear. The float, executive share options. A big payday would clear the Holts' debt and save their son's life, but it would never happen unless Bernadette's indiscretion was kept quiet, at least until the money came through.

'You still there, Jonesy?'

'Yes, sorry, Torrens, just walked outside. I think the reception's not as good on this side of the house.'

'Well, anyway, I wanted to ask you about the USB sticks,' he said, quieter this time, like someone might be listening. 'Did you hand 'em over to the cops?'

'No, I didn't.'

'Okay, but you didn't watch 'em, then?'

She was silent.

'Okay, okay. Don't answer me, I don't wanna know anyway. I just wanted to make sure you get rid of 'em, like I told you.'

'Yeah, yeah, of course,' she lied.

'Good. Well, I'll see ya at training.' He hung up.

She stood outside for a moment, the wind whistling in the branches of the mountain gum.

It seemed she may have found the final pieces of the puzzle.

CHAPTER 36

The days went by quickly. The Cats won their preliminary final by less than a kick—it was a shaky performance that left the whole town on edge. Mr Nicholls gave pimply faced Beasley the thousand-dollar man of the match award because, he said, none of the others had played to their capacity. Beasley had been over the moon—a scrawny kid who battled away in the back pocket getting the occasional kick, laying the odd tackle, but mostly just getting under the skin of the forwards, putting them off their game with his constant sledging.

Other than training, Clem had kept to herself up at the cottage, looking after Pocket and avoiding the Holts as much as possible, avoiding everyone really, including Rowan. She'd spent some time thinking, trying to decide whether she was doing the right thing. And she'd written a meticulous account, noting all the relevant information and then checking it thoroughly to make sure Torrens was protected. Then she waited. She wanted to be here for the grand final, but she'd be leaving as soon as the news was out. There was no other way around it. Once she had made her report, her secret would be public information, a field day, a smorgasbord for Tiny Spencer and every other journo with a page to fill. And when she reflected on it, everything had been pointing to that end anyway. The countless times she'd thought about leaving, starting again somewhere, were just a sign that it was the right way to go.

In the meantime, the police appeared to have the drug syndicate in their sights. It was the simplest answer: they assumed Clancy had got on the wrong side of the underworld, and all their lines of inquiry were in that direction. And with the police on their backs, it seemed the drug syndicate had gone to ground. But for how long? Clancy was still an unresolved fly in the ointment, capable of costing them hundreds of thousands of dollars in revenue. Clementine now too. Nothing had changed—the danger, the threat to their lives, remained.

She'd spoken with Clancy. He'd told Mel about Bernadette and she'd gone ballistic. But with Clancy having cheated death, survived to be a father to their child, and then the baby arriving, life had simply steamrolled all over Mel's hurt and rage. Clancy was upbeat, seemed to think things would come right between them. But he told Clem he was terrified of not being around to see his child grow up.

She told him her plan. He was all over it, thought it was the best way. The cheeky bugger had even given her a pep talk, straight out of her own playbook: 'This is it, Jonesy, this is what you've trained for. Now go ahead and execute. And whatever you do, don't fuck it up—bring that bloody trophy home to Katinga!'

The little shit. But they'd had a laugh at least.

And now the day had come, she was totally pumped for it. She would shine the clear light of justice on the darkness, indecency and corruption these powerful people had inflicted on Clancy Kennedy.

It sounded ludicrous: Clementine Jones, the bearer of truth. She wasn't even using her real name. She remembered what the managing partner had told her on her first day at Crozier Dickens: *You only have one reputation. Once it's gone, you may never get it back.*

She had lost her reputation, and with it everything she knew about herself.

But while it was ridiculous, preposterous in fact, that she would

267

be the one to shine the light of truth on Clancy's terror, she hoped there was at least a chance it needn't always be that way. If she just gave it time, surely at some point she'd have the strength to confront the truth about herself?

But that time was not now, and until it arrived—well, the rest of the world could bloody well wait. The last thing, the very last thing, she could endure right now would be her own story, out there in public, so that every time she encountered a friend, a colleague, a neighbour, a stranger in the street, the first thing they would think of would be her colossal, her contemptible lapse.

As she made her way into town, she felt none of her old confidence, the chutzpah she'd had entering a negotiation, a room full of lawyers, her clients hoping she could swing something for them. That was a memory of a different life now. But there was a composure and a calmness, as if she were about to finish a painting, filling in the last of the blue sky in the top-right corner.

Her phone started ringing. She let it ring out. She took the long way into town, so she could go past the oval. She wanted to see it, think about the team and the grand final that lay ahead of them tomorrow. She was almost at the clubrooms when the phone started ringing again. She swung left into the car park, pulled up in a space facing the oval. It was empty, quiet. Only last week it had been full with the sounds of the crowd, cheering, groaning, the pounding of feet on the turf, the thud of bodies, the sound of a sweetly timed kick, the slap of the ball hitting outstretched hands.

She picked up the phone. *Gerard mobile*. Her heart sunk.

The call rang out as she stared at the screen, then immediately started again. She pressed the green button. Whatever he had to say, she had already considered it, turned it over and over in her mind. She knew what she had to do.

'Hello,' he said stiffly. 'All ready for the big one tomorrow?'

'Yep. All set.'

'How's the ear?'

'Yeah. Recovering.' She wanted to say, *smaller, thanks to you.* No, actually, she wanted to scream at him, tell him never to speak to her again, but that would mean giving him the satisfaction of seeing her angry. 'What do you want, Gerard?'

'Well, it's just…well, we know you've been through so much, and we don't mean to intrude, but Bernadette and I, well, we really just need to know your intentions. It's important we understand where everything's at.'

'What do you mean?'

'The deal, Clementine, the deal. Now that you've seen firsthand the terror these people are prepared to unleash, you must know it's best to keep your head down, keep quiet about everything, let things play out without getting involved any further. God knows it's better to be in the audience at an execution than up on the gallows.'

He was creepy. He couldn't help it, even when he was trying to be persuasive.

'I have nothing to say to you, Gerard.'

He cleared his throat. 'Yes. Of course. I understand, I understand completely—you must be very shaken up. But please, if you wouldn't mind holding on a moment, Bernadette would like to speak to you.'

There was a pause while he handed the phone to Bernadette. Clementine waited, her jaw clamped tight, staring across the green of the oval.

'Clementine, thank you for taking our call. I'm so sorry about everything. I heard what you've been through, it's dreadful, it truly is. We wanted to contact you, but we thought you'd need some time.'

Her voice sounded strained. Clementine thought of the hurt Bernadette had suffered, her son's gradual downward spiral, the striving to make things right for him, running down alleyways after him, chasing every possibility in the hope of rehabilitation.

But Clementine had thought through all this already, and none of it changed anything.

'Bernadette, I hope you understand, but I'm not really up to speaking with you or Gerard.'

'Of course, yes, yes. So just let me fill you in on where things are, and I'll let you go. I have received a formal offer for the new role from head office. I will be accepting it today. The plan is that I start in Sydney in a week's time. It's good news, Clem, it means you and Clancy only need to keep our secret for a little longer.'

She hadn't mentioned the debt, thought Clementine, but that was to be expected. She didn't know that Clementine knew. But did this development change anything?

'Clementine. Are you still there?'

'Yes,' she said, 'but I want to ask you something. I want to know how you could possibly put Clancy through what he went through in the last few weeks, not to mention me and Rowan, for a promotion.'

The words hung in the air for a moment. 'Well, as I said, when I spoke to you in our front yard, there is more to the story, Clementine, but I just can't—'

'Bernadette, I know. I know about Nathan.'

A pause. She could hear Gerard's breathing. She realised she was on speaker.

'I know about Nathan's debt. Ambrose told me.'

Bernadette let out a short puff of air, like she'd been holding it in for a long time. 'So you know. Well, I didn't expect this, but it's actually a relief. I'm so relieved…just so relieved,' she said, softly.

It was hard not to feel sorry for her, but Clem pushed the thought away. 'Explain to me the terms of the offer, how you plan to clear the debt so quickly.'

'Well, my salary will be double what it is now—'

'How much?' Clementine knew it wasn't about the salary, but she wanted to know it all, to feast on the information, stack it all high, add it to the supporting evidence for her argument.

'Six hundred thousand.'

'And the equity component?'

'Well, it's confidential, Clementine, I can't disclose that.'

'If I can keep your little encounter with Clancy secret, I can keep your big payday a secret too,' she snapped.

Bernadette hesitated for a moment. 'I'll be allotted a hundred thousand shares in the company when it floats in three weeks' time.'

Clem did the maths. If estimates in the financial press were right, Bernadette's shares would be worth around $1.5 million as soon as the company listed on the ASX.

'But it's a paper profit, Bernadette, you won't be able to sell those shares until the trading window opens for executives. That could be months, maybe a year, after the float.'

'Oh, but you see, I've negotiated an arrangement.' She sounded pleased that Clementine was engaging in the conversation, hopeful that she would come around. 'You see, as a direct report to the CEO, I'm actually entitled to 150,000 shares, but there are special provisions in the employee share plan that allow early sale in exceptional circumstances approved by the company. So I'll only receive a hundred thousand shares, but it means I can sell straightaway. It's all been signed off. So you see we can clear the debt as soon as the company is listed. This is what Mr Macpherson was so keen to ensure, and of course—'

'But where does it end, Bernadette? Once an addict, always an addict.'

There was a pause. 'So you know that...well, that Nathan is in prison at present?'

'Yes.'

'Well, as hard as that has been, Clementine, it's given him a chance to complete his rehab. He's been clean for six months now.' She sounded buoyed, optimistic. What mother wouldn't be?

'So let me get this straight: Clancy and I are to stay silent about your sexual manipulation until the float. Then you sell your shares and pay the drug lords to clear Nathan's debt, and we all live happily ever after?'

'Yes, yes, that's right,' Bernadette said.

'And what if Nathan fucks up again, incurs some new debt? The crims will be on your case, wanting their money. The minute you lose your job, your cashflow dries up, and they know Clancy could bring you down anytime. They'll be lining him up like a rabbit in the crosshairs.'

'But Clancy only has to do one simple thing—how hard is it to keep what happened between us to himself?'

'So as long as he keeps on lying, everything will be sweet?' Clementine said bitterly.

'But it's not lying, he just has to remain silent. There's no lie in not saying anything.'

Lights flashing inside Clementine's head, sirens going off, loud and shrill. She knew this to be untrue. Her life was a lie. Every day she withheld the truth—about herself, who she was, where she'd come from, what she'd seen in life—was yet another lie, to herself, to those around her, the people she had come to love here in Katinga.

She allowed the thought to filter through her mind, watched it turn and twist, emerging as something completely different: if she could live like that, why not Clancy?

It only lasted an instant.

'And what about the people who know? Clancy's told Melissa now. Do you plan to kill all three of us if you get jumpy about your dirty little secret escaping?'

'No, no, Clementine. You must understand, that wasn't us. The creditors, the syndicate Ambrose worked for, they were nervous, you see, they know I need the promotion in order to make the payment, and Clancy seemed to be out of control—'

'Right, so we should expect another round of death threats and kidnappings if we fall out of line?'

'Clementine, we can assure you of your safety.'

Ridiculous, Clem thought. After everything that had happened, Bernadette still believed no one would be harmed. It was all a fantasy anyway, dependent on criminals and addicts doing the right thing, and minor things like justice didn't even factor—justice for a missing ear, a bullet hole in the leg, a deadly fall, and maybe never living long enough to meet your own son.

Dependent also on keeping secrets.

'You know, you once told me about sharks always swimming forward,' said Clem. 'Remember that? Don't you think the truth is like that, Bernadette? Like a great, relentless pressure that propels every living thing onward. And every time you try to crawl away from it, a little part of you is lost in the struggle.'

Bernadette was silent.

Clementine waited. Nothing. It dawned on her. *She knows. She knows who I am.* Gerard had completed his research on her. The hairs on her arms stood up.

Finally Bernadette spoke again. 'Clementine, I hear what you're saying, I really do, and I know it's not perfect, but we have the chance to save them both! Clancy *and* my boy'—her voice faltered—'my Nathan.'

'He made his choices, Bernadette,' Clementine said softly, 'and I suspect he could make another choice now, couldn't he? Dob in the big cheese higher up the supply chain, right? The cops would put him in witness protection. Why is that not a solution?'

'Because we'd never see our only son again,' she whispered.

'Bernadette,' said Clementine as gently as she could, 'you know they threatened Clancy's child as well, don't you? I mean, as hard as it is for you, you're not the only mother in this story.'

Bernadette was crying now. Clementine heard a few steps, then a click. She was off speaker now. Then Gerard's voice.

'Oh, bravo, Jones, bravo. Very helpful,' he snapped, 'and now that you've brought my wife to tears, it's time for you to wake up to something.' *Here it comes*, she thought, bracing herself. 'We know who you are, we know what you've done. *Joanna*. That name mean anything to you, does it? How about Joanna Clementine Jones, lawyer, Crozier Dickens? Oh yes, we know all about you.'

The name hit her like a brick between the shoulders. She had not heard it since the warden had called her to the gate on her last day.

'How about this one: Sue Markham. Remember Sue?'

Unbidden, the image was there again. Susan Markham, mother, wife. Her head lifeless on the steering wheel. Blood. Blood. Blood everywhere. Her eyes staring, so cold.

Clem gasped. 'No! Stop—'

'Shut the fuck up, Jones. You see this is only going to get worse for you now. This is a good deal—Clancy is safe, his child is safe, Nathan is safe, fuck, even your dirty little secret is safe! What more do you want?' He was seething. 'I'm going to hang up now, but you'll get another call in just a few seconds. I want you to take that call. I guarantee you will find it interesting, especially given your observations regarding mothers.'

The phone went dead. It sat in her lap like a ticking time bomb. She waited, her eyes closed, trying to prepare herself for whatever was coming.

The phone rang. She picked it up. An unknown number.
'Hello.'
'Am I speaking to Joanna? Joanna Jones?'
'Yes,' she said hoarsely.
'This is Jeremy Markham.'
Her mouth fell open, her breath caught in her throat.
'Are you there?'
'Yes, yes, I'm here.'
'I'm so sorry to intrude but I've been speaking to your boss. He tells me you're not doing too well.' His voice was just like she

274

remembered, in the courtroom, the victim impact statement.

'You spoke to Gerard?' Her voice sounded strange—little more than a whimper.

'Yes. You see he found out about my daughter's crowdfunding campaign. Sophie has a congenital heart problem. It's terminal unless I can get her to the States within the next six weeks. The treatment costs hundreds of thousands of dollars.'

She knew she should speak, say how sorry she was to hear about his daughter. She had taken his wife, the mother of his child... and now the daughter...Her mouth moved, but it was hopeless, nothing would come out. She tried again. 'I'm so sorry. So sorry about your daughter.'

'Thank you. But I didn't call about that, actually. Gerard asked me to call you, he said he was worried about you.'

'Worried?'

'Yes. Um, I don't exactly know how to put this, but he said you might be suicidal, with the accident and Sophie and everything. So I called to let you know how much I don't want to see that happen...' He swallowed, paused a moment. 'You see, during the trial I couldn't see anything beyond the price my family paid for your boozy night out. But then I heard your statement at the sentencing hearing. I heard your remorse and I could see it was genuine, and I could see how much you were hurting, and your family as well. I couldn't acknowledge it at the time, because, well, because my heart was breaking with grief for Sue. But I do want to let you know this: I have forgiven you. It was a momentary lapse, nothing more, and I just wouldn't want to see you...well, to see you do anything drastic to make the whole thing, well, worse... even worse than it is now, for your family.'

She was speechless for a long time. The seconds ticked by. Jeremy waited. 'Thank you,' she stammered, 'thank you...I am...I'm so sorry, I...well it's hard to take in...Thank you.'

'Well, I have to go now. Please take care.'

The call ended. She sat there, not moving, staring at the oval. It looked blurry, formless, like the ocean at night.

\|/

The phone rang again. She didn't hear it at first, her mind still far away. It kept ringing. She looked down at her lap at the phone.

Gerard.

She picked it up.

'Clementine? Joanna? I'm not sure which you would prefer,' he gloated. 'I take it you've spoken with Jeremy, then?'

'Yes,' she croaked.

'Okay, good. So we only have one more matter to cover, and that is this: Jeremy's crowdfunding campaign has raised twenty thousand over four weeks. He needs two hundred thousand before they'll even let Sophie in the country, and his daughter has only weeks to live. Are you doing the maths here, Jones? Now, Bernadette and I have agreed to fund the balance. The bank is prepared to extend bridging finance on the strength of Bernadette's new role. However, our support is entirely conditional. If Bernadette does not get the role, if, for example, anything about her—what shall we call it?—temporary lapse in judgement becomes public, then we will withdraw the funds. Well, of course we won't have any funds, will we, Jones, because the bank won't be lending to us in those circumstances, will they, and that'll be because Bernadette won't be getting the promotion in the midst of a scandal.'

There was a lump in her throat the size of a tennis ball. All the certainty, that feeling of composure she'd had, was disappearing.

'So you see, the equation is quite compelling, I'm sure you'll agree,' he said. 'On the one hand, we have Clancy, his wife, his child, Nathan, little Sophie and your secret, all safe. On the other hand, we have none of the above.'

Clementine could think of nothing to say.

'Oh, and before we wind up this call, just to let you know, I've drafted a summary for Tiny Spencer. In the event that you or Clancy divulge what you know, Tiny will know everything about your past, and how you destroyed the Markhams' lives.'

The phone went dead.

\\//

She sat there for a long time. A very long time. She watched a dog wander around the edge of the oval, stop just behind the goalposts, lick at an empty meat pie wrapper. Two crows landed on top of the scoreboard, cawed, ceaselessly, for ten minutes.

Her thoughts were going around and around. All her careful planning. Clancy's expectations. Nothing had changed but everything had changed.

She sat a little longer before she drove out of the car park and into town.

\\//

Clementine was standing in the phone box outside the Salvos, her backpack at her feet, a pair of latex gloves on her hands. On the shelf next to the phone was a small cardboard box, a roll of packing tape and a pair of scissors.

She checked the street again. All was quiet. It was early, the odd car and a couple of pedestrians down near the IGA. She took the roll of tape and the scissors, cut off four lengths and knelt down on the pavement, the cardboard box in her hand. She checked the street again, then taped the box to the underside of the shelf, stood up, put a dollar in the slot and dialled the number.

It rang twice.

'Hello, Crime Stoppers.'

'There's a box taped underneath the shelf at the public phone box outside the Salvation Army shop in Main Street, Katinga. It contains two USB sticks with CCTV footage and a note explaining their contents. The information is critical to the investigation into the abduction and violent assault of Clancy Kennedy and Clementine Jones, the shooting of Rowan Dempsey, the injuries received by Graeme Hardy and the death of Ambrose Macpherson.'

Kelsey Flood picked himself up from the soggy ground, a tiny trickle of blood creeping from his temple. He heard the wet thump of the ball as the Eels booted it out of defence and his opponent sneering, 'You just lost the premiership, ya useless lump of cat shit.'

He'd narrowly missed a tough chance at goal, on the run from the flank. With only minutes remaining, it would have put the Cats in front. Bent over, hands on his knees, gasping for air, ten seasons of humiliation thumped through his head.

The Eels' kick was haphazard, a desperate attempt to clear it out of their back line. It tumbled out of bounds just forward of the wing. Midfielders from both sides were rushing to the throw-in area, frenzied pointing and shouting from the Cats defenders, ordering each other into position, their voices edgy and flustered. With a two-point lead, the ball in their forward line and only minutes to go, the Jeridgalee Eels screamed at each other to maintain possession, slow it down, use up the clock.

The noise from the Cats' supporters was thick and hoarse now, an intermittent roar since halfway through the third quarter, when Richie Jones had snapped back-to-back goals in the space of three minutes, closing the gap and giving hope. The Plains mob had sent up a huge cheer as Richie had nailed the first one. And Clancy, sitting on the sideline in his wheelchair, unable to yell through cracked ribs, had broken out into a broad smile, gripping the arms of his chair and hissing, 'Yes, yes, yes!' Standing next to him,

Melissa had hugged their son tighter to her chest. She could feel Clancy's excitement spreading like a wave—he was like the Clancy she knew back in their schooldays, before everything got so hard, before all this. She wanted to share that excitement, transfer it somehow through the soft folds of the blanket to the tiny soul in her arms. Benjamin Jones Kennedy.

The umpire was jogging back to the point where the ball had crossed the boundary line for the throw-in. A giant figure in Cats blue and white was thundering towards the boundary, desperate to make it to the contest in time, mud flying from his boots, smaller players parting to clear the way. With fatigue twisting knots across every muscle in his body, Torrens slowed to take his place in the drop zone, then slammed a shoulder the size of a horse into the Eels' ruckman—a good three inches shorter, with a look on his face that said he'd rather not be there.

The umpire arched his back, heaving the ball over his head back into play. The crowd noise dropped as the ball curved in the breeze, the trajectory favouring Torrens' opposite number. Their bodies were locked in a battle for position, Torrens thrust his bulk sideways with an almighty grunt, nudging his opponent just enough to shift him from the prime piece of grass under the ball. They stood, two gladiators pushing against each other for territory, ball peaking and starting its descent, Torrens managing to hold the other man off for one more gruelling moment, timing his jump. Then, launching upward, his boots cleared the ground by just a few weary centimetres and his huge meat-boning mitt stretched up. His hand inches clear of his opponent's, Torrens tapped the ball straight down to the waiting Maggot Maloney, roving hungrily to his right.

Maloney's opposite number pounced, locking him in a bruising tackle. Maloney grimaced as he wrenched his arms out of his opponent's grip, up and free above his head. From the corner of his eye he caught a glimpse of a flying Cat, the glistening head of

Todd Wakely exploding from halfback, screaming for the ball. The tackle spun Maloney around in midair, his back to Wakely as he fell toward the ground. Arms still free, he lobbed a handpass high over his head towards Wakely's run as the tackle brought him crashing to the ground.

It was as if the ball was suspended, waiting for something. Wakely, legs flashing, arms pumping, elbows high, eyes wide with anticipation, ran straight onto it without breaking stride. A roar from the crowd as it snapped into his grasp. He stepped right, dodging a lunging Eels defender, accelerated again, heard his teammates yelling, 'Clear! Clear!' spreading his fingers wide around the ball in his right hand, curling it safely against his forearm. One bounce, stride, stride, stride, another bounce, all limbs, graceful, flowing—no one could catch him.

On the sidelines, John Wakely was in his Cats jersey, hands cupped in front of his mouth, yelling for all he was worth. 'Go, son! Go, you bloody good thing, go, son!'

Clem watched from the sidelines, checking on the forwards preparing for the kick, willing them to clear a space for Kelsey's lead. Richie Jones sprinted out from the pocket then darted right, towards the far flank, the ground opening up—a paddock for big Kelsey Flood to run into. The big forward jinked around his defender, set off towards centre half-forward like a galloping cement truck as Wakely dashed up the wing.

Eyes up and Wakely spotted him. He took one more step to steady, leant back, guiding the ball gently to his boot, right foot stabbing it sweetly, low and sharp, like a missile, landing with a loud thwack straight into Kelsey's outstretched hands.

The shrill of the umpire's whistle sounded the mark but was swiftly drowned by the thunderous boom from the Katinga crowd. The ball in the hands of their leading goalkicker directly in front of goal—this was it, the kick that could put the Cats in front with only minutes, seconds maybe, to go.

There was a hush as Flood walked back to take his kick, ball on his hip. And, in the stillness that fell upon the ground in that moment, came a tiny voice from the front of the Katinga crowd, beneath a hand-knitted blue and white beanie barely a foot above the boundary fence, like a fairy-wren chirping: 'This one's for Tom!'

A rousing chorus of 'For Tommy Lemmon!' rang out among the Katinga folk. Somebody squeezed her bird-like shoulders and Mrs Lemmon's smile lit up the space across the ground to where Kelsey Flood was going through his customary preparation, resting the ball on the ground like a fragile egg, pulling up each of his blue and white hooped socks.

The Eels defender manning the mark began yelling, punching the air, star jumping, anything to distract. Then, amidst the frenzied boos of the Eels crowd, Kelsey Flood cantered in his usual ten steps, leaned back and calmly booted a fifty-metre drop punt. The goal umpire shuffled towards the left-hand goalpost, crouched, watching it soar over his head, as the crowd held their breath. Then, standing tall, feet together, eyes forward with the deadpan face of goal umpires across the country, the man in white began to raise both hands, forefingers pointing, signifying the goal. The supporters were bewildered at first, unbelieving, then a deafening cheer rose directly from the hearts of the Katinga townsfolk, the glorious taste of triumph denied them for so long.

All eyes swung toward the scoreboard:

	Goals	Behinds	Total
Cats	12	9	81
Eels	11	11	77

Clem felt her ribs stretching and she couldn't seem to breathe out properly. Looking out, she saw the tiredness of men who had spent every cent of energy they had ever possessed, half of them with hands on their knees, bent over, gasping for air. She sent up a prayer for the final siren to come and then, with perhaps seconds, at most a minute left in the game, made her final substitution from the bench, sending a message to maintain possession at all costs.

As the field umpire jogged the ball back to the middle for the centre bounce, Torrens was struggling, barely able to lift his gigantic boots above the turf, in the downward gape of his mouth a look of utter exhaustion. He found the energy to give Todd Wakely a wordless pat on his bald head as he lumbered past. Todd turned, ran with the big man for a few steps, urging him on. 'C'mon, Mattie, give us one more, mate, you can do it.'

Clem had kept Torrens on the field unchanged for the last twenty minutes, with instructions to be at every ruck contest and get back behind the Eels' forward line to defend the high ball whenever he could. She would have liked to sub him off for a rest, of course, maybe she should have, but the Eels still had enough time for a winning goal. She needed one last burst. She just hoped he had the strength to give it.

The Cats supporters, sensing the situation, began yelling, 'C'mon, Mattie, get in there. One more, Mattie!'

Mick Torrens, standing next to Rowan, shook his head in disbelief. He'd driven down from Brisbane for the game, hadn't seen Matthew since he was eighteen. That was six years ago now. Mick had left town, too ashamed to face the father of the lad who'd had his arm broken by the teenage Matthew Torrens. Now—well, now he could hardly recognise this young man. A menacing, hulking presence still, but no sign of the cruel-spirited violence he'd once been renowned for. And here he was, playing with the heart of a lion, loved by his team, cheered by the townsfolk. Mick realised, with something of a shock, that tears were forming in his eyes. He brushed his sleeve across his face roughly, hoping no one noticed.

In the centre of the ground, the umpire was steadying for the bounce, midfielders jostling and shuffling for position around the circle, Torrens taking his place with his opponent inside the circle, both men crouching slightly, preparing themselves for one last clash.

The umpire stepped forward, banged the ball into the turf, bouncing it straight, true and high. Torrens took two steps and launched himself into the air, his body crashing into his opponent with a smack you could hear from the post office. Reaching above, he gave the ball an almighty thump with his closed fist, sending it as far as he could towards the Cats' forward line. It sailed twenty metres in the air, bouncing to the feet of little Richie Jones as he powered into the centre square. Jones gathered the ball smoothly but was immediately tackled by his opponent, and it spilled to the ground. A huge pack of players swarmed onto the ball, Eels grabbing for it, Cats grabbing at Eels, the ball completely invisible inside the heaving mass of limbs and bodies.

It never came out.

A loud blast sounded like a trumpet across the ground, time slowing as the noise went on and the realisation set in. The final siren calling time on fifty-three years of loss, half a century of disappointment.

Arms thrown jubilant in the air, blue-and-white-clad supporters flooding onto the ground, players lying exhausted in the mud, others hugging, Torrens kneeling inside the centre circle, his head resting on his arms, sobbing. Clem turning toward Clancy, wrapping both hands around his raised hand, her smile stretching wide across her cheeks, Clancy holding his ribs with his other hand, laughing, shaking his head.

People crowding around her, thumping her back, tousling her hair, then she felt her feet go out from under her, her body lifted high. She was looking down at John Wakely and Mr Nicholls from the IGA carrying her on their shoulders out onto the ground, the players flocking around, high-fiving her outstretched hand.

She glanced back at the boundary. The Eels supporters were still, hands thrust deep in their pockets, dejected players slumped on the ground. And there it was, a police car, half-hidden behind the sheds. Constable Miller was gripping Gerard's arm, marching him toward the car, Gerard's head turning towards her, a look of utter shock on his face. Sergeant Phillips opening the rear passenger door, Constable Miller pushing Gerard into the back seat, Bernadette standing there, one hand over her mouth.

CHAPTER 38

Clementine rolled up a pair of jeans and shoved them in the open suitcase. The faded yellow bedspread was strewn with clothes, a bulging garbage bag sat upright under the open window, one arm of a white shirt flopped over the lip. Pocket limped into the room and sat near the door, watching quizzically, his bandaged leg resting lightly on the timber floor.

She bent down and ruffled the tuft of fur on the back of his neck. 'It's okay, mate, you're coming too,' she said. His tongue flopped out, his mouth in a wide grin, his tail like a windscreen wiper. She pulled open another drawer, scooped up an armful of T-shirts, pushed them roughly into the case.

Pocket's ears pricked up and he clamped his mouth shut, then scampered away up the hall, squealing with eagerness. Then she heard it too. A car coming up the driveway.

Oh God. She rushed over to the window. She just saw the back end of a green Holden station wagon behind the plum tree in the front yard before the corner of the house obscured it from view.

She hadn't seen the car before. No one came out here. Someone lost, she thought? Someone from next door? Not Jim, he drove a Landcruiser. Her heart started pounding. Ambrose's gang mates? No, she could hear Pocket yelping at the front door. It was his welcome noise.

A knock at the door. Pocket ramped up the excitement, barking wildly.

She put the clothes down on the bed, walked up the hallway to the door, her socks making no sound on the floorboards. Pocket's tail was wagging furiously. Definitely a friend. But she didn't want visitors. Not now. Not ever.

She approached the front door, slowly, peering at a shape through the frosted-glass strip running down one side of the door. A stick? Not a stick, too straight, too uniform. She took a step closer. Crutches.

Oh God. Rowan.

Another knock. Pocket was going crazy.

'Clem, it's me,' Rowan shouted.

He knew she was home—her car was in the driveway. She would have to open the door. Just get rid of him fast, make something up.

She opened the door halfway. He was grinning at her, the same grin he'd flashed through the car window when they first met after she'd smashed into his van. His three-day growth, the short, clipped hair, everything about him the same as it had been then.

'I bloody hope that car's an automatic,' she said. Dempsey's Handyman Van had been impounded as evidence.

'Yeah, well, it's only my left leg that's bung. You gunna invite me in or what?'

He was wearing a tailored shirt, tapering in close to his waist, the dark blue of the collar framing his jawline. It occurred to her that he'd put his best shirt on for this visit. She was dismayed.

'No, sorry, I'm not.'

'Oh, come on. You have to now. Can't let me drive in this condition.'

'Look, Rowan, I can't. I'm in the middle of something.'

'I'll give you a hand.'

'No, really, I don't need any help.'

'You heard from the evil drug lords again or something?' he asked. Now that Gerard had been arrested, the word was out about Ambrose and the drug ring at the centre of the horrifying events in the Arkuna National Park.

'No, no. It's all fine. But I really can't talk right now.'

'If it's about the other day, at my place—' he said.

'No, no,' she stammered, looking at the doormat, 'nothing like that, I just...' She looked up. 'Actually, yes, it is.'

Rowan looked away, the crutches splayed either side of him, his bad leg resting forward. 'Maybe I shouldn't have—'

'No, Rowan, it's fine...really.'

'I shouldn't have...shouldn't have mentioned Kate either,' he said, after a long pause. 'It was just the way you...just someone caring, you know. But it's not anything to do with Kate. I don't... you two are so different anyway...'

He was trying hard, this man of few words, this big-hearted man who'd saved her life.

She cleared her throat. 'Well, I'll see you around, okay.' She started closing the door. He stuck out his right crutch, jamming it in between the door and the doorframe. Pocket saw this as an opportunity, squeezed through the gap and trotted off towards the shrubs around the side of the house.

'Hey. Hang on a moment,' Rowan objected. 'This is weird. This is so not you, Clem. What's going on? Is there someone here? One of those thugs?'

'No, no,' she mumbled, her heart thumping. This wasn't what she had planned. A quick, invisible getaway, no goodbyes. She had managed to hold it together, but now she could feel it unravelling. 'Please, Rowan, leave me be.'

This only seemed to embolden him. He pushed his shoulder against the door, opening it enough to swing his left crutch forward into the hallway and push his way in.

She backed off, not wanting him to fall over on his crutches. He started down the hallway to the kitchen, yelling, 'Whoever's here, I'll deal with you right now. I'll fucking smash your brains out.'

288

He stuck his head in the kitchen, the front room, the lounge room.

'I'm telling you, there's no one here,' she said.

He was charging back up the hallway. She blocked the way. He pushed past her, his eyes blazing, came to the bedroom, stopped in his tracks.

There was a silence as Rowan took it in. The half-packed suitcases, the garbage bags.

'What the bloody hell is going on here?' he said slowly.

She didn't answer.

He hobbled further inside the bedroom, as if he might find more information there. Clementine took a few steps into the room behind him. He turned around to face her, bewildered.

'You're leaving?'

She nodded.

'Why?'

She couldn't speak.

'Have they threatened you?'

She shook her head.

'You moving into town?'

'No, I'm leaving Katinga.'

'But I thought you liked it here. Your cottage and all.'

She couldn't argue with that. It had started out as a place to end the days of aimless driving, a temporary refuge. It had become a sanctuary.

'And the team? What about the players?'

She shrugged. She hadn't planned for this, hadn't concocted a story or figured out a way to explain.

'Something is seriously wrong here. Tell me what the hell is going on.'

He took a half-step forward on his crutches, reached his hand out, gently touched her arm.

She was staring at the rug on the floor; his touch on her arm had started something. She fought to stop it taking over. 'Rowan, I can't…I can't tell you…you'll find out soon enough, and that's fine, but I don't want to be here when you do.' Her voice was choking. 'I've got to leave.'

She stepped around him and went to the chest of drawers, started flinging clothing into the suitcase.

He took a step towards her. She felt his hand on her shoulder, gently pulling her back, guiding her to the edge of the bed. She sat, her head bowed, fists clenched on her knees and a tremor running through her arms all the way to her shoulders.

He eased himself down next to her, letting the crutches fall with a thud on the floor. He took her hand in his. She felt the sudden warmth. Then he gently lifted her hair from across her face and tucked it behind her shoulder.

'Clementine, please, I can help. You can tell me.'

She could not stop the sob that surged out, her whole body shuddering.

Rowan took her in his arms. 'Shhhh. Shhhh. It's okay. I've got you.'

She sat, his arms around her, weeping freely. After what seemed like an eternity, the sobs eased. She felt him brush a tear from her cheek. Every muscle in her body, every bone, every sinew screamed at her: she needed someone to know the truth. The long lie was coming to its end. She had to tell this man.

Raising her head, she looked through her tears into his eyes. She felt the months of grief, the weeks of torment, the long days living with the shame piled high. She felt every moment of guilt like a knife in her side.

Softly, in a whisper, she said the words.

'Rowan. I killed someone.'

DANGEROUSLY ILL GIRL TO FLY TO USA
Tiny Spencer

Sophie Markham, the four-year-old from the Sydney suburb of Coogee with a rare congenital heart condition, is going to America. As reported first in the Valley News, doctors in Sydney have exhausted the treatments available in Australia, and without lifesaving surgery from cardiac specialists in California, Sophie is not expected to live. Since we featured the story two weeks ago, Sophie's crowdfunding page has soared from $20,000 to over $250,000 and arrangements are now being made for her to travel to the United States.

Sophie lost her mother in a tragic car accident involving grand-final-winning Katinga Cats coach Joanna 'Clementine' Jones.

Sophie's father, Jeremy Markham, thanked the Katinga Cats Football Club for their support in garnering over $100,000 in donations from Australia's country football leagues alone.

ACKNOWLEDGEMENTS

Lapse was conceived at a time of high excitement at the prospect of a great sea journey. The first draft was completed before that journey began, but now I have both the book and the sea, and a lot of crew to thank along the way.

First to ship's captain, Dean. Thank you, for making not just one but both of these odysseys possible. When you read that god-awful second draft and excitedly declared it to be a masterpiece, it was all I needed to keep going. And thanks to your limitless technical knowledge, I've never had to research car models, car chases, tyre behaviour, driving fast, and other fun details like how to get over a tall fence without a ladder, or destroy a letter box. But most of all, thank you for your boundlessly creative and adventurous spirit and your long-suffering support throughout the entire undertaking.

Secondly, my most expert and unexpected mentor, award-winning writer Michael Collins. I can never thank you enough for your encouragement and your perceptive and forthright coaching. That you volunteered to review and comment on the entire third draft over the course of that pipe-freezing Indiana winter still leaves me speechless—it was an act of pure generosity and, quite simply, a priceless gift.

And next, to my astute, well-read neighbours: the Commodore-driving, Harley-chasing Donna, a (slightly) more mature version of Clementine Jones; and our very own storytelling, laughter-filled, bright-eyed man on the street, Vaughan. I awaited your responses with bated breath. When I saw your joy in the reading of it, my heart nearly burst. Thank you so much for taking the punt...could have been very awkward around the neighbourhood if the story was a dud.

Thank you also to Dean's mum and my friend, Lana, who read an early draft of *Lapse* in between snorkelling and fishing and sailing on our catamaran, Live Louder. Your feedback and support was much appreciated.

To my agent, Gaby Naher, for so many things beyond the simple, joyous fact of believing in me and my writing, including your hard-headed industry experience, your unquestionable know-how and your ten-point list of brilliant ideas and insights on the manuscript. I count myself very lucky to have you at my side.

And finally, to the champion team at Text Publishing: thank you to each of you for your exuberant support, your confidence in my story, your hard work and, more generally, your commitment to Australian writing. Special thanks also to my painstaking and talented editor, Elizabeth Cowell, who not only helped me add extra polish and flow to the manuscript but also taught me so much about good writing.

I am immensely thankful to each of you. And to jump from sailing to footy—because now the damned thing's finished, I'm allowed to mix a metaphor—each of you have played an absolutely essential part in coaching me, cheering me on and helping me to kick this almighty fifty-metre goal. C'arn the mighty Cats!